WOMEN
LIKE US

WOMEN LIKE US

A NOVEL

KATIA LIEF

Atlantic Monthly Press
New York

FIRST EDITION

Published simultaneously in Canada
Printed in the United States of America

This Book was set in 11-pt. Janson Text by Alpha Design & Composition of Pittsfield, NH.

First Grove Atlantic hardcover edition: June 2025

Library of Congress Cataloging-in-Publication data is available for this title.

ISBN 978-0-8021-6492-6
eISBN 978-0-8021-6493-3

Atlantic Monthly Press
an imprint of Grove Atlantic
154 West 14th Street
New York, NY 10011

Distributed by Publishers Group West

groveatlantic.com

25 26 27 28   10 9 8 7 6 5 4 3 2 1

For Maïa Hunter and June Shadoan,
sister and aunt,
in gratitude for their constancy and love.

"People, feelings, everything! Double! Two people in each person. There's also a person exactly the opposite of you, like the unseen part of you, somewhere in the world, and he waits in ambush."

—Patricia Highsmith, *Strangers on a Train*

Prologue

There were different ways you could tell trouble was coming: You'd see it or hear it or feel it. When Joni was young and her mind was clear those senses ran parallel, with one just slightly ahead of the other, sending off alarms, begging reaction. But her thinking had grown murky over the years and murkier still as society's signals counterposed her instincts. And then, when her husband died—when she killed him—her inner wiring went haywire.

She no longer automatically trusted people. That was true.

Sometimes, she didn't trust Val, her closest friend.

But the crux of it was that she distrusted herself.

Five years ago, she'd imagined that with Paul out of the picture she'd be able to think straight and feel resolved. But no. How could she ever feel secure now that she had crossed that stern red line and done the unthinkable? How could she believe people didn't look at her and somehow know? It was always there, that doubt bubbling under the surface, hard as she worked to push it away.

PRODIGAL BROTHER

1

Joni plunked herself down at the desk of her home office and searched for the Zoom link. She was twenty minutes late for a meeting she was supposed to co-lead. She slashed on some lipstick (red) and joined the meeting in progress (*too* red, she noticed when her sun-washed face appeared on the screen). A dozen thumbnails smiled and waved. She waved back in her little square, startled at the sight of someone just behind her on-screen: a serene-faced woman with a disheveled head. But it was just the goddess planter with its flowering cactus, aloe spikes, and dripping ivy. She'd moved it into the sun yesterday without realizing that it would look like a medusa on her shoulder.

In the chat, she messaged Chris, her daughter and second-in-command of the television production company they ran together: Sorry. Traffic. Grr. She saw Chris's attention drift down and then her slight nod.

No worries, Chris messaged back. Everything's under control. Btw move the flowerpot it looks insane.

Chris shared her screen, pushing the faces off to the side. A post-production schedule appeared. They'd revised it just that morning and, as agreed, Chris was presenting it to the team, which meant that Joni could take a moment to gather herself.

She turned off her camera so now just her name and title filled her square: Joni Ackerman, CEO & Executive Producer, Sunny Day Productions. She'd dropped Lovett from her name five years ago, the moment Paul Lovett, her husband and the company's founder, was gone.

She crossed the room to place the (creepy) goddess head planter (a gift from her friend Val) out of sight. Then she found her comb, ran it through her shoulder-length hair, and was about to rejoin the meeting when the doorbell rang.

Standing on the front step, blocking the clear blue Malibu sky, was a man Joni didn't know . . . until a snap of recognition: It was her brother, Marc. Bearded. Grinning his old grin. A bulging backpack hanging over one shoulder. Flanked by a carry-on roller suitcase, its handle pulled up at the ready.

Stella came bounding to the door, barking at the sight of a stranger, but calmed down when Marc offered a hand to smell. Wagging her tail, she allowed him to pet her before posting herself at Joni's side. Joni was amazed by how quickly her Goldendoodle took to this unknown person.

If the wiry young man Joni remembered as her brother was buried somewhere in the potbellied, middle-aged person on her doorstep, she barely saw him—unless she looked at his eyes. The brown color was the same, of course, but so was the glint that used to mean he was up to something. The smile was his, too: warm but, once you knew him, complicated. When he was younger, he'd been capable of springing anything on you at any time. Like showing up on your doorstep unannounced after a decades-long absence.

She shook her head. "Wow, *Marc.*"

He opened his arms first. They hugged crisply, more like old acquaintances than sister and brother. He had a cinnamon smell that was new, at least to her—she liked it. She found herself gently patting his back like she used to when he was a baby and she pretended he was her doll. Feeling blindsided, confused—she didn't know this person—she pulled away, folded her arms over her middle, looked at him and didn't know what to say.

He tilted his suitcase and wheeled it into the foyer. "Sorry to just show up like this—I hope it's not a bad time." He dropped his backpack on the floor next to the suitcase, then turned to close the door behind him.

She ground her teeth and felt a sharp pluck in her jaw. Then, on cue, the wicked itch in the unreachable middle of her back ignited as if her jaw and spine were connected by an electric thread. Not an itch, but *itch*, according to the dermatologist, a mysterious condition that would either resolve itself or last forever.

Joni was trying to think of what to say to this man who had just deposited himself in her house when the sound of footsteps turned her attention to the stairs. Her assistant, Blair, paused halfway down and stopped when she saw there was a visitor. "Oh. Sorry."

The distraction was a relief. "This is my brother, Marc."

"I didn't know I had such a gorgeous niece."

Blair's freckled face pinkened to her blond hairline and she repressed a smile.

"No. Blair's my assistant. My daughter's Chris—she's in a meeting."

"Ah," Marc said. "Of course. I remember now. Hello, Blair."

"Hi," Blair greeted him. Then, turning to Joni, she said, "Val just called—you left your phone upstairs and I heard it ringing so I answered, hope that's okay. I know you guys have been playing phone tag."

"Is she still on the line?" They'd been missing each other all day. An earlier message had said there was something Val wanted to discuss but she hadn't specified if it was business or personal. Val was her oldest friend. Once she'd left teaching and joined Sunny Day as a producer during the pandemic, their conversations had become a complicated meshwork of work and friendship. It could have been anything.

"Her flight was taking off so she had to go. She said she'd try again from Alaska but I told her good luck with that. Last time they were shooting in . . ."

"Yakutat," Joni filled in the blank with a wry smile that lifted one side of her mouth. The name of that remote Alaskan town had always amused her.

"Last time, there was no internet for, like, a week."

"I remember that." If it was important, Val would try again. Otherwise, they'd connect next week. "Would you let Chris know I won't be back in the meeting?"

"Sure." Blair jogged back upstairs where the three women Zoomed from separate rooms.

Joni turned to her brother. "I can't believe you're really here."

"Me neither." He looked at her, nodding. "You look great."

Bullshit, she wanted to say but didn't. She'd combed her hair, but her lipstick was overbright. And the rips in the knees of her jeans had appeared of their own accord and not as a fashion statement.

"Where are you staying?" She glanced at his suitcase. It was black, gleaming, with crisp store tags still dangling off the handle as if he'd bought it and left in a hurry.

The answer she wanted was a hotel, an Airbnb, anywhere but here. But she knew him; she used to know him. They were both so much older now, dinged up by life—he had to be wiser now, better. He couldn't possibly still be the heartless manipulator who used to torment her when they were young. She reminded herself that she didn't know him anymore.

"Hey, I'm sorry to show up like this but I wanted to surprise you."

"You did."

"Too much time has passed, sister, and neither of us is getting any younger."

"That's for sure."

"I just wanted to put all that behind us and see you. And get to know my niece!"

He hadn't answered her question about where he planned to stay. "Well," she said reflexively, "we have a guest room. You're welcome to it if you don't have other plans." She felt a pang of regret the moment she made the offer and hid it behind a smile.

"That would be great. Thank you."

And that was that. He was her guest now. Her brother, of all people—standing right there next to her—a middle-aged man. Despite her misgivings, she decided on the spot that it was only fair to give him the benefit of the doubt. He was her only sibling, and both their parents were gone. Maybe it was about time they gave what was left of their family another chance.

Leading them into the living room where they could sit comfortably, she asked, "What brings you to LA?"

"I retired recently. I've been traveling around, looking for the perfect place to park myself for the foreseeable."

"What did you do?"

"Information technology."

"You're young to retire," Joni said. He was younger than her and she didn't feel anywhere close to being ready to stop working. His having retired made her feel old and she didn't like it.

He smiled gently, reading her, and agreed. "Much too young. I took early retirement. It was a good package, too good to turn down. I was burned out, anyway."

Joni smiled in return. It *did* make sense. And it didn't make *her* old. "So how long are you in town?"

"You know," he said, "I haven't seen Chris since she was, what? Five years old?"

"That sounds about right." He'd avoided her last question, and he hadn't mentioned Paul. She remembered that about him: how he'd been good at steering conversations and avoiding land mines. Unless he wanted to step on them; then he'd step hard. Was it possible he didn't know? He must have known. He'd found her, and the minute you googled Joni Ackerman Lovett the scandals and tragedies floated right to the top.

From the sounds of footsteps and voices overhead, Joni knew the meeting was over. She texted Chris to come meet her uncle. While they waited, Blair came downstairs looking at her phone. She'd brushed out her luminous hair and slathered her lips in gloss. She'd told Joni earlier that she had a date that evening and hoped to leave work on time.

Joni smiled. "Have fun tonight."

"He *just* canceled." Blair trilled her lips, clocking a fresh disappointment.

Again, Joni thought, but didn't say it. Whoever this new guy was, it was obvious he wouldn't be around for long.

"Guess I'll go for a run instead." Blair headed to the powder room to change into the running clothes she carried, just in case, in her backpack.

Chris appeared moments later, jogging barefoot down the stairs, already smiling. Her strawberry bob was pushed behind both ears and her eyes were bloodshot from looking at a screen all day. Zoom ready from the waist up, she wore an elegant gold necklace and cream silk blouse over frayed cutoffs. She stood in the foyer with her hands on her hips and stared at their visitor.

"Uncle Marc? Damn, I remember you!"

He got up and kissed her cheek. "And I remember you, little girl."

"Wait," Chris said. "Is it Marc or Marco? I used to call you Uncle Marco, right?"

"Right." He laughed at himself. "Just Marc, these days."

"I also remember a Maximillian." Joni grinned.

"Right." He grinned back. "Max. One of my many alter egos. Can't say I'm not embarrassed about all that now."

"Oh, *please*," Chris said. "Who doesn't look back at their teenage self and cringe?" She pushed up a sleeve to show the *Aidan* tattoo on her shoulder, having at sixteen inscribed on her skin the name of her first boyfriend.

Marc's laugh sparked delight in Joni. She remembered that about him now, the warmth of his laugh, and how his first-ever baby smile had been for her.

"I'm starving," Chris said. "Anyone else hungry?"

"Now that you mention it." Marc patted his belly.

"I'll make dinner," Chris offered. "Let me see what we have in the kitchen."

Marc smiled. "I'm a great cook. Come on, we'll figure something out."

Blair emerged transformed, wearing spandex shorts and a cropped running top, hair now pulled back into a high ponytail. Her backpack was slung over her shoulder, presumably to drop in her car before she went for her run. Joni stopped her.

"Stay for dinner," she insisted, pained at the thought of Blair spending another night alone in her cramped Santa Monica studio apartment. Ever since her engagement had broken off a few years ago, Joni had sensed her loneliness.

"You sure?"

"Stay," Chris echoed.

"Okay." Blair smiled and put her bag down beside Marc's suitcase. "I'll help."

"Take your run," Chris insisted. "You can be on cleanup."

"Deal." Blair waved, then disappeared through the front door.

Marc followed Chris into the kitchen and soon there was an eruption of cupboards opening, ingredients being discovered, and pots and pans being taken out. Joni watched from the doorway. They wore the matching orange-and-white-striped aprons Joni had bought on impulse during the first and scariest pandemic lockdown. She and Chris had spent an extravagant amount of time cooking and baking together, creating feasts too big for just the two of them, redirecting their energy somewhere, anywhere but into the abyss of anxiety about what was happening to everyone in the entire world at the same time. That was before their exercise phase when they sought to fit into their Before Times clothing—free weight routines, yoga Zooms, and long rambling walks with Stella. Which was before Chris took up knitting and Joni discovered the addictiveness of eBooks.

It was all that reading that led Joni and Sunny Day to the subject of her new project—a narrative pilot called *Hear Me Out*, based on the lives of two women in the 1950s who started Caedmon Records against everyone's advice, recording LPs of authors reading their own work and seeding what became a booming audiobook industry. The goal was to finish the pilot, get a partnership development deal with a premier network, like HBO or Apple TV+, and then go back into production on the first season. Joni and Chris had emerged from the pandemic over-rested and energized, with projects bubbling on all of Sunny Day's burners.

The exercise routines had mostly stuck, but the clothing never made it out of the closet since elastic waists and sneakers were too comfy to give up, ever. Joni wondered if Marc had acquired his potbelly during lockdown. She felt a wave of compassion for him, imagining that he'd gone through the worst of the pandemic alone—but, of course, she had no idea how he'd spent it.

Her brother was right: They did have a lot of catching up to do. Dinner was a good start.

The roasted vegetable frittata was delicious, better than you'd expect for a last-minute dinner party. It felt like a party, Joni realized, with the unexpected company. Joni and Chris had shared many meals with Blair over the years, she was practically family at this point—she'd started a decade ago as a junior assistant, rose to become Paul's right hand then stayed on as Joni's. But Marc, who *was* family, felt like . . . what? Not a stranger, exactly. More like a new neighbor who'd swung by for introductions and stayed to eat. And Joni realized as the evening wore on—as the parbaked baguette from the freezer was warmed, ripped, and devoured, as the frittata was reduced to a bare plate and the salad bowl emptied—she was glad to have him.

They brought bowls of ice cream to the cool evening deck while sunset blazed just beyond their sloping hill. Joni relished the taste of the cold creamy chocolate on her tongue and the glowing sorbet of the red and orange sky while she listened to Marc tell them about his itinerant life as an information systems engineer on cruise ships.

"Twenty years," he told the girls (*the women*, Joni corrected her own thought; Chris and Blair were grown women). "I sailed the high seas for longer than I ever thought I would."

"Ahoy, matey," Joni joked.

"Seriously, though," Blair asked. "Were there ever any pirates? I mean, the new kind they have these days."

Joni chuckled, but Marc's tone sobered. "There were a few near misses, but no onboard incidents. Every ship I worked on had top-notch security."

"Sorry," Joni said. "I went right to eye patches and peg legs. I didn't realize—"

"Pirates are no joke," Marc told her. In the dimming twilight, his skin looked fresh, almost damp, and his forehead looked broader than before, as if his hairline had just receded another quarter inch. It was strange how sometimes you saw more clearly in a duller light. His brown eyes looked browner out here. As Joni looked at them now, they fused with the taste of the chocolate ice cream, and she remembered something from their childhood. When he was a baby, their mother used to cradle him and coo, "Look at those deep dark chocolate eyes."

He smiled, returning his sister's gaze. "What?"

"Were you ever married?" she asked.

"Never got lucky enough."

"So, no kids?" Chris asked.

He grinned, and Joni braced herself for the creepy old quip so many guys fell back on: *Not that I know of.* But he didn't say that. "No," he answered simply, with a tinge of regret. Then he added, "I've been a lone wolf for a long time, which is why I'm moving around now. With my line of work, it got to the point where I didn't bother keeping my own place anymore. With no wife or kids, it was easier. But now I will. Now I'll find out where I want to settle down. Maybe I'll stay here, near you." He looked at Joni and she reached out her hand. He set down his nearly empty bowl to take it. A sensation of familiarity washed over her at the warm, dry feel of his hand in hers, squeezing. They smiled at each other in a moment of easy silence.

Stella took the opportunity to leap from Chris's feet to Marc's side on the chance she'd get to the melting chocolate in time, but Joni was too fast.

"No way." She dropped Marc's hand to grab the bowl and lofted it above her head.

"My family had a dog die once from eating chocolate," Blair said. "It was the middle of the night. We didn't find her till morning and then it was too late."

"That's so sad," Chris said.

"Just terrible," Marc agreed.

Joni finished her brother's uneaten ice cream, then stacked all the empty bowls and brought them to the kitchen. When she returned, she said, "I didn't want to be a bummer earlier, but I need to tell you why I was late to the meeting." To Marc, she clarified, "I took Stella to the vet earlier today and was late getting back."

"Ah," he said.

"I thought you said traffic." Chris looked squarely at her mother, expecting either confirmation or explanation.

Joni wished it was as simple as just traffic. "It was slow getting back, that's true. But that's not the only reason I was late. I had to stay and talk with the vet. Stella, well . . . there's a reason she's been lethargic lately."

Chris and Blair traded worried looks. They both loved Stella almost as much as Joni did.

"It's nothing dire," Joni clarified, "but it is serious. She has heart disease. The vet said it's common in older dogs. She'll have to take a pill twice a day for the rest of her life."

"Oh." Chris's face relaxed. "That doesn't sound *so* bad."

"It isn't," Joni said. "Not really. But she'll sleep more now. We should expect that. And we have to be careful not to overstress her."

Blair got up and crouched to nuzzle her face in Stella's thick fur. "I'll take good care of you while Mommy's in New York," she promised. A trip to visit Sunny Day's headquarters was scheduled for the following week.

"You're going to New York?" Marc asked.

"Next week. Chris and I are both going. For work."

"Okay." He nodded. "I'll be out of your hair by then."

Chris glanced from Stella to Joni. "Actually, Mom, wouldn't it be less stressful for Stella if she stayed here in her own home instead of going to Blair's? Maybe Uncle Marc could dog sit? I mean," she turned to him, "if you don't have other plans."

Joni looked at Marc, her kindly new-and-improved brother, holding out his fingers for Stella to sniff and lick. He'd been great with dogs as a kid, she remembered now. Bad with people back then, but good with animals. "Can you?" she asked him.

"Absolutely. Happy to."

"Thank you," Joni smiled. "Look at how great this is turning out."

Over the weekend, Marc was a model guest. He made himself useful around the house, did small repairs here and there without being asked (tightening a loose toilet paper holder, quieting a squeaky door, fixing a kitchen drawer that kept falling out of its tracks), told jokes over dinner, offered to take over the shopping and cooking as long as he was there so Joni and Chris could focus on their work. It seemed he'd grown up, was worn at the edges by life, and was softer and nicer than she'd ever imagined he could be. If at moments a speck of darkness pulsed into view, in a glance or an edge to something he said, it erased itself instantly. He was like a cloud with a silver lining that had devoured its own dark heart.

2

Music emanated from the living room speakers and drifted upstairs to Joni's office. As she looked away from her screen and tried to identify the song, her gaze fell on the paperweight Chris had commissioned an artist to make for her distraught mother five years ago—after Joni's infamous meltdown and Paul's famous death—the curled lock of brown hair tied in a pale ribbon, floating in a crystal orb.

Alex's hair. Alex's ribbon.

Was it really twenty-five years since the coroner clipped it as a keepsake for them?

Chris had found it in her father's things when she was clearing out his dresser. He'd never shown it to Joni or even told her about it; he must have felt it was too morbid for her to handle, given how young Alex was when they lost her, their second child. He was more right about that than he'd realized. Chris insisted her mother keep the paperweight in view as a reality check—a reminder of Alex's life and her loss, the horribly sad fact of it—thus sealing off the rabbit hole of magical thinking Joni had once lost herself in. The reminder was stark and effective: Alex was long gone; Chris was an only child; they were strong women, they were.

Looking at it now, a reflection coalesced on the surface of the glass, a distortion of herself. She sat back quickly, and the reflection evaporated.

She got up from her desk and went downstairs to follow the music to its source. It was Joni Mitchell's "Chelsea Morning." As a teenager, she'd checked out Mitchell because of their shared first name and the sweet, soaring voice and soulful, quirky lyrics had captivated and held her. Soon preteen Marc was listening with her, and they both loved her; they loved her together. Finally, there was something for the siblings to share. It had been years since she'd purposefully listened to a Joni Mitchell song and now, coming downstairs into the fullness of the sound, she recalled another thing she'd long forgotten. At one time, when they were children, and before their relationship soured, she and Marc had felt a genuine connection. It had crystallized through this music.

Seeing him sitting beside Chris on the couch, the two of them knitting together—knitting of all things—brought it all back. The music and the memory, her brother beside her daughter, the tenderness between them as her slender steel needles and his fat wooden needles clacked beneath the song's harmony, made her glad that Marc was there. It was at that moment that any lingering resistance to his visit fell away.

Joni stood in front of them, smiling. "I don't know where to begin."

"I'm teaching Uncle Marco to knit," Chris said.

"So I see." Not, *It's Monday, a workday*. Because work was coming along fine, and this was interesting.

"It's easier than I thought," he said, guiding the right needle into the stitch on his left needle, pulling a strand of chunky green yarn from back to front, guiding off the new stitch. "And it's relaxing. I had no idea."

"That's why I love it," Chris said, her hands moving swiftly, producing stitch after rapid stitch, the start of a yellow sweater. "It's like meditation—your hands are busy but your mind goes free."

"Pull up some needles and join us," Marc said.

"Thanks, but it's not for me." Joni sat down with them and allowed herself to soak up the relaxed mood.

After a few minutes Stella came over, stood in front of Joni, and woofed. She knew what that meant. She got up, found Stella's leash, and hooked it to her collar.

"How about some company?" Marc put down his needles in a tangle of yarn. "I need some exercise—gotta work off this beer belly."

"Sure. Chris?"

"Nah. I only exercise when I pay for it." Chris went to the gym three times a week like clockwork and left it at that.

Joni grabbed a hat from the eclectic collection hanging by the door, mostly broad-brimmed sunhats and baseball caps. "Want one?" she asked Marc.

"Not a hat guy, but thanks."

Once clear of the driveway they turned onto Idlewild Way and followed its gentle downward slope edged with clusters of palm, arroyo, and walnut trees separated by asphalt drives that tongued from the houses. The houses along this road were a mix of modest and spectacular, depending on when they were built. She loved these sunburnt windswept hills and sudden clearings with sweeping mountain views. If she was feeling energetic on her daily long walk with Stella and had the time, she'd keep going once she reached Newell Road and follow it to Corral Canyon Road and wind all the way down to the beach. There was a dog park near the beach where Stella loved to run off leash and fill up on water, returning to lick Joni with long, languid swipes of her soaked tongue. Joni would have to restrict her running time now that she had heart disease.

"LA sun is kind of raw, I've noticed," Marc said, shielding his eyes with a flattened palm.

Joni nodded under the shade of her sunhat.

"I don't think I've walked this far down yet." His cheeks were turning red.

They were approaching Newell Road. She asked, "Want to turn back?"

"Maybe."

At the rumble of an approaching car, they retreated to the side of the road. The green VW bug zipped by them, stopped, and slowly backed up.

Joni was already smiling when Blair's window scrolled down, releasing a puff of cool air. Stella leaned into the window for the flurry of greetings she knew Blair would offer. When the dog licked the young woman's face, Joni felt a spark of jealousy, which she buried in a smile.

"Am I early?" Blair asked.

"Are we meeting today?" Joni asked. "I thought it was tomorrow." A few times a week, Blair came to the house so they could work in person. The schedule was never the same and sometimes there were mix-ups.

They both took out their phones to check.

"Shit, you're right, it's today," Joni said. "I'd say let's do it, but I haven't gone over the stuff you sent me yet. Sorry, Blair."

"No problem. I can come back tomorrow. Want a ride back up to the house?"

"Yes, please!" Marc was shading his face with both hands now.

"Thanks, but I'll walk," Joni said. It was an especially nice afternoon, and she wasn't ready to go back inside to face her work.

Marc slid into the passenger seat and as the car took off up the hill Joni could see through the rear window that they were talking animatedly. Marc was good with women, it seemed. Joni thought about that as she continued to the intersection of Corral Canyon Road, where she decided to turn around.

She started to wonder if it was women Marc was good with or young women in particular. There was a jocular ease to his relationship with Chris, the way they cooked and knitted together like a pair of chummy old friends. With Blair, Joni sensed a flirtatious edge that felt inappropriate given their age difference and it put her on alert. She told herself that she was imagining it but knew she wasn't when, the next day, Marc appeared in shorts, a T-shirt, and a baseball cap and announced that he was going for a run. Joni nearly burst out laughing at the thought of her portly brother *running*. Having finished their work, Blair had changed into her running clothes and joined him at the door where he waited, smiling, sucking in his gut.

A dozen quips popped into Joni's mind. *You're kidding! You'll have a heart attack! What about your knees?* But she held them back because she didn't want to embarrass him. Instead, she told them, "Have a good run," and watched from the top of the drive as Marc huffed down the hill beside the trim, golden young woman.

When Joni got back to the house, Chris was standing in the front hall, smiling.

"If he thinks he has a shot at her," Joni said, "he's out of his mind."

"Maybe if he lost the belly."

"He's too old for her," Joni said.

"Don't be ageist, Mom."

"Oh, come on."

"Marc's cool."

"Cool? Guys his age who go after young women are nothing but old horndogs."

"Mom!"

"It's true!"

"Sometimes, but maybe sometimes not. I guess if I were your age, though, it would bother me, too."

"It's not because of my age that it bothers me." But as soon as Joni said that she regretted it and now the words she couldn't unsay prickled with a bitter defensiveness. She wondered if Chris had a point. Younger women had an obvious sexual edge over older women and maybe, in a way, Joni was envious of that simple animal force.

And resentful.

And frustrated.

And worried.

When men did their thinking with their penises and women felt empowered by that, the women usually lost when things went off the rails. In the end, men still held most of the power. When they got sick of those women, they still tossed them out like garbage and society still snapped on the lid.

She recalled a headline from last year that had stunned her and still disturbed her whenever she thought of it: "That's a Wrap on #MeToo." It was a reaction to the verdict against Amber Heard that found she'd defamed Johnny Depp, her violent movie-star ex-husband whose monstrous behavior toward her was judged more acceptable than the "damage" he suffered from her essay revealing his outsize role in their toxic relationship. What damage? What suffering? Joni knew as a fact that he had prestige projects in the pipeline that were going full steam ahead. And now Heard was an outcast who owed her abuser fifteen million dollars.

Joni recalled how her stomach sank when she witnessed the social media pile-on recasting Heard as a viper and Depp as her prey.

She recalled feeling lucky that she'd made it out of her own debacle, five years ago, innocent in the eyes of others.

In her case, she'd kept quiet and gone into hiding—far, far away in Bali. Her pulse raced even now, thinking about how close she'd flown to the sun in the months after Paul died.

Devil's ivy. Hearts of Jesus. Someone had a morbid sense of humor when they planted Joni's Balinese terrace. But there were also banana trees, palms, banyans, ti plants with their long needly red leaves, frangipani with their pretty flowers, and an abundance of glorious hibiscus. She would sit at the small table that straddled indoors and out and gaze on to the sun-drenched vegetation of her hideaway. Her villa—really one large room—had its own small pool where she swam every morning. Stella sometimes swam with her, or she'd jump in later and paddle back and forth, then lie in the sun to dry.

Joni ate all her meals at that little table. It was where she finished her screenplay, wrote emails, shopped online, and fell down countless rabbit holes that started with searches of her husband's name, career, and death. His transgressions had spawned their own cottage industry of gossip, and as she had nothing but time and was all alone at first (before Chris joined her), and because she was terrified, she read everything, then regretted reading it, then numbed herself with drink. She was still afraid she'd be discovered. The thought of the shame and the punishment she'd suffer for what she'd done to Paul became a labyrinth of long nights and wicked hangovers.

In the wake of her husband's sudden death, Joni was in shock from what she was learning about him. What he'd done. But that was just the tip of an iceberg that reared over time to show its ugly shape and enormity. The worst of it was buried deep in his past: the predation, with Lou Pridgen, on unconscious (in too many ways) women. Paul had stopped before, or when, he met Joni; she wasn't sure. But

Lou continued, and as the two of them rose through the industry in stature and power, they became a paired beast, sharing a circulatory system that fed on each other's secrets. Little in Hollywood went untouched by some tendril of their complicity. After it all came out no one questioned that Paul would want to kill himself; you could only wonder why Lou, rotting in prison, hadn't done it first. What quickly overwhelmed Joni during those first weeks in Bali was how she'd become associated with her husband's guilt.

The media's vitriol was swift and vicious, a self-perpetuating frenzy of schadenfreude that pulled down everyone it could. Joni watched the news with her heart in her throat as they came for her— and they came for her right away.

She was Paul Lovett's wife; one of his victims had been her best friend: How could she not have known?

They had some of it right and some of it wrong, but it didn't matter.

And Chris: They came for Chris, too. That nearly killed Joni, eight thousand miles away, as her daughter struggled alone, no mother, no father, no sister.

Val was the one who picked up the phone and told Chris to get on a plane and join her mother in Bali where they could sit out the worst of it together. Then she advised Joni to hire a lawyer and work with a publicist. Maris O'Connor built a legal scaffolding around Joni, doing all the right things at the right time. Candy Sonnenfeld swooped in, reshaped the story, and generally kept the wolves at bay. And Blair jumped in with social media posts that beat the drum of Joni's innocence.

Post by post, tweet by tweet, Blair hit home runs for Joni.

She declared herself a feminist for the first time in public.

She aired and deconstructed the sins of Paul Lovett from a perch of knowingness as his longtime assistant.

She became a voice of reason as to why a scumbag like him would kill himself.

She gave ballast to the reality of how someone so close to a predator (Joni) could be so thoroughly fooled.

Then, after Dallas Miller's article came out in *Vanity Fair*—making a strong case for disbelief that a husband could hide all that from a wife in a marriage of their duration, that anyone blind enough to live with a monster would understandably be enraged enough to kill him when she finally opened her eyes—Blair tweeted a lengthy cri de coeur that knocked Miller's argument to its knees. The tweet went viral as people, mostly women, rushed to Joni's defense. There were letters to the editor. The magazine printed an apology and fired Miller, who was also promptly canceled.

Joni remembered how shocked she was to read Miller's article. After evading his requests for an interview, she'd finally spoken with him briefly at Paul's funeral. That was when she planted her seed about the suicide, the seed that multiplied and scattered and flowered. She hadn't reckoned with the strong possibility that Miller, though he spread the seed as she'd hoped, was never himself convinced.

Later, after Joni took the reins of Sunny Day and returned to Malibu, Blair told her something she couldn't have anticipated would one day work so brilliantly in her favor.

When Dallas Miller had first wanted to interview Paul for a feature article about the great man's new studio and how his arrival in New York marked a sea change in the industry, his way in was to befriend Blair. It was an old trick. Assistants were always the key you wanted in your pocket. Her Instagram feed showed where she took her daily runs. It went from there. He didn't treat her like a booty call, and she liked that. She thought they were dating. She thought there was something good happening between them. She got him the interview with Paul, which secured the assignment with the magazine.

She encouraged him to keep trying to interview Joni, as well, after their appointment was canceled—at first, he wanted to interview the great man's wife at home; then, when the scandal broke, he persisted because he thought there might be more there than met the eye.

He was right.

After he finally got to Joni, Dallas Miller ghosted Blair.

"I showed that fucker," Blair told Joni, cheeks pink from the relentless southern California sun. She got him canceled for what he did to her. The byproduct, for Joni, was freedom.

And now? After all that, how much had society really changed? Had history just looped in on itself? Was it back to the inevitable ending for women: be quiet or be destroyed?

Or maybe it wasn't society or history. Maybe Joni was just bitter. Bitter with the dark realities that had surfaced in her marriage. Bitter that, through it all, she became so distorted that she was capable of murder. Bitter that she had to live with herself now, knowing how dangerous she could be to the people she loved. She had wanted to know what it felt like to be a character in a Patricia Highsmith novel, what it felt like to not just imagine but *do* the forbidden deed—and now she knew. In winning her dangerous game she'd also lost by revealing a truth about herself that it still hurt to think about, so she tried not to.

All that had happened a long time ago and she'd moved on, fortified a stronger self, carved out a new career. She was a better person now, a good person; she proved that every day in how she lived her life. The darkness of that time did not need or deserve a second look. She'd put it away. It was resolved. Over. She reminded herself to keep it sealed in the distant past where it belonged. Like her brother, she had grown and changed.

"Why does it bother you, Mom?" Chris asked, closing the door on the disquieting view of Blair and Marc jogging down the hill together. "I mean, really, think about it."

"I don't know if I want to think about it, to be honest," Joni told her daughter. Thinking about it only brought her back to a lifetime of disappointments. Thinking about it felt bad. Thinking about it frightened her. Thinking about it was a waste of time because it didn't change anything.

Anyway, there wasn't that much to think about. Marc was too old for Blair, it was that simple. And Blair could do better than an unemployed, potbellied, middle-aged man like Marc, wonderful though he was now in contrast to the self-absorbed bully of a little brother he used to be.

3

Early Wednesday afternoon, Joni remembered that Val was due back by now. She swiveled away from her laptop, dialed, and clicked speaker. Val answered right away.

"Welcome back!" Joni said.

"Thanks! But can I call you later? We're just making dinner."

The royal *we*. Val and her husband had grown inseparable these past few years, ever since the first lockdown threw them together twenty-four seven. Even now their work remained mostly remote. Their closeness irritated Joni. It was obvious Russ didn't like her. Joni pictured the Williams family in New Jersey, in their newly renovated kitchen with its glowing cabinets and marble countertops. Val's memoir, *Behind the Curtain: Why I Kept One of Hollywood's Worst Secrets*, had been a bestseller and afforded her this new kitchen along with a sense of possibility that grew just as her love of teaching vanished into a suddenly online pandemic classroom and propelled her to Sunny Day and closer to Joni.

"Sure," Joni said.

"Never mind, it's okay. Russ said he'd do it himself."

Big boy, Joni felt like saying, but didn't.

"How was the trip?" Joni asked.

"Remind me why I wanted to shoot in Yakutat."

Joni chuckled. *Yakutat.* "Because you're making an amazing show with incredible locations and backstories."

"We could have built a set."

"Not really." Not if they wanted the full impact of that magical place. Val had brought her production—*Me, Myself and I,* a time travel series about a girl who experienced life in three different centuries—along beautifully so far, on budget and on schedule. Talented as she'd been as an actor, back in the day, her instincts as a producer were impeccable.

"I've been dying to talk to you," Joni said. "You won't believe who's here."

"Who?"

"*Marc.*"

There was a pause. Joni could practically hear Val trying to figure out who she meant; it had been so long since they'd even mentioned Marc, at least a dozen years.

"My brother," Joni jogged her friend's memory.

"You mean Marco? *The* Marco? He's *there?*"

"Yup. He showed up on Friday afternoon. Out of the blue. I didn't recognize him at first."

"He's been there for *six days?*" Every time she'd visited the Ackerman house, back when they were in college, Marc had been a torment.

"Believe it or not, he's actually grown up. He's a decent guy now. It's been nice having him here."

"This is nuts."

"Tell me about it."

"You know what's really weird? Last week I was sure I saw him at one of Zeke's soccer games."

"Marc? In New Jersey? At a kids' soccer game?" Joni laughed.

"Yeah, Russ didn't think it was likely, either."

For once, here was something that Joni and Val's husband could agree on. Val's long habit of claiming she'd spotted someone out and about—an old acquaintance or a celebrity—almost never bore up to reality. It had become a joke, but Val couldn't resist describing these encounters with relish.

The man smiled and looked at Val like she was some random soccer mom who was bothering him. Bothering *them*. The woman beside him—a brown ponytail and full makeup under a lime green baseball cap—was watching a short, muscle-bound, dark-haired boy dribble the ball across the field. "Excuse me," he said, irritated, "but we're trying to watch our son play."

"It's Val, Joni's friend," she tried again. "Come on, Marc. Seriously?"

The woman sighed and looked at Val, then at Marc, her husband—they wore matching gold wedding rings, though hers was drowned out by a second ring with an ostentatious diamond.

"I'm sorry," he said. "I'm not . . ." He pretended he couldn't remember his own name.

"Marc."

"Not Marc." He smiled, and there was the familiar gap in the front teeth. It was definitely him, just older—he had the same ruddy, squarish face, the thick, short beard now speckled with gray, the same brown eyes with that menacing squint that stared you down and made you want to squirm.

"I know you haven't talked to Joni for a long time, but I assume you heard about Paul?"

He shifted forward in the lawn chair and wove his fingers together so both hands made a single fist. "I told you, I'm not him. I guess I've got a look-alike. My name is Arno van der Beek."

Val raised her phone to take a picture of him but stopped when the woman stood up with her hands on her hips. She was short but foreboding, with a gleaming silver fanny pack strapped to her waist. "Will you please give it a rest? We're trying to watch the game." A diamond tennis bracelet that must have cost as much as Val's new kitchen sparkled on not-Marc's wife's wrist.

"Okay." Val slipped her phone into the back pocket of her jeans. "But this is . . ." *Bullshit*, she stopped herself from saying. Across the field, Russ was watching her. She crossed back to join him.

"He didn't seem very friendly," Russ said. The top of his head, where he'd lost a lot of hair, was red from too much sun. Val took the baseball cap from his chair and put it on him.

"He wasn't. He acted like he didn't know me. He says his name is 'Arno' something-Dutch-sounding. Van der Beek." Val laughed loudly, hoping that Marc, *Arno*, would hear her over the noise of the game, that her laughter would irritate him. "What an asshole."

They laughed together when Val finished telling the story.

"Arno van der Beek," Joni chuckled. "Even the old Marc couldn't make that one up."

"You're probably right."

"You might want to find that Arno guy and apologize."

"I feel like such an idiot."

"You're not an idiot."

Russ's voice rose in the background. Val said, "I have to go. Talk later."

"Keep it cool, lady. Love you. See you in New York next week."

"Can't wait."

* * *

Marc dropped them at the airport. Stella was with them and didn't seem to mind when Joni and Chris got out of the car. When Joni turned before going through the revolving door she saw Stella in the front seat, licking Marc's face while he reached his arms around her for a hug. Joni felt reassured that Stella was in good hands. It had worked out well with Marc staying to care for Stella in her own home where she'd be calmer, instead of displacing her to Blair's small studio apartment or asking Blair to stay at the house, a blurring of boundaries that Joni preferred to avoid.

Waiting at the gate with Chris to board their flight to New York, both women bent over their phones, thumbs dancing. Joni texted back and forth with Val. They agreed to meet at Joni's apartment first thing in the morning for coffee.

Joni and Chris made themselves comfortable on the plane, side by side in their roomy business seats. The trip was scheduled to last a little over a week. Sunny Day's East Coast headquarters, at Steiner Studios in the Brooklyn Navy Yard, had been up and running as a hybrid workplace for over a year now. Joni had visited occasionally but she hated occupying what she still thought of as Paul's office with its views of the bustling lot and crowded shelf of awards. Living and working out of the Malibu house had served them well through the worst years of the pandemic. But lately their "remoteness" (which colleague had called it that, stingingly, in a recent meeting?) was becoming harder to sustain. Much as Joni wanted to stay home in Malibu, working remotely and popping over to New York now and then for meetings and reviews, it was time—beyond time—that she parked herself at the studio's Brooklyn headquarters and really got to know everyone there as a 3D human being. If they decided to do post-production for her show in New York, a clear staff favorite in every recent meeting on the subject, they'd have to find a post house that could accommodate them on the soon side. That would be the price of Joni's ambivalence about breaking out of her comfort zone and returning to New York for more than a brief visit. Chris had arranged several post house tours, just in case.

The thought of living in New York again—the scene of the crime—sparked Joni's itch. Wiggling against the seat didn't do it, so she turned her back to Chris and asked, "Please, honey." Her daughter's hand slipped under her shirt, found the spot, and scratched gently with a fingernail. Relief fanned as the itch abated.

"Better, Mom?" Chris asked.

"Yes, but just another minute, please. Scratch harder. Yes, good, good." She wanted Chris to scratch so hard she opened skin, that's what she wanted. Chris scratched a little harder but was too kind to go deep enough to excise the itch. As if anyone could. Joni suspected she was stuck with the discomfort for life and if she was, so be it. She'd earned it or deserved it—maybe both.

4

———————

"Excuse me."

Val turned from the shelf crowded with all kinds of cookies and there she was: the woman from the soccer game. Not-Marc's wife.

"You spoke to my husband a couple of weeks ago at our son's game?" The woman's tone, this time, was cowed, almost questioning, with none of the diamond-bangled hip-handed belligerence of their last encounter when she'd basically ordered Val to *get lost*. Her face was naked and sad and tired.

"Yes, I remember."

"I'm Louisa Singer."

"Val Williams." She offered a hand and the woman, Louisa, held it, in her own sweaty hand, for a moment too long. Val pulled hers away. She took a package of McVitie's biscuits from the shelf and dropped it into her cart. Joni's flight was getting in late that night and Val thought these would be good with morning coffee—Joni always had a sweet tooth when she was jet-lagged. They planned to meet first thing tomorrow, at the company apartment.

"I'm sorry to ambush you like this."

"That's okay. How's . . . Arno?" Val asked because she didn't know what else to say. Marc's look-alike was Arno. Marc was in Malibu, dogsitting Stella.

"Who?" Louisa's rage-stiffened smile, an upside-down frown, sent a shiver through Val. There were dark circles under Louisa's eyes, pupils floating in bloodshot. She tried to laugh, but it didn't work. "I'm sorry, I've been a mess ever since that day."

"No need to apologize to *me*." Val felt an urge to get away from this agitated person and reached for the handle of her cart.

"You called my husband Marc."

"I thought—"

"You thought he was someone named Marc Ackerman."

Had she mentioned Marc's last name at the soccer game? Val wasn't sure. She let go of the cart handle. "That's right."

"I've been looking for you. A friend at the soccer association gave me your info. I was going to ring your bell but when I got there you were driving off."

"You followed me here?"

"I'm sorry."

"You could have called."

"I tried a few times, but you never answered, and your voicemail was full."

Val never answered unknown callers, it was true. But still. She felt stalked. Cornered. She didn't like this. "I'm sorry but I have to go."

"*Please*. I really need to talk." Something in Louisa's tone shifted; she sounded scared. "Now, or some other time? I could give you my number. You could look me up. I swear, I'm not a danger to you."

Val glanced at her cart. "Let me just grab one more thing and I'll pay. We could go next door for tea."

They sat across a tiny round table. Even at this time of day, on a weekday evening in a suburban shopping mall, the café was busy. Val was grateful to be surrounded by people and felt somehow safer than if they'd been alone. Louisa's hand trembled when she pried the plastic lid off her latte, releasing a cloud of steam. Val had opted for chamomile tea since it was getting late and she hoped to sleep that night.

"My husband lied to me," Louisa began. "We were married for eight years, and he lied to me the whole time."

Val nodded. She basically knew what was coming; all she had to do was wait for the details to be filled in. She wanted to grab her phone and warn Joni: *It* was *Marc. He hasn't changed at all. Run for the hills.* But Joni was midair right now.

"We met at the Museum of Modern Art. He told me his name was Arno van der Beek. I had no reason to think that wasn't true."

"Of course not."

"It's such a good name, isn't it?" Louisa smiled wistfully as if hearing it for the first time again. "I mean, who could make that up?"

"The Marc I knew could have."

"In retrospect, it should have been a red flag."

"Everything's clear in hindsight," Val said. "That's the problem most of the time, isn't it?"

Louisa sighed. "You knew it was him the minute you saw him."

"Yup," Val said. "But hey, he was convincing—he even convinced me. When I walked away that day I was angry, but when I calmed down I figured I'd made a mistake." Val recalled how Russ dismissed her. How when Joni laughed at her she felt so stupid.

"It's his confidence," Louisa said. "He's a con man. That's what my lawyer told me. He's seen it before. And my private investigator—"

Val leaned forward, buzzed by a sensation she couldn't interpret yet: worry, excitement, something else. She said nothing, just listened as Louisa told her story.

* * *

Louisa Flores Singer turned forty less than a year after her divorce from Marshall Singer. He'd been unfaithful, she couldn't bear it, their marriage of sixteen years ended, and she came away with an abundant divorce settlement thanks to her husband's success as a commercial real estate developer. Marshall moved to Manhattan. Louisa stayed behind with their six-year-old son, Lawrence, in the Colts Neck house.

Well, *house*. There were three floors, eleven bedrooms, two servants' suites, a pool, and a tennis court. They couldn't see or hear their neighbors through the dense woods surrounding their enclave. No one could get through their front gate without permission, to protect both their privacy and their world-class art collection. The size, amenities, and remoteness of the house seemed ideal at first; Louisa's plan was to fill it with a big family. But she never got pregnant a second time. And now Marshall was gone. Eventually, after the divorce was final, he admitted that he'd had a vasectomy soon after Lawrence was born.

In the weeks after Marshall left, Louisa took a part-time job at a gift shop in town just to get out of the house, which had started to feel like an echo chamber of loss and disappointment. One by one, her local friends, all parents from Lawrence's private school, abandoned her. Marshall was a better bet; he threw great parties and the invitations from his Upper East Side penthouse had already started to arrive. Meantime, in Colts Neck, housekeeper Elfrieda and nanny Rose, both of whom lived-in, held down the fort.

With Marshall gone, Louisa often absent, and a six-year-old child whose life needed to be arranged and, more importantly, lived, the two women began to run the house like an entrepreneurial enterprise upon which they unleashed their creative energies. Louisa was grateful at first. But later, having lost control of her marriage and now her environment and her son's schedule and even, she worried, his affection, she realized she'd made a mistake taking her hand off her life's only remaining rudders. Motherhood. Home. She fired the two women, brought in some part-time help, and devoted herself to her new life as a single parent. Except for biweekly weekends with his father, Lawrence loved having Louisa all to himself. But she was lonely, and forty loomed.

She first saw Arno van der Beek standing in contemplative repose in front of Jackson Pollock's *One*, an enormous canvas of black-and-white chaos on a dull beige canvas that felt, unnervingly, like a reflection of her own inner life right after Marshall left. Something about the gravity of the man's gaze made her feel seen and understood. She was immediately drawn to him. He struck her as grounded, intelligent, insightful, attractive.

In their final argument, that bitter hour when he transformed from Arno to Marc, he admitted that when she stood next to him in front of the painting, the first thing he'd noticed was her diamond earrings. He knew they were real, just looking at them: three-carat studs set in platinum. Her jeans, sneakers, and leather jacket were also expensive. A young boy held her hand: She was a mother. There was no wedding ring.

When he smiled at her, she knew he was also interested. A wave of questions rushed over her: Was he married, was he single, did he have children, did he *want* children, what did he do, where did he live?

In the whirlwind weeks that followed, she learned all the answers, and each one felled a potential obstacle. He was about her age, single—once engaged but never married—with no children but a yearning for a big family. He was an independently wealthy investor who, having recently sold his apartment faster than expected, lived alone in a temporary sublet—subpar, but it belonged to a friend away on sabbatical, thus making for an easy transition as he searched for a new place. His requirement of outdoor space narrowed the possibilities and slowed the search.

He got it—and more.

Arno moved into the Colts Neck house six months later. They married in a small ceremony beside the pool. He bonded with Lawrence, and they became a family. They tried to get pregnant right away, but to Louisa's disappointment, it never happened. Eventually, she would learn that he'd known all along he was infertile.

The night after Val approached them at the soccer game, Louisa brought up the awkward encounter. Wasn't it strange how sure the woman was that he was someone else? Were look-alikes really a thing? Could two people ever resemble each other that closely? Arno discounted the woman as "crazy," and a bell went off in Louisa. The woman had been energized but not crazy. By then, Louisa knew her husband well enough to sense that he was avoiding something. The less he wanted to discuss it, the more she needed to. Finally, he admitted that Arno van der Beek wasn't his real name.

"There's still plenty I don't know," Louisa told Val. "But the fake name, that was all I needed to hear. Our marriage fell apart like *that*." She snapped her fingers. "Like it was spun from sugar. It just collapsed."

"Jesus." Val was shocked but not surprised. This was Marc they were talking about, Marco, Maximillian. Maybe he *had* changed; maybe he was even worse than he used to be.

"He married me for money. He isn't who he said he was—I don't know who he is. We can't find much of anything on him. It's been a nightmare. I can't sleep anymore. I can hardly function. My son is drifting away . . . he spends every weekend with his father now, by choice."

"This is awful." Val leaned forward and asked, "So, how much did he steal?" hoping the damage wasn't too bad.

"He can't get at my money—not much of it, anyway. When we got married my lawyers made sure he only had access to one joint account and my accountant never kept that much in it." She shook her head. "It pissed me off at first. Made me feel so controlled. But now I'm grateful."

"I bet."

"I need to serve Arno, whoever, divorce papers—but I can't find him. My investigator can't find him. It's like he just disappeared—his phone number, his email, nothing reaches him anymore. That's why I hoped to talk to you."

"I understand."

"Do you have any idea how to reach him? Or that other person you mentioned at the game that day; I can't remember the name. It was a woman's name, I think."

Val answered, "His sister—" then stopped herself. She wasn't sure how much to share. The situation felt complicated and before she said too much she needed to speak with Joni. Joni and Marc had grown close recently, and she'd likely want to give her brother a chance to defend himself. Maybe his side of the story would be just as disturbing; maybe he'd run from Louisa for a reason.

But.

That malicious boy Marc/Marco/Max flashed in Val's memory, and her suspended disbelief buckled. Of course what Louisa said was true.

But.

Val thought of Russ, her good husband, who always stood up for the men who had been wrongly accused. In recent years, so many men had been thrown under the bus without a chance to offer a nuanced explanation that it was—well, it was noisy with indignant cries in the bowels of hell.

"Sister?" Louisa repeated. "He told me he had no one, no family. He said he was . . . Just listen to me. What an idiot. Like anything he ever said to me was even a little bit true. I'll never trust another man. I've had it." Her eyes closed and her mouth tightened, her face cinching like the knot of a balloon, puckered around all that bursting hurt.

Gently, Val asked, "Did you have him sign a prenup before you got married?" At least then the damage would be limited.

Louisa shook her head almost imperceptibly as if she hoped not to be noticed. "I couldn't bring myself to ask him. That's why my lawyer and accountant clamped down so hard on the other stuff." Louisa felt ashamed; Val saw it: the waves of self-blame radiating off this poor (rich) woman who'd been love-bombed and scammed. Not scammed but robbed, robbed in the flesh, *of* the flesh. She'd loved him, slept with him, married him, let him parent her child.

"This sister," Louisa said. "Would she know where he is? All I want is to find him and get this over with."

5

———————

As soon as they landed in New York Joni's phone lit up with texts.

Blair was feverish with Covid and was isolating in her apartment.

And Val had texted several times before giving up.

I need to talk to you. Call me if it's not too late when you get there.

It's eleven. I'm still up.

It's midnight. I'm going to sleep. See you in the morning—I might get there a little early. We really need to talk.

Joni texted Val back but knew that she wouldn't see it until the next day. No matter. If it was an emergency, she would have waited up.

It was two in the morning when Joni and Chris stepped out of an Uber in front of the gold awning on Henry Street in Cobble Hill. Sunny Day kept an apartment in one of the modern towers sprouting up everywhere to the dismay of locals and the delight of real estate developers. It was meant to be a base for both staff and company visitors—but mostly it was Joni's apartment, much as the nearby Vinegar Hill mansion she'd shared with Paul had been a business property as well as their home. The building had an in-ground pool that was a rare amenity in New York City; it was one of the things that had sold

Joni on the place. Plus, it was fairly close to the Brooklyn Navy Yard and Steiner Studios where Sunny Day was based. The pool was only one of the unusual amenities that had drawn her to the building: There was also an in-house doggie daycare, so Stella wouldn't have to be left alone if Joni had a busy day and couldn't bring her along. She felt a sharp pang of missing Stella; she hated to be away from her sweet pup.

The marble lobby was quiet, with just Billy, the night doorman, behind the desk.

"Long time, Mrs. Ackerman," Billy greeted her. He'd always called her that, and she never corrected him. Joni hadn't liked being called Mrs. Lovett back when she was married, but that wasn't Billy's problem.

"How's the baby?" Joni asked.

"Walking like a champ!" He smiled.

"Hey, Billy," Chris said as they passed him on the way to the elevator. "Just got off the plane and totally wiped out but I want to see pictures tomorrow, okay?"

"You bet. Sleep tight, ladies."

Just as the elevator doors were about to close, a man jammed in a red sneaker to stop them. The doors cranked back open and in walked an older man in jeans and a down jacket. He was striking, with his lush silver hair and bright blue eyes. Chris must have noticed Joni noticing because she leaned against her mother and surreptitiously winked. Lately Chris had been urging Joni to date or, as she put it, "Get out there again." Out there. *No thanks*. Again. *No way*. The mere thought of it made Joni panic.

The man eyed their luggage. "Arriving?" He had a nice, deep voice.

Genius guess, Joni almost quipped but stopped herself. "Just flew in from LA," she answered politely.

"That's a long flight, as I recall. I haven't been on a plane since before the pandemic."

"Were you here the whole time?" Chris asked. It was a fair question; everyone knew the legends of early-lockdown New York City when it was the ghoulish epicenter of a terrifying new disease.

He nodded. "Not in this building, of course." The building was new; it only opened a year ago. "But in the neighborhood." The elevator stopped at the eighth floor and, again, he held the door open with his foot long enough to say, "Nice to meet you. I'm Griff."

"Joni," she reciprocated. "And Chris."

"Sisters?" A glint in his eyes.

"Ha!"

"See you around." He smiled and the elevator doors sealed them in.

"He's cute," Chris said.

"You can have him."

"Not for me—for you."

"Now you're my pimp?"

"I'm your yenta."

"Good luck with that."

The elevator dinged when it reached the top floor. The doors slid open on to a small foyer and a single door with a brass sign stamped Penthouse. They hauled in their luggage, and there it was, just beyond the sliding glass panels that separated one whole wall of the spacious white living room from a broad terrace: lower Manhattan shimmering in the night like stacks of jewels.

It was almost ten when Joni opened her eyes. She'd slept right through her alarm after lying in bed for hours before sleep came, wired from the flight, restless, overheated. Once she cracked a window to let in some air, she'd finally relaxed.

Waking up now, groggy, she forced her eyes to stay open by staring at the white rectangles of the window shades. Occasional sharp breezes pulsed the shade over the open window: *Get the hell out of bed, don't waste a minute, go, go, go.* Yes, she was back in New York City. She'd only stayed in this new apartment once before; she tried to recall the view from the master bedroom but couldn't. She got up, pressed a button, and both shades rolled up simultaneously.

A blue sky mottled with thin clouds. The Statue of Liberty. The southern tip of Manhattan. A ferry slicing through the river toward Governors Island. A helicopter circling down. A sailboat, a speedboat, a canoe.

Mornings in New York were crisp and clear, and they beckoned you, unlike the lemony, sweet mornings back home in California that tricked you into thinking you had all the time in the world. Ironically, in Malibu, she was always up early and got more done before noon than she did when she was in New York with all its distractions. There was a bluster about the energy here. Out west, she was propelled from a quiet place deep within herself and moved forward with a steady ease.

She heard voices in the living room: Chris and Val. And she smelled coffee. Val had kept her promise and arrived earlier than their ten-thirty appointment.

Joni pulled herself together quickly and emerged barefoot with a big smile and her arms wide to greet her friend.

Val. There she was. More brightly blond in person, having recently decided to color her shoulder-length hair, erasing all those lovely strands of silver. And she was wearing makeup—why? What could she conceal that Joni hadn't already seen on that deeply familiar face?

They hugged. Val was slightly taller, allowing Joni to nestle her face into her old friend's soft neck. She smelled like herself: like laundry and breakfast and memory.

Val pulled away so she could look directly into Joni's eyes.

Joni knew right away that something was wrong. "What is it?"

"Sit down," Val ordered. "I have to tell you something."

Joni looked at Chris, who shrugged—she had no idea what this was about. "I'll get you some coffee, Mom."

A plate of digestive biscuits waited on the table. Joni let the steam from the hot coffee warm her face a moment before taking a first sip.

"Brace yourselves," Val said, and told them everything.

6

_____

Chris and Val sat across the table from Joni so she could FaceTime Marc as if alone. She worried that if they were all on-screen together, he'd shut the conversation down immediately. She tried to stay calm but she was nearly shaking with rage as the call rang through.

The moment he answered with a bright hello, Stella jumped onto the couch beside him and copiously licked his face. Who had paid for the iPad he was using? For the pricey diver's watch he could wear "in the shower, isn't that incredible?" For the high-end running shoes? For that new suitcase he'd rolled in two weeks ago on a wave of hot air? Details that had seemed innocuous or even charming now flashed like warning lights. He'd been paying for some of their groceries, a gesture Joni appreciated even if it wasn't necessary—but with whose money? The new Marc, who'd developed like a shiny new skin over the despicable old Marc, shimmered a moment and went poof.

"We need to talk," Joni told him.

She saw a flicker in his eyes, a recognition that something had changed.

"I was just about to head out for a run," he claimed. But he never ran without Blair; Blair was why he ran, obviously.

"Hang back a minute," she insisted.

He glanced at his chunky black watch. They both knew he had nowhere to be.

"Louisa Singer," Joni said.

He looked at her impassively as if that name meant nothing.

"Lawrence Singer."

His jaw tensed. He leaned slightly forward, as if to stand up, but didn't.

"Colts Neck, New Jersey."

He sat back and folded his arms over his belly, which, she noticed only now, had shrunk since he'd first arrived.

"What is this, Joni?"

"You tell me."

"Who did you talk to?"

"Why does it matter? I can't believe it, Marc. You marched into my house like you'd changed but all you've done is lie to us."

"Okay, okay, but my life has been really complicated, I needed to get away and think, figure stuff out. I never meant to lie to you. They weren't lies. They were—"

"Shut up. You lied."

"What I mean is I didn't want to hurt you guys. I didn't want to lie. I just needed time to think things through on my own, without, you know, any interference. I wanted—I want—to come to a clear decision on my own, without anyone's feedback. So I kept things simple. But they're not simple; they're anything but."

"Decision about what, Marc?"

He crossed his legs. With his arms folded, he looked like knotted yarn, like a tangle of his own poor knitting. Looking at him like that, Joni felt a pang of sympathy. Her brother had always been his own worst enemy. To get to his age and still be twisted up in himself was really sad.

"Talk to me. I'm listening." She would hear him out before she gave him the boot. Anyone deserved that.

He gathered himself like picking up items from a dropped bag: back straightened, knees aligned, hands folded on lap, a deep breath in and out. "I am married. I told you I'm not, but I am. And I have a stepson. And we live in New Jersey." With each admission, the sweat stains under his arms spread farther down the sides of his T-shirt.

"And you called yourself Arno van der Beek." One side of her mouth crooked up a moment before she forced it back to neutral. "Don't leave that out."

Color rushed to his cheeks. "God, I regret that," he said. "It was stupid. When Louisa and I met, I had no idea it would turn into something. I thought I'd have some fun, like I used to, and she really liked that name; I could tell the minute I said it. So I stuck with it. It got to the point where there was no turning back."

"You got married under a false name. Isn't that illegal?"

"Nope." He repressed the glimmer of a nascent smile. "You marry a person, not a name."

He'd researched it. She was appalled. "How did you get a marriage license?"

"I had some ID made so I could, you know, be Arno." He'd *prepared*.

"Fake ID."

"Yeah."

"Like some idiot teenager." She glared at him. It was worse than that. A regular person of any age wouldn't have been capable of doing what he'd done.

The red in his face burned brighter. "Joni, I know I've always been an asshole. I can't get out of my own way. It's been one stupid mistake after another my whole life. I wish you could understand how embarrassed I am."

"Why didn't you just tell her right away? She might have understood."

"Louisa? I doubt it. She's the most reactive person I've ever known. She's intense. I liked that about her. She had all this energy, and she was fun. I fell in love with her. And if she knew my real name, she'd have googled me and found out I was a big nothing. I was broke. I wasn't sure what I was going to do. That's why I went to the museum when we met, because I needed to get my mind off how I was going to pay my rent."

He would have been in his forties by then. The thought of being that unmoored at that age made Joni even sadder. She wondered if he really had worked on a cruise ship or if that, too, was a lie. She asked, "What happened? Did you lose your job?"

"What job?"

"Oh no."

He nodded sheepishly.

"Marc, please don't tell me you lived on the inheritance all those years." He was only twenty when their parents died together, asleep in their bed, in a carbon monoxide leak. All their assets—house, car, retirement funds, investments, life insurance policies—were liquidated and divided between the two siblings. Joni had used hers to finance her first film. Until now, she'd never known what Marc had done with his.

"Guilty as charged."

"It wasn't enough to live on forever."

"I found that out."

"Oh, Marc."

"Yeah, like I said, I'm an idiot."

"You're not an idiot. You're just—"

"A fool."

She smiled. "You *are* a fool."

They both laughed but there was no joy in it. He was right. He'd made a series of bad choices. He'd done nothing with his life. It had to feel awful to be him.

"Louisa filed for divorce," Joni told him.

He winced. "That was quick. But I get it. Okay. Okay."

"She can't find you. You ghosted her, she says. She needs an address to send the papers. Should I give it to her?"

"Doesn't she have it? Doesn't she know I'm at your place? You're not exactly hard to find."

"She doesn't know you're there. She's been talking to Val. No one's told Louisa anything yet."

"I'll call her," he said. "I'll tell her where I am."

"Really?"

He nodded, ashamed and serious, and said, "I will."

Across the table, Val was shaking her head; she didn't believe him. But Joni was determined to give her brother the benefit of the doubt, however slim, until she heard the entire story. She knew in that moment that she had to meet Louisa in person, to see her and hear her out. Then she'd decide who to believe.

"I can pack up and leave tonight," he offered. "But what about Stella?"

Blair was in Covid isolation, sick with a fever, and it was well known that pets could catch the virus from people. She'd have to think of someone else to ask or find someplace for Stella to board at a kennel, which Stella hated. The problem was that Stella was notoriously fussy about who she was willing to be left with; she trusted the people she already knew but with most others she became a barking machine no one could tolerate. That she'd accepted Marc so easily had been kind of a miracle.

"I'm not sure," Joni said. "Do you have somewhere to go?"

"No, but I'll work something out."

How? He was broke. He had no job. He was still her shithead brother—not that man who she'd imagined in a haze of wishful thinking had actually grown up to become someone else.

"Stay there for now," she relented. "Blair's sick but as soon as she's better she can take Stella. By then you'll have arranged something else. Right?"

"Yes. Thank you. I don't deserve you."

"No, you don't."

After the call, Val and Chris, released from silence, burst into talk. But Joni's mind was too crowded to think clearly. Stella, Marc, and a woman in Colts Neck angling to serve her ridiculous brother with divorce papers and nail him to a cross if she could. He deserved to be nailed up . . . but was it Joni's job to deliver him?

"I want to meet Louisa," Joni said. "I need to hear her side."

"Right," Chris agreed. "That's a good idea."

"I have her number," Val said. "Should I call her now?"

"Hold on." Chris clicked open the calendar on her laptop. "The calendar's pretty packed. We're at Steiner Studios this afternoon to meet with staff, drinks tonight with . . ." Their busy schedule went all the way through an end-of-the-week dinner meeting. "So, Mom," Chris concluded, "you and I are pretty busy through Friday."

"Then I'll reach out to Louisa Singer for a Saturday meet or Sunday if she can't do Saturday," Val said. "Does that work?"

Joni nodded. "Either day is fine."

"We'll do it near my house, "Val announced. "And then both of you are coming over afterward for dinner. Period. No arguments."

"Am I meeting with Louisa, too?" Chris tucked her hair behind her ear with its trio of gold hoops ascending the lobe. "I'm not sure I want to."

"Up to you," Joni said. Chris was clearly reluctant to give up the bond she'd formed with her long-lost uncle, and Joni didn't blame her.

Val nodded. "She's a little high-strung, so it's probably best if it's just me and your mom, anyway," she told Chris. "You can hang at my house. Wait till you see Zeke. He's so tall!"

"I hope he doesn't think he can beat me at basketball now," Chris said.

"I'm sure he thinks he can beat you."

The women shared a smile, remembering Zeke before his most recent growth spurt, more effort than skill on the driveway court.

"Okay." Chris steered them back to business. "So now, looking to next week . . ."

Luckily Chris was an excellent planner. Joni couldn't concentrate. Stella. Oh, Stella. How could her Stella be old enough for heart disease? Why was she in California when Joni was in New York? How could Marc have lied to her? Why had she believed he'd changed?

The rest of the morning was spent on the welcome distraction of tweaking the wish list of all they hoped to accomplish during their stay in New York. There were new staff to meet. Old staff to catch up with. A meeting with the company's CTO to address technology upgrades. The following week would be devoted to familiarizing Joni and Chris with all the East Coast productions—there were four in progress and two about to start—and also pinning down post plans for *Hear Me Out*. The way Chris talked about it reminded Joni of her daughter's determination to accommodate the majority of staff who wanted to stay east. Joni was proud of her daughter, who was a good manager and learning to be a thoughtful leader.

"Lunch?" Joni asked Val when they were done with the calendar. There was so much to unpack about Marc, Louisa, everything. Joni needed to process it all. And she needed to vent—she needed to talk with Irene, her therapist. A quick text exchange set an appointment for that evening.

"Sure. Then I'll drive us to the Navy Yard."

"We can grab an Uber." Joni didn't want to inconvenience Val, who had already sacrificed half a work-from-home day to greet them in person after their long separation.

"No need. I'm going anyway. Since I'm here, I'll check in with my crew. We've got a shoot tomorrow, so."

"Sounds good." Joni stepped close to Val and couldn't resist touching the bright hair. "So pretty."

"Not too yellow?"

"It's perfect."

"You don't like it."

When did Val become insecure?

"I love it." But Joni didn't like it. She wished Val could relax into her age. Her own hair had turned silver at the temples. She gathered it in her hands and pulled it back to show Val. "Check out my racing stripes."

Val said, "I wish I had the courage."

"It's not courage, trust me." But it was courage, the kind when you stood on a cliff and decided to let the wind just blow you. Since the moment she tipped the antifreeze into Paul's cocktail she'd embraced a new kind of recklessness she would have hated to see form in anyone else. If this was courage, it had been honed on a sharp inner blade that lingered. Sometimes Joni wondered if anyone was safe around her, even the people she loved the most. But she worked hard to push against that thought. What happened to Paul, what she did to him, was an anomaly. She was a good person. She could be a good person. She just had to keep reminding herself that it was a choice.

"I really do love your hair," Joni said a little too insistently.

The way Val looked at her, without smiling, was like the moment you realized you'd just drunk curdled milk, but it was too late. So you swallowed.

7

After lunch Val drove Joni and Chris to the Navy Yard's massive complex that hulked on the edge of Wallabout Bay, a bend in the East River that had been the site of a shipyard for nearly two hundred years. In its modern iteration the Navy Yard was a bustling creative and technology hub and housed the biggest movie studio outside Hollywood. They parked in one of the spaces designated for Sunny Day.

As they stepped out of the car into the crisp spring afternoon, Val realized that she had mixed feelings about Joni spending more time here, and it surprised her to feel that way. Joni had a lot of emotional baggage and helping her carry it could be exhausting. There was always so much to "process." Well, now Val had something to process: the way, last week, Joni had automatically assumed that Val had imagined seeing Marc at that soccer game. Joni and Russ hated each other but they always united on laughing at Val's reports of sightings in the wild. No one was laughing now. They should have listened to her. Joni, especially, should have listened to her and confronted Marc before she left for New York . . . before she left her sweet dog in the care of that awful man. And there was also this: Joni was the boss. They were no longer equals. Val loved her new career as a producer but sometimes she wasn't sure she'd made the right decision to work for her friend. No, *with* her friend. *No*, for her friend.

They parted ways with kisses and promises to touch base when Val heard back from Louisa Singer about meeting that weekend, then they headed in opposite directions. Since she was here, she decided to drop in on the cyclorama stage *Me, Myself and I* had booked for tomorrow. If she was lucky, it wouldn't be in use today and she could see with her own eyes that there wasn't a single nick or scratch in the paint, otherwise the visual effects editor would be faced with unnecessary challenges. Cyc shoots tended to be fun at first but quickly became tedious. The background, green in this case, fused floor and walls, and everyone who ever worked on one started off charmed by antigravity play. Once the magic wore off it was just work. The lead actor, Nadia, who was only twelve, had been a pleasure to work with and Val was sure she'd have a ball. But her mother, Esther, was another story. Val had made it her business to go above and beyond to circumvent potential problems before they occurred to ETR—Esther the Relentless—as they'd privately dubbed her.

Val stepped through the door to Stage 11 and was disappointed to find that the cyc stage was in use. A man in tap shoes, smiling and holding a toothbrush, danced across the field of green to bouncy jazz. She'd have to send someone over late tonight to make sure the repainting was thorough.

On her way to the *MMI* production office her mind kept going back to Joni's comment about her hair—she obviously hated it.

Val had been to the colorist yesterday because she was excited to see Joni and wanted to look her best. The color had come out a little too bright, too yellow. Val knew it and wished Joni had just said so the way she would have when they were young. As the years piled on, as secrets deepened and understandings grew obtuse, it had become harder to be straightforward with each other. Joni probably thought Val was trying too hard to look young but was afraid to say it.

Val had been thinking a lot about that lately, how she didn't want to worry about getting older, and yet she did. Val was five years older than Russ and, truth be told, the closer she got to sixty the more it worried her that he'd look at her one day and see an old woman. For Joni the decision to age gracefully was conceptual: She was "intentionally single" and "past men," or "beyond men," or "finished with men," or however she described herself on any given day. Empowered. Enabled. Free. Just that morning when Chris told Val about the cute guy in the elevator and Val asked if Joni had seemed interested, Chris rolled her eyes and quoted her mother: "Not going there." Well. It was probably true that being single was a form of freedom. "Racing stripes." Huh. Joni could glance at a mirror and not wonder what the person she slept with saw when he looked at her. Val didn't have that luxury. So she colored her hair. So what?

What did Joni know about good marriages, anyway, when hers had been such a disaster? Val couldn't truly fathom what it must have been like to be married to Paul. That horrible man.

Her skin crawled when she thought of him, what he did to her thirty years ago—to Val, drugging her, participating in the attack she slept through (was that *sleep*?) when they were all young and new to Hollywood. It still confounded her how deeply memories could be buried and how they could spring at you so suddenly. How, years later, a red carpet shot of shining, successful Paul Lovett could trigger a dormant memory, and she knew. She knew. She knew that one of the men who'd raped her had gone on to marry her best friend. What a horrible moment that recognition had been, that plunge into a part of herself she'd closed off. Her desire to tell Joni. The attempts that faltered. Her decision, after little Alex was hit by a car, that it was too late—she couldn't level another blow on her already devastated friend.

And the way Joni snapped when she found out. Did she snap? Or was it really a coincidence that Paul died the same night?

Poor Joni. She survived that marriage, at least. Paul didn't. Another thing Val couldn't understand about Joni was how a person could bring themselves to kill someone. A wife to kill her husband. If that's what Joni did. To this day, Val wasn't sure. She'd never brought it up because she didn't really want to know. Sometimes she sensed that Joni wanted to talk about it, but she couldn't tell. It was up to Joni to bring it up because once that Pandora's box was opened there'd be no closing it. That box of snakes was Joni's box to open, not hers.

Val had been aware, back when she asked Joni to bring her into Sunny Day, how packed with resonance that choice would be for both of them. She'd toggled between thinking it was a bad idea and a good one. She'd be working in the company founded by her rapist—how macabre. But then again, she was the only person who knew—did she know?—how that monster really died. Joni would fear her, and that fear would allow Val more creative agency than she'd have anywhere else.

So her hair had come out a little too yellow. So what? Joni shouldn't have said anything; that was unkind.

Passing through the bustling lobby to the elevator bank, Val smelled the sweet warmth of her favorite almond croissants. Damn that bakery, setting up on her route to the office. She sidetracked to pick up half a dozen for her team upstairs. Her thoughts turned to the catering for tomorrow's shoot: Had she reviewed the final menu? ETR had recently announced that she didn't want Nadia eating sugar on set.

Val's phone shivered, and she looked at it: Louisa Singer was free on Saturday at noon. Good. Joni had her appointment. She asked and she received, as usual. The key was to keep her boss-friend happy because Joni on a rocking boat was, well. Let's just say that you tested her at your own risk.

8

"We gaslight ourselves all the time," Irene said, floating in her square on the monitor, in response to Joni's anger at herself for having bought Marc's lies when she knew he was a liar.

Irene was young, maybe, or maybe she wasn't. Her round Black face was broad and friendly and open, with big green eyes, smooth skin, and a quick smile. She paid close attention, always. If not for the flecks of gray in her pulled-back hair, Joni might have guessed she was Chris's age. The gray added ten years, maybe twenty. Back when they first worked together, at the start of the pandemic, Joni had stopped trying to guess her age. She was just Irene, wonderful, warm, wise Irene.

"The difference between gaslighting ourselves and other people gaslighting us is that once we catch ourselves doing it, we can stop. We do stop. We improve. Recognition is forever. Other people, we can't control."

"Thanks for reminding me of that," Joni answered. "I cut Marc off years ago because I understood that about him. I guess time made me soft."

"Soft is good." That bright smile. "Soft is human."

They'd talked a lot about that: being human in relationships with a gaslighter. That you can't control the other person; what you can do is name the lies, "See what you see," in Irene's words, and walk away.

Joni had walked away from Marc before, and she could do it again.

"I imagine this must resonate," Irene ventured, "with your feelings about Paul."

"Uh, yeah—but I think the word here is detonate."

Irene laughed. Joni loved making her laugh.

They'd spent a lot of time in their sessions on why Joni had taken so long to recognize her husband for the predator he was. How she didn't see it until it was presented to her in hard, cold facts. How she didn't have the chance to make the choice to walk away because Paul died first. But the deep, dark truth of it was that she could have walked away but she made a different, crucial choice. She lost herself in her anger and her rage and she . . .

Irene interrupted Joni's spiraling thoughts: "Dealing with grief, especially in the first year or so, can be like a hall of mirrors. Old stuff comes back, front and center, looking bigger than it really is. It's the same as PTSD; it *is* PTSD. It's just your mind playing tricks. It'll do that to you."

"But it's been *five years*." It still amazed Joni how powerful the feelings were when they reared up. His death, she accepted. But her role in it had claws that only got sharper and when that hand gripped her, it gripped hard.

"Even years later it'll pop up. I'm here to remind you not to pay it too much mind when it does."

"Paying mind" was something else Irene talked about a lot. "When you pay mind, you add value," she'd explained in a long-ago session.

"Value to what?" Joni had asked.

"Whatever it is. Fear. Anxiety. In your case, grief, guilt. Because Paul fell down the stairs when you were asleep."

Guilt. That was the stickler every time this came up, and it came up a lot. That wasn't exactly how it had happened, but how could Joni explain it to Irene without ending up in prison? Right after the party that night, she'd passed out the moment her body hit the mattress. When she found Paul on the stairs the next morning, she immediately knew why he'd lost his balance. She knew. The first thing she did before she called the police was clean up the evidence. Joni wished she could share all that with Irene. She felt awful that she had to misdirect, deceive, gaslight her own therapist when they talked about the thing that troubled her the most—the gem of violence she'd discovered within herself, discovered and excavated, cut, and polished. Her choice to weaponize it against her husband. To kill him. That was her choice. That was who she was—who she chose to be. That was what animated her gnawing guilt. It was what she needed to talk about and what she couldn't talk about and so, as usual, she talked around it.

"If I hadn't gone to bed first," Joni said, "maybe he wouldn't have killed himself." That was the party line in a nutshell. Joni had stuck to it through the press-scandalized year in Bali and ever since. It was the corner she'd superglued herself into the moment the police arrived at the house alongside the ambulance: shocked, remorseful, clueless widow.

"Maybe. Maybe not. You can't know that."

"Right." Wrong. Joni did know that. She remembered thinking, in the morning, sober: *What have I done?*

"If staying up with him that night might have stopped him from drinking the antifreeze, it might not have stopped him the next day. In fact, he might have been more determined in the light of morning when the truth of what was about to happen to him really sank in."

"True." Not true. Paul had no shame. When the news hit and the scandal broke, he would have fought back. He would have hated every minute of it but he would have done everything in his power to win the argument, in public opinion and in court, that he'd never teamed up with one of Hollywood's most notorious predators to drug and attack women. That he'd buried his crimes so deeply in his past that even his wife and his surviving child never knew. Joni felt certain that by the time he had wanted to kill himself it would have been too late; he'd have been locked up by then, dethroned and defanged, alone in a cell.

"Repeat after me," Irene said: "I am not responsible for my husband's suicide."

Joni sucked in a breath. It was not the first time Irene had required this of her and she hated it. "I am not responsible for my husband's suicide."

"Exactly. *That* he died and *how* he died. While you were asleep in bed, not there to prevent it or help him. You're human, Joni. It's very clear to me from everything you've said here that you would have helped him if there was any way. Then you would have followed through on your decision and ended the marriage. His death was not your fault."

"Right."

"No one holds you responsible for any of that. You're not responsible for that. Say it again."

"Really?"

Irene nodded.

"Okay, I'm not responsible for that."

"For what?"

"For Paul dying."

"What else?"

"For his crimes."

"Good."

There had been moments when Joni considered telling Irene everything: how she'd succumbed to her rage, how she'd imagined herself a character in a Highsmith novel and fantasized about killing Paul and methodically planned it and actually (drunkenly) done it.

Then she could also explain that only Val knew the truth, or might know—it was unclear what exactly Val understood about how Paul had died—and that it was causing a frisson in their friendship. That for the past five years it had been a sword of Damocles hanging over Joni's head.

But she didn't tell Irene. She couldn't. She stuck to the under-belly of those things, the grief and guilt but not the remorse for having done such a terrible thing; the fear and anxiety but not the real consequences she'd face if Val ever made her suspicions public. Irene was great, and therapy was helpful, but it could only go so far if Joni couldn't be honest, and how could she be? Val was the only one she could conceivably talk to about what happened, but in the years since Paul died they hadn't openly discussed it even once. It was *the* hot potato. Neither of them wanted to touch it so they let it hover between them, radiating hazard.

Joni wanted so much to dig into her guilt and remorse in therapy, but she could only scratch the surface. The first time it had occurred to her in those terms she'd thought, *Oh, shit.* Her itch first appeared in Bali, the year she hid from the law, the press, the world, herself. The itch that couldn't be reached and wouldn't go away. The itch no one could see.

Discussing Marc was easier because Joni had no secrets about him. Marc was the conniver, full of his own secrets. And now, with his latest veil having been pulled back, the session had a focus that was new, concrete.

"I'm just so disappointed," Joni said to Irene. "It makes me feel foolish that I believed him. When he first showed up, it took him like ten minutes to get me to let my guard down. I was actually willing to believe that he'd lived all those years we were apart as a bachelor working on a cruise ship. I actually believed he'd become a decent man."

"Guess that wouldn't take much since your bar for him was pretty low."

"Growing up, he was an asshole and a loser, as far as I was concerned."

Irene frowned slightly. "How would you describe him, back then, if you used other words?"

Joni cringed. She'd been judgmental and "in the room" you were expected to channel your best self. She felt a stinging awareness that channeling her best self for Irene when she couldn't face her worst self made her a hypocrite.

"Okay," she tried. "He was manipulative and dishonest and cruel."

"Cruel," Irene repeated. "That's heavy. Cruel, how?"

"Well, for example, when we were young, he'd twist the skin on my arm really hard, like it was a game. He held me down and peed on me. He took money out of my dresser drawer. He'd raid my Halloween bucket. One year he ate my Easter bunny. When I was applying to college, he hid my mail so I wouldn't know where I got in. Our father nearly killed him for that."

A chill hung in the cyber air. Irene's green eyes blinked. Joni heard her words resonate in the silence.

"What did your father do to Marc?"

"He beat him pretty badly." Joni remembered how the beatings would focus on Marc's torso so the bruising wouldn't show in clothes.

"How did your mother react to that?"

"She didn't. She stayed in bed, where she usually was."

"I'm sorry you had to endure that kind of trauma growing up," Irene said.

"I guess it was worse for Marc. I got out of there—I left for school. My life came out okay. Until. Well. Alex. Then Paul."

"Keeping this at Marc for the moment," Irene said, "what I'm hearing is that, as an adult, in hindsight, you're able to feel compassion for him despite his behavior."

"Maybe. I guess so."

"But you're back to feeling he can't be trusted."

"Because he can't be."

Irene nodded. "We're out of time. There's a lot to talk about next week. Don't be too hard on yourself, okay?"

"Okay."

"Try not to overthink it."

"I won't."

But she did; she couldn't help it.

Like a bag of trash you set outside the front door until morning, inevitably the night animals get in—not just get in but rip it open and devour every morsel. There was a lot of garbage in that old sack and by morning, instead of rested, Joni was exhausted from turning it all over—and over and over—in her mind.

9

The hours and days in New York blurred past in a quick succession of appointments and meals and drinks . . . well, not drinks for Joni, not anymore, but she'd gamely sip her sparkling water with its wedge of lemon or lime as if it contained the old magic. It was exhausting being back in the city but also exciting. When she'd lived here with Paul he was always busy and she'd had too much time alone to think, imagine, wallow, plan, and plot. It was not a good time and, obviously, it ended badly. Now, this felt electric in contrast to the deadening loneliness of being Paul Lovett's wife. She was CEO of Sunny Day and, just as in LA, here she had more than a voice in every meeting; hers was the final word, and that made all the difference.

Joni was starting to adjust to the idea of a long stay here. In truth, it would be a relief to ditch all that LA traffic, and she'd enjoy walking in the city, the shops, the people, other dogs for Stella to greet and sniff and circle and lick when they were out. She realized that the locus of her unease had shifted and now what loomed was the meeting with Louisa Singer.

When Val called to confirm their appointment with Louisa on Saturday, they agreed that whatever happened they would not tell her where Marc was, not until they'd had a chance to digest everything she had to say. Marc was still her brother and Joni couldn't deny a sense of loyalty even if it was unearned or misplaced.

By Friday, Joni found herself wondering if Louisa would tell her things about Marc that she'd rather not know. Did she really *want* to meet with her? *Should* she meet with her? Maybe it was a bad idea to open another can of Marc-worms.

En route with Chris to their last post house tour, Joni reminded herself that disappointment had for so long been the foundation of her relationship with her brother that there probably wasn't much left that would really surprise her. Yes, she did want to meet with this woman who'd had the misfortune to marry Marc. Joni knew what it was like to be on the wrong side of a marriage to a bad man. Her impulse was always to leap forth to help the wronged woman, but wasn't it an assumption that the harm had gone only one way? Could anyone really know what went on inside someone else's marriage?

She'd go to the meeting open and curious, a listener.

A red mailbox hung beside the gate that led to Red Chair Post. They'd already visited Nice Hat Post, Post Participle, and Good Trick Post, all in Manhattan, all medium-to-large facilities suitable for their needs even if they were corporate and antiseptic. Red Chair was not only in Brooklyn, but it was close, right there in the neighborhood, just a short walk from the apartment. On that merit alone Joni favored it.

Chris rang the bell and spoke into the intercom when a deep voice asked who was there. There was a buzz, and the gate opened. Joni followed her daughter down a long bluestone path to a five-story brick building with two doors: one faced with wood planks that blended into the matching wall and gave it the feel of a secret, or private, entry; the other a glass door that swung open.

They were to meet with a man named Franklin Lipstadt, but a young woman appeared to greet them. "Hi, I'm Sam—I work with

Frank." She was tall, hipless and very thin, with thick brown hair in the kind of feathered cut Joni hadn't seen much of since her childhood. She was a six-foot Farrah Fawcett but not quite: She had an Adam's apple.

After introductions Sam led them into a ground-floor office that was bright and welcoming. A white couch sat in front of a broad window overlooking a garden with clusters of daffodils and, soon, tulips around the trunk of a tree whose branches bristled with green buds. Colorful paintings lined the white walls of a large open space with long wood-plank tables set up as shared workspaces. A heavy-duty printer sat beneath a bright orange wall cabinet upon which several Emmy awards sat among other, less easily identifiable awards. One stood out: a clay concoction replete with fingerprints and slashed-on paint that had clearly been made by a young child. Joni smiled, recognizing the touch of self-deprecating wit in placing that among the shiny totems of success.

"Those are Frank's," Sam told them. He started as an editor but these days he mostly runs the business. He's on a call right now—he'll be out in a minute. I'll show you around."

Joni and Chris glanced at each other: Could this charming place be for real? It was a far cry from the bland post houses they'd already toured. Sam opened the door to a small room just off the main area, with dark gray walls hung with more art and a desk with two large monitors.

"This is one of the edit rooms," Sam said. "We have four."

Both monitors were on and one looked busy, a disembodied editor at work.

Chris asked, "Is someone working remotely?"

Sam nodded. "When the pandemic started, Frank set us up for that. At one point he had ten projects going at once and he was the only person in here. It was surreal, he said. Amazingly, he kept the business alive during all that."

Joni remembered that difficult time when productions ground to a sudden halt until everyone figured out how to get back to work. By the time they were ready to post again, hardly anyone went in person. It was nice being back in a real post house, but not. This place had captured the perfect balance of office and home. There was even a fireplace.

"Most of the staff is freelance. Some work in-house now and some still work remotely, depending," Sam explained. "What are you looking to do?"

"Most likely we'll want to work in person," Chris answered. "We'd need an edit room and space for two producers and two assistants."

"I assume you have your own staff?"

"Except an editor."

"We can hook you up. Also mix and color if you need."

"We'll see," Joni said.

"Shall we?"

They followed Sam through a small kitchen, down a flight of stairs, along a hall and to a sound mix studio that doubled as a screening room. It was as high-tech as what they'd seen in Manhattan and as good as, if not better than, some of the LA post houses Joni had worked in.

"We have Dolby Atmos surround sound in here. You can't see them but there are sixteen speakers—some are embedded in the ceiling and walls," Sam explained. "Frank's always updating everything. Don't tell him I said so, but he's kind of a tech nerd. And he's a perfectionist. If something's not working on a Sunday at midnight, he's in here fixing it."

"Himself?" Joni asked. She would have been alarmed at Sam's comment—just how obsessive was this Frank?—if not for the warm note of affection in her tone.

"If need be. He has a lot of tech experts on call. They all love jumping on a crisis."

There was also a vocal booth, another edit room, and a color room that overlooked another garden. Every room had at least one piece of art decorating the walls.

"What about security?" Chris asked. They'd need to meet high security standards for the top streaming platforms they were targeting.

"Yup," Sam said. "We meet every standard and beyond. Cameras everywhere. Every room is secure, with fingerprint access. Sometimes I can't even get through these doors." Sam chuckled. "Luckily Frank lives in the building so he's almost always right here."

Following Sam back upstairs, Joni and Chris glanced at each other—the place was impressive. Now it all came down to cost and, of course, the owner: If he made it clear that it was his way or the highway, like one of the people they'd met the day before, there was no way they'd work here.

And then a door opened and out walked Frank: tall and thin, handsome and bald, with a face that emanated good cheer. When he stood beside Sam, Joni saw that they could have been related: father and son, no, daughter; man and child, or maybe not. It didn't matter.

"Sorry about that." Frank had a nice voice, medium-pitched and grainy. He extended a hand to Joni first, then Chris. "We've got projects going in LA and London right now."

"Overlapping time zones," Chris noted. "Yikes."

"It's pretty much nonstop."

Joni knew what that meant. "So you have, what—four good hours when nothing's happening to catch some sleep?"

Frank laughed. "Sometimes, unfortunately, yes. So, Sam gave you the tour?"

"Nice place," Chris said. "You sound busy. Does it get crowded?" It was a good question; the place was on the small side.

"Not usually," Frank answered. In good weather things tend to spill to the outside areas—the gardens have their own high-speed

Wi-Fi nodes, by the way. But so many people work remotely that it's usually pretty quiet around here."

A rich smell of coffee drifted into the main room and Sam appeared from the slip of a kitchen bearing a tray with three mugs, a pot of coffee, a pot of tea, and a plate of scones. Joni felt trapped—they were here for business, not a tea party—but the scones ignited a wave of hunger. She'd had coffee on her way out the door but no breakfast.

"Can we tempt you?" Frank offered. "A cup of coffee or tea, at least?"

Sam carefully set the tray on the low coffee table, then stood and smiled. "Frank made the scones," she beamed.

"Wow." Chris sat down on the deep cushioned couch and picked up a scone. It crumbled as soon as she bit into it. She caught the fallout with a cupped hand and moaned, "Yum."

"Some people find them too dry," Frank said.

"I love a dry scone." Joni sat beside her daughter, placed a scone on a napkin, and lifted it to her face before biting in. There was a hint of orange, then a pop of sweetness from a currant. She smiled and nodded her approval at Frank.

"The trick is to replace a third of the flour with ground oatmeal," he said. "Coffee?"

"Yes, please."

"I'd love some tea," Chris said.

Sam poured while Frank sat on one of the chairs opposite the couch. "Do you bake?" he addressed them both.

"Not me," Joni answered. "But Chris does sometimes. I see there's a bakery right across the street—why bother?"

"Oh, I'm a good customer there—I have a sweet tooth. But during the pandemic I needed something to do."

Joni laughed. "We went a little crazy in the kitchen, too, during lockdown—but more on the savory side."

"Cooking and baking are *relaxing*," Frank said.

His emphasis on the word made Joni realize that she hadn't felt relaxed since learning the (latest) truth about Marc. But she felt relaxed now. This place. The scones. The easy talk.

They chatted for about fifteen minutes, then Frank led them outside where he told them about the garden—he knew every plant by name. He was partway through installing an irrigation system that he seemed as proud of as he did his sound mix room. He clearly loved it out here and grew so comfortable that a potbelly appeared where it hadn't been before. It was a sign of age that Joni found charming: the letting go of pretense, his belly, her racing stripes. She had a feeling he did the gardening himself but didn't want to ask too many questions about his personal life. This was business. And she liked him. Already, she worried that she might like him too much, too fast. She almost wished he was an arrogant control freak instead of this attractive and warm and successful man about her age with a good sense of humor and, stop, no. She did not want to go there. Sam had mentioned that Frank lived in the building. Joni glanced up at the stack of three broad sets of casement windows above the two office floors, hoping to glimpse another person, a wife, a husband, any kind of life partner that would deter her from even thinking about him in anything but professional terms. The windows gleamed mirror-like, offering nothing but an amplification of her own thoughts.

This place was perfect.

She didn't trust perfection.

Something had to be wrong here.

It would be the money. The cost of working at a post house this near and dear would be sky-high.

Somehow, it would never work.

"Thanks for your time," Joni said, walking up the path toward the gate, expecting Chris to follow. They'd had their tour and now it was time to leave. Once all the bids came in, if the decision to post in New York became final—and it looked like it would—they'd end up at one of the two bland post houses of the three they'd toured in Manhattan that were acceptable. Joni knew it. She felt so relieved, she smiled.

Frank smiled back. "My pleasure."

"I'll send you our project specs this afternoon." Chris stood in front of a rose bush whose branches climbed an arbor that arched over the path. In a couple of months, it would be covered in flowers. Joni wondered what color the roses would be, then stopped that thought. It didn't matter. They wouldn't be there to see it.

"We better get moving," she prodded Chris.

Without even glancing at her mother, Chris told Frank, "We'd like an estimate for edit, color, and sound."

Joni faked a smile. Chris was moving too fast. They needed to discuss this.

"We'll get it to you by tomorrow." Frank was still smiling.

"Just to be clear," Joni said, "we'll be getting several bids."

"Of course." He sucked in his gut. "Just let us know what you decide."

Joni struggled to get to sleep that night. She couldn't stop thinking about Frank Lipstadt, how friendly he'd seemed, how his post house was just what they needed, how it was only a short walk away . . . how delicious that scone was. And he was single, damn it—she'd looked him up. He'd divorced three years ago and their children, a son and a daughter, were grown and gone. Everything about him bothered her; he seemed too good to be true. She wanted to trust that her impression of him was accurate but how could she, after Marc?

After Paul?

For twenty-six years, she was married to a man she didn't really know. She'd sustained a warped reality when anyone else might have noticed inconsistencies, if not deceits. To this day, she felt ashamed for her long-held willful blindness. Ashamed and bewildered.

Her thinking was murky when it came to the men she loved. That was obvious. And it was her answer. Feelings for Frank Lipstadt or any other man were warning signs telling her to keep away. She would cut the feeling loose and let it drift so far into the distance she could no longer see it.

Finally, she slept, badly and not enough, but it was better than no sleep at all.

First thing in the morning, Chris knocked on her door, announcing coffee and reminding Joni of the noon appointment in New Jersey with Louisa Singer. Joni rose with a sense that by the end of the weekend things would be clearer.

She'd know what to do about next steps in New York.

And about Marc. From their conversations, it sounded like he was taking good care of Stella. Growing up, he was always better with pets than with people. She trusted that he still was—why wouldn't he be?

Because he was Marc. Or Marco. Or Max. Or Arno.

He was whoever he said he was.

Trusting him was an act of wishful thinking.

Panic spiked, remembering that.

Blair was still testing positive but feeling better. It had been agreed that as soon as she was in the clear she'd swing by and get Stella. When Joni found herself frustrated that Blair was taking so long to recover, she checked that feeling. Blair had been a stalwart support for a decade, and it wasn't her fault she was sick. As Joni thought about that, a back-of-mind decision began to gel—Blair's reliability in all things needed to be rewarded, not just acknowledged. When all this was done, when post was settled and Marc had moved on, Joni would turn her attention to promoting Blair or giving her a raise or both.

She tried not to think about Marc on the short train ride from Penn Station to Maplewood, but it was hard since he was the reason she was meeting with Louisa Singer.

His wife.

Damn Marc, the liar—*his wife*.

Chris worked on her laptop while Joni looked out the window, failing to calm her anxiety as she watched the industrial landscape fade to a suburban sprawl of towns linked by a series of same-store strip malls that were as comforting as they were weirdly menacing in their bleak ubiquity.

10

Though it was chilly out, Louisa had booked them an outdoor table as if afraid of what they carried with them and how they might infect her. Somehow, this put Joni at ease: She wasn't the only one nervous about the get-together. She pulled her spring coat closed, wound her linen scarf around her neck and tucked the ends into her collar so they wouldn't blow around in the stiff breeze. Val had been smart to wear a baseball cap; the sun was bright where they sat, near the curb of the town's Main Street, just outside the bistro that looked so warm and cozy inside. Joni tilted her head to position her eyes out of the direct sun. Louisa sat across from them, zipped into a light down jacket, wearing sunglasses, her face fully made-up and her straightened brown hair pulled back neatly by a tortoiseshell barrette. She'd arrived in the armor of a woman on her guard.

Joni followed Val in ordering French onion soup and iced coffee. Louisa ordered a Cobb salad and hot tea. Even in what and how they ordered there was a sense of searching for a footing. When the waiter left, Louisa lifted her napkin and placed it on her lap. She wore several bracelets but no rings.

"Thanks for agreeing to meet," Joni began.

"I'm glad you asked. There's so much I'm trying to understand."

Joni leaned back and folded her arms. She was relieved that Louisa hadn't come right out and asked where Marc was. "This has been a real surprise for everyone. I wanted to meet you. To hear you out."

Louisa nodded. "Well, I have plenty to say."

"I can imagine," Val said warmly, an attempt to pull down barriers that Joni appreciated. "I was thinking on the way over about what we should call him—Marc or Arno? I mean," she said to Louisa, "you always knew him as Arno."

"The Bastard," Louisa said. "Let's call him that."

That did it. Everyone smiled. "Is this what it's like to have a sister?" Joni asked.

Louisa looked at her, a subtle glow in her brown eyes. "Eight years," she said, "and I never knew you existed," shaking her head, voicing a mantra that must have been haunting her.

"I didn't know about you either," Joni said.

"I guess I'm not surprised by that."

"I'm so sorry he did this to you."

"It's not your fault."

"I know, but still, he's my brother. This is all a reminder of why I didn't talk to him for so long."

The iced coffees and hot tea arrived. Louisa dipped her teabag into the mug of hot water, releasing steam into the air.

"When we ran into each other I told you I'd hired a private investigator." Louisa looked at Val, then turned to Joni. "Well, I've found out more since then."

Joni sipped her iced coffee. It was delicious, cold, bracing. She said, "Okay."

"Honestly, I just learned most of this over the past couple of days and I'm still processing it. I'm sure you'll understand why I need to find him." She took a breath. "Here goes."

Joni reminded herself to keep her mouth shut and listen. Just take it in. Process it. Then allow Marc a chance to rebut. She looked at Val, who offered Joni a subtle smile, just enough to seal their pact of silence. They were good at that.

"It's funny," Louisa began, "well, not funny, but I remember this: The day we met at MoMA it was my fortieth birthday. I woke up that morning with a strong feeling that something was about to happen—something good, I assumed. I was so bored and lonely and broken. The world was going to give me a present to make up for how bad the last couple of years were after my husband left. My son, Lawrence, hated going to museums but he agreed to come since it was my day. We'd have a day in the city together doing whatever Mommy wanted." Louisa smiled, remembering, then the smile faded.

"The minute Arno and I looked at each other, I knew this was my present. I hate myself now for thinking that when the real present was the little boy holding my hand. Anyway, that's how it started. He fed me a lot of bullshit and I ate it right up. But now, thanks to Roddy—my investigator—I know who he really was before we met. I wasn't his first wife, it turns out. Did you know that?"

Joni and Val traded another look, this one less composed.

"Who is she?" Joni asked. "How long were they married?"

"Her name was Carolyn Knudson. That's all I know at this point." Val leaned in. "Was?"

"Turns out, when we met, he was a widower." Louisa stirred her tea, then locked eyes with Joni. "She'd been dead all of two months."

The brown eyes drank Joni in and stole her breath. Her emotions tangled with this news, and she couldn't think. She felt Val bristle beside her.

The food arrived. They waited in silence for the waiter to leave.

"How?" Joni asked. "How did Carolyn die?"

"A heart attack," Louisa answered. "She was thirty-eight. Who has a heart attack at thirty-eight?"

Val asked, "Was she rich?"

"What do you think?" A bite in Louisa's tone. "Sorry. Yes. Family money. But there was an airtight trust the Bastard couldn't touch."

"Was he Arno with her or Marc?" Joni asked.

"Neither. He was Tobias Boyar. Roddy's having a hard time finding anyone with that name on the internet or in public records, except in connection to Carolyn. That's how we know it was him. Your brother is good at this."

Joni felt sick. She looked at Val; she could see that her friend felt just as stunned. Marc was worse than a liar—he was a grifter. How could this feel like such a shock when it shouldn't have been a surprise? Because. Because this was Marc. Because he was *good* at this. Ever since they were children her brother had always managed to disarm her before he played his trick.

"There was a life insurance policy on Carolyn," Louisa said. "It never paid out. There were questions about how she died. But we only know that because of the records on *her*. And we only found her by tracing his financials before he knew me. There were a couple of things that pointed to her, not much but enough."

"Wow," Val muttered. "Wow, wow, wow."

Joni's eyes locked with Louisa's again and for another frightening moment they fell into each other. Louisa blinked. Joni plunged her spoon into her soup, pushing down the blanket of cheese. But she couldn't eat.

"You said certain things in his financials pointed to her," Joni said. "What, exactly?"

"Two large transfers to Arno's account—early on, right after we met—from someone called Tobias Boyar. I didn't know who that was, so I googled him. He was married to the late Carolyn Knudson, but that's all there was about him online, nothing else, and that was strange. So, Roddy dug in." She raised the perfect crescents of her tweezed eyebrows. "Turned out, Tobias Boyar was fourteen years old when the account was opened. It was a custodial account controlled by Marco Aker, another fake name, and that account led to your brother. He was easier to find online; there wasn't much, but we didn't need much. An old picture told us it was Arno. It seemed complicated to me, but Roddy says it's not that uncommon. It's a low-level shell game people use to hide money."

"Oh, my god," Joni moaned. She felt hot, like something had detonated inside her. Panic. She needed to get Stella away from her brother. She needed him out of her house.

"He killed her," Val said, then looked at Joni with a cool flash of recognition.

Maybe it ran in the family.

Joni's panic tightened and she felt—almost heard—an inner snap: her long-held seal breaking, the ooze of shadows from her past gushing out.

Maybe it did.

"You have to wonder," Louisa said. "*I* wonder. But no one will talk to me until the divorce is in motion. No one trusts me. It's like they think I work with him, like we're a team. I cannot be married to that man for another minute."

Joni could feel Val percolating, ready to tell Louisa where to find Marc. She feared that Val's new insecurity was driving her in directions that were undisciplined—she was too eager to please, too ready to believe what was said on the first hearing. Joni reminded herself to be cautious. They didn't know Louisa, not really. What if none of this was true? What if Louisa was embellishing and dramatizing so she could win the divorce, whatever that meant for her? Money? Revenge?

Something else? Joni knew how well a wife could spin a story when she was motivated. She needed to hear and see and feel her brother's reaction to all this and then she would know who to believe.

"Please," Louisa said. "If you do know where he went after he left your house, I hope you'll tell me. Roddy's guy in LA has been everywhere, but no luck. I feel like I'm losing my mind."

Joni stared at Louisa. "You had someone go to my house?" As she said that, she realized, *of course*. Her address was easy enough to find. Louisa wouldn't have hesitated to look for Marc there. Why hadn't she thought of that?

"Roddy did. Right when we learned about the first wife. I'm sorry, but I didn't think you were going to tell me yourself, and I had to know."

"When?"

"Tuesday."

That was four days ago. Joni's mind spun. She'd spoken with Marc since then and he'd acted as if he was still at home.

"Maybe he was out when the guy showed up," Joni suggested.

"He went back three or four times at different times of day. He even went in the middle of the night. He talked to a neighbor who said they hadn't seen anyone there for days."

"What about a dog? Was there a dog there?"

Louisa tilted her head as if this was the first she'd heard of it. "No one said anything about a dog barking."

He must have taken her with him. Marc loved dogs and he loved torturing Joni, still, to this day.

Then a new thought wormed in: What if he hadn't taken Stella with him? Who would want a dog along when you were on the run? What if she was quiet for some other reason?

Her heart drummed. The suspended disbelief she'd held in place these past weeks ruptured in a firework of panic.

Panic and shame for her gullibility. Stupidity.

Why couldn't she stop tricking herself into believing what she wanted to believe?

Marc wasn't capable of loving anyone, not even a dog.

He would do anything.

Joni felt herself keeling, heard the scrape of Val's chair and felt arms around her, steadying her.

11

As Val drove them to her house, Joni's hands were shaking and sweat-ing, too slick for her phone to register touch. She stabbed the screen again and again, trying and failing to activate FaceTime, then threw the phone behind her into the back seat and roared.

Val slowed and pulled to the curb. Three houses up, a man mowed his lawn. A girl on a bike rode past them. Joni didn't understand how the world could look so peaceful when an earthquake was happening inside her.

Val reached into her purse and found a small Ziploc bag half-filled with gummy bears in a variety of bright colors. She pulled out a red one and handed it to Joni, saying, "This will calm you down."

"Can't I just have a drink, please?"

"How hard do you want to fall off the wagon?"

"Will this make me high? I don't want to get high."

"No, just calm. Take it."

Joni popped the edible into her mouth. It was sweet, chewy. "How long does it take to work?"

"Not long."

"I didn't know you used this stuff."

"I started a few months ago."

Val had never mentioned that to Joni, which surprised her. New hair. New anxiety. Joni searched her friend's face for answers.

"Are you alright?" Joni asked.

Val sighed deeply. "Let's not open that can of worms right now." She got out of the car and went around to the back seat to retrieve Joni's phone.

Opening FaceTime, Val clicked Marc's number, then handed the phone to Joni. She rolled up the windows and kept the car in park. "I want to hear every word," she said. "Keep it cool. If he answers, and he has Stella . . . well, don't let him know we know anything or he'll slam the door."

Val was right: Joni shouldn't make him so defensive that he wouldn't care about keeping Stella safe. He'd put himself first. Who knew what he'd do with, or to, Stella, if he hadn't already crossed that line? She raised the phone to face level and waited while the ringing thrummed through three cycles before Marc picked up.

"Sister!" he greeted her. He was on the move, face bobbing up and down, breath raspy.

Holding the phone so Val could see but not be seen, Joni asked, "Are you running?"

"More like speed walking." He laughed. "Look who's keeping up with me like a champ."

The camera swerved down to show Stella trotting along beside him. Her tongue was out. It must have been a hot day there.

Flushed with relief, Joni said, "I'm not so sure that's good for her heart." She heard the tightness in her voice as her words spooled out, too late to relax the thread.

"You okay?" he asked.

"Fine. I just don't want Stella overexerting."

"Don't worry. The minute she slows down, we stop. Trust me, I'm paying close attention."

"Where are you?"

"Corral Canyon Road, almost at the beach."

The background was a green-blue-brown-gray blur; he was moving too fast for Joni to recognize anything. She steeled herself for what she had to say. "Listen, Marc, I have to talk to you about something."

"Sounds ominous. Should I hang up now?"

"I hope you won't but you're not going to like it."

"Ugh."

Off-screen, Joni reached for Val's hand. They squeezed. "We just saw Louisa," Joni told Marc. "Val and I. We had lunch with her."

"Wow. Huh. You're right. I'm not in love with this."

It was unnerving the way his face kept jumping around as he walked. "Could you sit down somewhere, please? I just want to talk to you calmly for a few minutes. Okay?" As soon as she said that she realized she was feeling less agitated. The gummy was keeping its promise.

Marc's background swirled and tumbled while he found a tree to sit under. When he came back into focus he was on the ground, leaning against a trunk, with Stella panting by his side. Had he thought to bring her water?

Marc asked, like it was nothing, "How's Louisa doing?"

"You told me you were going to get in touch with her."

"I did."

"No, you didn't."

"I called her. Twice. She never called back."

"Did you try texting her? Emailing her?"

"Of course."

"Marc, please stop lying to me. Just . . . please."

He lifted his phone, and his face filled the screen. His skin was damp, sweaty from running, blanched by the sun. He hadn't shaved. "I'm not lying to you. I tried to reach her."

He sounded sincere but Joni didn't trust herself enough to read him accurately. She told him, "She hired a private investigator. He found out some pretty surprising stuff. And he sent someone in LA to stop by the house to look for you."

"Whoa." His chin cocked in defensively, then he shook his head. "Well, I've been here, but I'm not a prisoner. I go out sometimes."

"She said he went over a few times, including in the middle of the night."

"That's weird. Did he ring the bell? Maybe I didn't hear it. I sleep with earplugs."

"Just stop. Please."

"Joni, I've been here. I went to the store a couple of times, but I've mostly been hanging out with Stella at the house."

"Marc."

"One of the reasons I left Louisa is that she lies."

"Says Arno."

"Fair enough. But it takes two, Joni. You were married for a long time. You should know that better than anyone. It's not like I was Mr. Shit and she was Miss Perfect. She lies and manipulates with the best of them. Trust me, I know. She wants to slam me in the divorce so she's building up her story and she's using you. She's using you, Joni. Don't let her. You're my sister. If you have to take a side, take mine."

"I want to believe you." Which was true. She did. But she also wanted the truth. Both feelings pulled hard at her; she didn't know what to think.

"You don't know her like I do."

Joni realized that he'd bypassed the "surprising stuff" she'd mentioned and fixated on the investigator's visit. She steered things back: "Here's the nut of it."

"*She's* a nut."

"Marc! Listen to me, please."

He fell silent. His nostrils flared. Joni recognized the front edge of his anger. If she confronted him with Louisa's claim that he'd had a first wife, would he hang up and . . . what? Cut her off? Run, if he hadn't already? Feeling queasy and unbalanced, she shifted her focus from his face to the striated tree bark. She had to be careful what she said to him, so he wouldn't panic, so he'd keep Stella safe until Joni got back to the West Coast. She took a breath. Steadied, she looked back to his face, that sweaty, effortful face.

"Stella's getting her meds twice a day?" she asked, instead of the real question: Were you married before Louisa? Did your first wife die? Was she also rich? Who are you? *What* are you?

"Yes. You need to stop worrying so much. Okay, sister?"

"This is . . . exhausting." *Terrifying*, she'd wanted to say.

"Don't let her get into your head, okay? As soon as we're off the phone I'm going to call her again, and when I talk to her, I'm going to tell her she can have whatever she wants. I won't contest the divorce, and I won't ask for anything. Then she'll stop the bullshit. Okay?"

"I'd really like to see you do that."

"Then she'll leave you alone. And she'll leave me alone. And everything will be okay. Stop worrying. I'll see you soon. You'll be back Thursday, right?"

Joni nodded. "See you then."

"Say bye-bye, Stella."

The phone switched off on a view of Stella gazing at Marc, wet tongue hanging sideways. Joni felt a pang of longing. She missed her doodle's wet kisses if that's what they were—she'd once read that when dogs licked, they were trying to find out what you last ate. No. They were kisses. Kisses for Joni. She couldn't wait to be reunited with her sweet, slobbering pup.

Joni stared at the screen a moment after it blacked, feeling depleted, flattened. She asked Val, "Do you believe anything he said?"

"Nope."

"I want to."

"You need to go home right away."

"I know."

It took five minutes to book the first available flight, later that night, out of Newark airport, which was less than half an hour from Val's house.

Val started the engine. "Come on. I marinated chicken and Russ is going to grill it up. I'll have you at the airport in plenty of time. Chris can stay over if she wants, or Russ can drive her to the train station."

"I can't believe this is happening."

"What's happening?" Val put on her blinker and paused at a stop sign before turning. "Breaking news: Marc Ackerman is still a piece of shit. You'll go back, kick him out of the house, hop into bed with Stella and life will go on."

"What about Louisa?"

"Yeah, that's a tough one. I feel for her."

"It didn't seem like she was lying."

"No, it didn't. But there's no way to know what goes on inside a marriage."

12

Val plunged her hands into the bowl of chicken that had been marinating in the refrigerator overnight and moved the slimy pieces around, redistributing the herbed olive oil that had pooled at the bottom. Through the kitchen window, she watched Russ start the grill. He wore only a T-shirt and must have been cold, but she knew that if she asked him, he'd deny it. Lately, if she said red, he said blue; up was down; wrong was right. It had been going on for months now. She had started to wonder if he was having an affair or if it was something else . . . but what? Every day she thought about asking him and every day she chickened out. Was she a chicken, quartered and marinated like this one? It took several minutes to rinse the grease off her hands.

"That's disgusting," Zeke told her, coming into the kitchen for an apple. He'd recently become a vegetarian. Not just a regular, quiet vegetarian but a "devout" vegetarian. She wondered if he bullied his friends about their eating habits the way he did her (though not so much Russ) but doubted it, and that thought made her feel better. As long as it was only her he persecuted. As his mother, wasn't it her job to endure whatever his developmental stages offered up? Didn't her lack of reaction show the fortitude of her love?

Didn't the simple fact that Russ was still here, with her, in their home show the depth of his commitment?

"Your turn!" Chris called out from the living room. They were playing Battleship. They hadn't known each other as children but had made up for it in recent years and had taken each other on—as Val and Joni once agreed, under their breath, with deep satisfaction—as surrogate siblings. "I sunk your destroyer."

"Fuck!"

For a vegetarian, he was quick to use the ugliest words.

Joni was upstairs, resting in the spare room, but Val guessed she was really pounding the internet for any information she could wrest out of it about "Louisa's story," as Joni called it before heading upstairs. Val was glad that Joni was flying back to LA that night. Whatever the truth was, she would find it there. Val didn't trust Marc, not for a minute, but she understood why Joni felt so conflicted—she knew her brother was trouble, yet she'd always been susceptible to him, which was at the root of why she'd kept him at a distance for so many years.

Zeke refused to set the table, by dint of inaction after Val asked him twice, until Chris got up to help, then they swam through it like a team. It was nice having the five of them together for a meal. Val felt less lonely and, realizing that, decided that tomorrow she would ask Russ if he wanted to do something with her. Go to the city, to a museum, or take a walk in Central Park. Or they could pile into the car to drive Chris back to Brooklyn—she'd decided to spend the night with them—and then they could all do something together. She was pretty sure he'd agree to that.

Joni came down and they gathered at the table.

"The chicken is delicious," Chris announced. "Can I have the recipe?"

"Do you cook?" Val asked.

"Do you have a grill?" Russ asked.

"Yes. And not here but at home we do."

"We still have the fancy grill Paul bought," Joni added.

Val thought the huge stainless-steel grill that dominated their Malibu deck was ridiculous but had to admit that it turned out an excellent steak.

"I'll email it to you," Val promised Chris.

"What time does your flight get in, Mom?" Chris knew the whole story. They all did, having been barraged with it the moment the women came into the house.

"A little after three in the morning," Joni said.

"So," Chris calculated, "you'll get to the house around four."

"I hope it turns out okay," Russ said. Val noticed that he was eating his chicken with enthusiasm, though he didn't say anything to her about it even though it was the first time she'd tried this marinade.

"Oh, God," Joni moaned, "I can't think about this anymore." She turned to Russ: "How's work going?"

"Pretty well. The firm's been expanding—don't know if Val mentioned it."

"I'm sure I did," Val said. "Didn't I?"

"You did," Joni said. "But remind me.'"

Joni was covering for her. She'd been so preoccupied with *MMI* that she probably hadn't mentioned anything about Russ's firm doing well enough to grow. Val smiled at her friend and reminded herself for the umpteenth time how much they owed each other.

"We've got five architects in-house now," Russ said. "Up from three before the pandemic. With all the staff, we had to rent more space. Some of us are working hybrid now. Personally, I haven't taken the plunge yet, but I'll have to sooner or later."

"Congratulations," Joni said. "You made it through the pandemic and then some."

"Cheers." Val lifted her water glass.

Everyone lifted their glasses and toasted Russ's success, even Zeke. Val noticed that he'd already finished his grilled portobello mushroom; she should have made him two.

Russ adjusted his glasses and smiled. Val loved seeing him smile. They'd been together over twenty years, and he'd softened like good suede, still attractive but seasoned, with a body she still desired. They hadn't had sex in half a year. Whatever was going on with him, she reminded herself, he was still here with her, with them, gathered at the family table with friends. Smiling.

At the airport, Val pulled up at the curb outside departures.

"It feels weird without any luggage," Joni said. She was traveling with only the clothes she had on and whatever was in her purse when she left the apartment that morning.

"They'll probably think you're a terrorist."

Joni's eyebrows shot up. "Women like us would make the perfect terrorists. No one would expect it."

"Ha. You're right." Val leaned over to kiss Joni's cheek. "I'll wait out here for a few minutes in case you need me."

"Oh, I need you," Joni reassured her.

"At least someone does."

The door half open, Joni turned to her. "There isn't time, but I have to ask—what's with Russ?"

"You noticed something?"

"He seems a little, I don't know, stiffer than usual."

Than usual. Val was well aware that Joni and Russ were not exactly soulmates but there was no point in dredging that up now.

"He's been kind of distant lately," Val said. "It's true."

Joni leaned to kiss Val's cheek and promised, "I'll call you tomorrow."

"You better. If you don't call me, I'll think you're dead." Val meant it as a joke, but it landed hard. As in: Maybe Marc had killed her. Because it ran in the family. She hadn't meant to imply that so openly.

Joni laughed it off and pushed the door all the way open. "Here we go."

"Text me as soon as you get to the house," Val ordered. "Don't worry about the time. And here." She handed Joni the baggie of edibles to take with her.

"Thanks." Joni smiled, dropped the baggie into her purse, and was gone.

13

Except for the glow from a living room lamp that Joni kept on a timer year-round, the house was dark when she arrived at ten past four in the morning. Moonlight cast a vague silver hue. The quiet that normally would have felt delicious instead felt like emptiness.

Her car was in the driveway, parked at Marc's angle: askew, rear wheels too close to the border of the cactus garden. The little blue ball Stella liked to nudge with her nose for minutes at a time sat on the path leading up to the front door.

The familiarity of the lock turning to her key, the tumble and crack, was succor. She breathed deeply. Home.

She hung her purse on one of the hooks by the front door beside all the hats and several of her and Chris's light jackets.

The wheat-colored throw was draped, unfolded, over the arm of the dark blue couch that dominated the living room. A mug puddled with old coffee dried to a hard sheen sat on the glass coffee table along with a couple of magazines and a thick coating of dust.

Stella's downstairs bed was in its usual spot by the fireplace.

A few dirty dishes were stacked in the sink. She opened the dishwasher and saw that it was half full of dirty dishes. Something bothered her; she wasn't sure what it was. Then she realized there was not a drop of water on any of the surfaces—not in the dishwasher, not in the sink. It was as if everything had sat there long enough for all traces of water to evaporate. But couldn't that happen overnight? Joni wasn't sure.

She turned to Stella's bowls, normally stationed against the far cabinet wall. There they were—but the water bowl was also bone-dry.

The house felt warm, which was strange since it was chilly outside. Not warm but closed, stuffy. She opened the window over the sink to let in some air. It poured in, sweet and cool.

At the foot of the stairs, on her way up to check on Marc, find Stella, and throw herself into bed, she realized that she hadn't noticed the leash on the hook where they kept it by the door right next to the hats.

She turned to look.

It wasn't there.

She reminded herself that Marc didn't do everything the way she did. He was messier and put things in different places.

She hurried up the stairs, flicking on lights as she went.

The doors along the hall—three bedrooms, a study, and two closets—were all closed.

One by one, she opened them. Turned on the light. Stepped inside and called, "Marc? Stella?"

She left each door gaping in her wake, revealing another empty room.

The bed in the guest room, where Marc slept, was unmade as usual. But the things he kept on the bedside table weren't there: his reading glasses, the book he read to relax before sleep, his phone charger. The dresser drawers were empty. His shirts no longer hung in the closet. The shiny black suitcase he'd arrived with was missing.

In the door of her home office, she paused. Her chair, which she always pushed in when she left her desk, was angled. She'd left her papers and notepads neatly stacked, topped with the glass paperweight in which Alex's ribboned lock of hair floated, and now the papers were in disarray—he'd searched through them. And the paperweight was off to the side—he'd touched it, held it, displaced it. She strode into the room and grabbed the paperweight as if snatching it away from her brother. The glass orb was cool and smooth in her hand. She would take it back to New York with her. Then she noticed the goddess head flowerpot, neglected but thriving on the sundrenched windowsill, more florid and spiked than ever. As soon as all this was over, she'd get rid of that fatuous flowerpot, that stuck-in-place fertile head that grew relentlessly and never lifted its dead gaze. No, she wouldn't wait; she'd hated it for too long. She cranked open the window, lifted off the screen, and pushed the thing out. She heard it land and break and felt a tremor of satisfaction.

By the time she reached her room at the end of the hall, she could hardly breathe. Her bed was neat as a pin. The clothes she'd flung over the back of the armchair were exactly as she'd left them.

Stella's upstairs bed, rarely used but ever-present beside the dresser, was gone.

IF YOU DID IT
I'LL NEVER TELL

14

The empty Malibu house reminded Joni that, in the five years she'd spent rebuilding her life, she'd built an armor, not a core. And just like old times, no one could dismantle her armor like her brother.

She desperately wanted to believe that wherever Marc was he was taking good care of Stella.

"So believe it," Val told her over the phone—breakfast time in New Jersey, still middle of the night in Malibu.

Joni could hear the ocean through an open window. Or maybe it was the gentle wind that blew through the hills at night. It had been a long time since she'd been awake at this hour, alone in the house. She'd forgotten how slippery darkness could be.

"You have to believe something," Val insisted. "So choose the one that worries you the least."

"Okay. And Alex is still alive. And I never . . . And Paul is alive, too."

"Forget it. It was a bad suggestion."

"Fantasy is what I need to *not* engage in," Joni said. "I was out of my mind to leave her with him."

"No, you weren't." Val infused certainty into her tone, the tinny certainty of an actress missing her mark. "You didn't know the half of it when you asked him to watch her. You didn't know he might have . . ." Her voice trailed off.

. . . *killed his first wife.*

That Val couldn't bring herself to speak those words worried Joni more than if she'd said them aloud.

"He was always an asshole," Val tried, picking up the thread in a different spot. "And he was always great with dogs. Of course you trusted him with Stella. Stop beating yourself up."

Yes, he was always an asshole and always good with dogs, but he was never, maybe, a killer. Like his sister. A family of . . .

"But we don't know what he's capable of now," Joni argued. "We never knew, did we?"

"Take a gummy," Val ordered.

She was right. Joni got the bag from her purse, plucked out a green bear and chewed it.

"Did you take one?"

"Yes."

"Good. Now let's make a plan."

Joni called Chris and ran through a calmer version of the same conversation, minus the dread: Marc was gone and he'd taken Stella with him; nope, she wasn't happy about it, but she was sure everything was fine. Then she took a shower and waited for the sun to rise and businesses to open.

The first thing she did was arrange to have the locks changed.

Then she called Stella's vet and learned that her prescription had been refilled at an online pharmacy that wouldn't divulge the delivery address. Joni clung to that. Wherever they were, he'd brought enough of Stella's medication for another month.

"See?" Val said when Joni called her back to report in. "He's taking care of her. It's not wishful thinking."

It was a step toward rational thought, that was true.

Chris contacted the microchip service to report Stella missing and was reassured that they'd call if anyone reported finding her on the chance that she got lost or was abandoned.

Would Marc do that? Abandon her? Joni didn't think so, but how could she be sure?

"Definitely no way," Blair insisted. She'd finally had a negative Covid test and so joined Joni at the house first thing with breakfast she'd intuited would be needed. She was right. She set out bagels smeared with cream cheese, cut in half; half a dozen peeled hard-boiled eggs; plastic cups of fruit salad; cardboard cups of coffee—as if Joni couldn't make coffee in her own home. But the truth was, she hadn't. She'd sat there, stupefied, since finding the place abandoned.

Blair insisted, "He'll take good care of Stella. He's a good guy at heart."

He wasn't. But Joni was touched by her assistant's warmth and generosity—the food was helping. And reliability—she was here, as usual, parsing the situation with her anxious boss. If only Blair had tested negative a week ago she could have intercepted Stella. *If only*. Joni closed her eyes and stopped herself from spiraling.

When they finished eating, Blair made a move to clean up. Joni stopped her. "Wait," she said. "Sit down. There's something else I want to talk to you about."

Blair sat down quickly, obedient Blair. A flush of color rose beneath her isolation-faded tan, darkening her freckles like a night-scape of inverted stars.

"Don't worry," Joni assured her obviously worried assistant. "It's a good thing."

Blair smiled. "Phew." But she kept the balled wax paper from the bagels squeezed in one hand.

"I have to start by apologizing."

Blair reared. "Why?"

"We've all relied on you for so long. First Paul, then me, and Chris, too. But you're much more than an assistant. I hope you know that."

"I think I do," Blair said. "The raises have helped."

"It wasn't enough."

Blair shifted in her chair, actively listening. She probably expected another raise and the thought of it pained Joni because it really, really was not enough. They'd trained her to accept morsels and never ask for more. She was the kind of assistant everyone wanted on their team, someone who grew in competence but also internalized limitations enforced by habit, work culture, comfort zones, all the elements that had held women back forever. Joni hated herself for not seeing this sooner; she'd noticed it but kept her eyes averted because it was easier not to really see. It wasn't just the corrupting forces of gender but of power. Joni had abused her power with willful blindness. No more.

Joni wove her hands together on the table and sat forward. "I'm giving you a raise and promoting you to assistant producer on *Hear Me Out* for the period of postproduction."

Blair's eyes widened.

Joni went on. "Once we sell the pilot and lock down a season, you'll be an associate producer on the project with another raise. Starting with season two, if we're so lucky, you'll be a full producer starting at the salary you would have had if you'd been a producer for five years."

"Wow!"

"And if we don't sell the show, we'll fast-track you to producer on another show. How's that sound?"

Blair's smile pushed her cheeks wide, stretching her freckles. "That sounds amazing! *Thank you*." She stood up and opened her arms. "Can I hug you? Is that appropriate? I really feel like I need to hug you right now."

As they embraced, Joni felt how soft Blair's face was and picked up a sweet scent in her hair. "Do you use lavender shampoo?"

Blair pulled out of the hug with tears in her eyes. "I do."

Joni also teared up. "I'm sorry this took so long."

"No, this is great."

"It should have happened years ago, Blair, when you worked for Paul. At least when I came on board. There's no excuse."

"My therapist says to 'always go from here.' To 'go forward, don't look back.' Let's just do that."

"Deal."

So now, suddenly, Joni knew two things about this person with whom she'd coexisted for years. Up close she smelled like lavender, and her still waters ran deep enough to require a therapist.

"When do I start?" Blair asked.

"Right this minute. Start by finding us a new assistant."

"Us." Blair grinned. "I am so on that. But for here or New York?"

"Good question. I guess we should wait to confirm where post will be. Do you mind—"

"Not at all. I'll do both for now. It'll only be a few weeks."

"Thanks. Order yourself some new business cards and start using them."

The truth was that Blair's new job and her old job had already blended in reality. The difference was in the reframing and the young woman's improved attitude. Joni realized that by promoting Blair, she'd be infusing her own days with a bright new optimism.

Between them, they decided that Marc would treat Stella well and that whatever he was up to wouldn't last long. That was the party line, but beneath the surface Joni couldn't help worrying. It went against her grain to sit back and wait for Marc to come around.

She called Louisa and apologized for not telling her where Marc was as soon as she'd asked. By the time she was off the phone, she had Roddy the investigator's number. She called him right away and offered to retain him on her own to find Marc and Stella. Roddy refused to accept double pay for work he was already doing for Louisa. She caught herself thinking that he sounded like a nice guy, then reminded herself not to jump to conclusions. Nice was such an overused word. People had called *her* nice, but she wasn't, not really. He said he'd contact her the minute he knew something and told her not to worry in the meantime.

Everyone was telling her not to worry.

But wasn't that what people said when there was something to worry about?

15

Joni waited in Malibu for a week before she was willing to budge without Stella. But once post was confirmed to take place in New York, it was time to leave. She and Blair flew east together. Chris, meantime, arranged everything: The team would gather every morning at Red Chair and Frank Lipstadt would be their editor. Afternoons would be spent at Sunny Day.

And so Joni went back to work full throttle. But every minute that she didn't know where Stella was, she ached. The dog's absence left a hole in her life larger than she'd imagined it could be. She was a dog, but not just a dog. She was a steady, loving, beloved presence, needy but also needed. Through years of tranquility, turmoil, solitariness, activity, uncertainty and flight, and a long (in so many ways) return home, Stella had been the one constant in Joni's life. Now they were apart because Marc—Marco, Max, Tobias, Arno . . . and who else?—because her psychopath of a brother had taken her for himself like she was a prize.

But she wasn't his prize, she was Joni's—and that's why he took her. He knew how much Joni loved her and he exercised his power over her by not caring how it would hurt her.

Or maybe he did it specifically to hurt her.

Maybe that was it.

Frank Lipstadt must have sensed something was wrong because he paused behind her one morning where she sat at the long table alongside Blair and the other *Hear Me Out* staff imported from Sunny Day. There was longtime producer Mike Payne, a married father with young twins who lived farther out in Brooklyn and who was noticeably warm and conscientious in person. And there was his assistant Diana Valdez, newly hired, a small young woman who was professional and efficient but always five minutes late. Frank's assistant, Sam, occupied a corner table-desk across the room beneath the orange cabinet atop which the awards collected glances and dust. It was late morning and Joni felt herself slumping when she felt a presence hovering behind her. She turned and saw Frank looking as if he'd been about to offer her a reassuring pat on the back but thought better of it and instead put his hand on his opposite shoulder as if protecting his heart.

She smiled at him; it was impossible not to. "How's it going in there?" she asked. Frank worked in one of the small edit rooms in the back. He'd made it clear that he did his best work without "company," which Joni understood to mean creative interference. He preferred to work without a producer hovering.

"Got a minute?" he asked. "I was hoping to get your eyeball on something."

She followed him into the small room with its graphite walls and quirky Wilco posters. He sat at his desk with two angled monitors and an Avid editing keyboard whose multicolored keys looked like candy. He indicated the pair of comfy armchairs facing a large monitor suspended above his desk. She took a seat.

He pressed a button, leaned back, and winged his arms behind his bald head. Seated behind him, she could see the ringed shadow where there would be hair if he didn't shave the little he had. It was better that way, to make oneself cleanly bald instead of living the half-truth of a half head of hair as if begging you to imagine him shaggy. Seeing him at this angle, she liked him even more for his bald honesty, his frank honesty. She wondered what had led to his divorce and told herself it wasn't her business.

Joni shifted her attention to the large screen as shots she recognized appeared in a fresh sequence. Her characters, Barbara and Marianne, two properly dressed young women circa 1952, hatted, heeled, and gloved, hauled a hand truck loaded with boxes across a midtown Manhattan street during a bustling workday. Over honking horns and pedestrian chatter, the lyrical Welsh voice of poet Dylan Thomas intones his epic *A Child's Christmas in Wales.*

> "One Christmas was so much like the other, in those years around the sea-town corner now, out of all sound except the distant speaking of the voices I sometimes hear a moment before sleep, that I can never remember whether it snowed for six days and six nights when I was twelve, or whether it snowed for twelve days and twelve nights when I was six."

Because Joni had secured the rights to tell the story of Caedmon Records, her characters weren't *characters* but real people, Barbara Holdridge and Marianne Roney. Newly minted graduates of Hunter College, just twenty-three and bored by their low-paying secretarial jobs, they'd scraped up fifteen hundred dollars to start their own publishing house when they went to hear Dylan Thomas speak at the 92nd Street Y. They decided on the spot that their first project would be, instead of a book, a spoken word recording that captured the poet's magnificent voice. Worried that his brief visit to New York would end before they managed to pin down the slippery author, they called him at his hotel at five in the morning and finally got through—he was still up after a typical late night of heavy drinking. Sure. What the hell? He'd meet them the next day for lunch and talk it over. They spent their entire savings on that first recording and made such a large profit that, suddenly, just like that, Caedmon Records was born. Next, they hunted down the author Colette and, when they located her, flew to Paris to record her just weeks before she died. Other literary luminaries followed. The list went on and the years flew by and by the time they sold their thriving company in 1970 they'd given birth to the audiobooks industry.

Joni had never heard of these women until one of them died and she happened to read an obituary. How had she not known they existed? That they'd done this? As she dug into their story and discovered how little had been said about them, she decided to tell the story herself. Barbara was still alive. Joni found her phone number, called her, and within a week a rights license was in-process.

Once she got her footing as Sunny Day's new CEO, she turned her attention to writing, producing, and directing the pilot. Her vision was to focus on the women's ambition, creativity, and pluck as they founded a company in an industry that didn't yet exist. At the start of the hour they're a pair of girls searching for a foothold; at the end of the hour they're women who know they've created something special. Plus, they're making money. People start to appreciate them.

Joni wanted the show's tone to be light yet serious and capture the mood of its era. A significant portion of the budget had gone to a production designer known for his lush period sets. When the pilot was finished, they'd pitch a ten-episode open-ended series in the vein of "*Mad Men* meets *Mrs. Maisel*."

Her hope, if this worked, if a season was ordered, was to hand the CEO reigns to Chris so Joni could focus just on this, on filmmaking, television making—so she could remake herself as a mature version of the young auteur she'd started out as way back when. Back when she burst onto the scene with an award-winning independent film and then vanished after her single studio project. Before life derailed her: the death of her beloved Alex at only six, her marriage to a rapacious man she fooled herself into not seeing for who he was, her alcoholism, her descent into rage, into murder.

No.

No.

She was not a killer.

She was a creator.

She would be this: a woman who excavated the forgotten lives of other women and thereby saved herself.

Sitting in the dark room with Frank, she could feel the fresh energy of the two women on the screen: young, brilliant, hopeful. Laughing as they strode across the street, hauling their pile of boxes, a conspicuous run in Barbara's stockings. *Good,* Joni thought; that's what she wanted, to feel the energy but also see the fault lines as they forged ahead. Because success didn't come without a cost.

She remembered the post-college apartment in West Hollywood that she shared with Val. They were twenty-two and they were going to conquer Hollywood, whatever that meant—for Joni it meant becoming a director, for Val a star. They had shitty jobs that paid the rent while Joni wrote her first script and Val went on auditions. It was harder than they'd thought and was taking longer than they'd counted on. Joni remembered staying up late one night with Val, debating whether she should dip into her inheritance. When her parents died soon after she graduated, Joni and Marc each came away with nearly two hundred and fifty thousand dollars.

Joni recalled being stunned by all that money and hating that it had come through her parents' deaths. It felt tainted, somehow. Her parents had never understood her desire to be a filmmaker; her father went as far as to ridicule her and her mother just wouldn't listen. Joni resolved to save her inheritance to make her first film, to prove herself and spite them, if it was possible to spite people who were dead. They'd been terrible parents; the atmosphere at home was one of insidious trauma, being housed and fed and schooled while being mocked and denigrated, Joni for thinking too much of her potential, Marc for his love of negative attention.

It was Val who reminded her, again and again, to stick with the plan and not bow to the temptation to pay rent with the funds. It was Val who kept Joni focused and strong during those early lean years when it would have been so easy to live off that money, which Marc did without a thought, squandering his windfall in a matter of a few years.

Flung from Caedmon history to personal history, sitting in Frank's darkened editing room, Joni did the math between their parents' deaths and Marc's first marriage. He'd have run out of money about the time he found a wealthy wife. It made her sick to realize that.

Something else occurred to her for the first time, another if, but a big one.

If Marc *had* killed his first wife, if that possibility was true, what if it wasn't the first time he'd killed for money?

What if he'd caused the toxic leak that took their parents' lives?

It would have been simple to plan it. An investigation had found that a stove burner was left on without the pilot light. Their parents had been aware of the problem; they'd ordered a new stove, but it hadn't arrived yet. They were always checking the burners to make sure they were turned off. Marc still lived at home, but he stayed over at a friend's that night—a stroke of blind luck.

Or not.

"What do you think?" Frank asked.

Joni returned to the moment, confused at first—he was asking her if she thought Marc had killed her parents. How could he know what was going through her mind? She caught herself and smiled. He wanted to know what she thought of *Hear Me Out*'s opening cut.

"It's rough, obviously. But does it set the tone you're looking for?"

"Yes," she told him. "Perfectly." He'd taken her footage and created an opening for the pilot that was compelling, nuanced, evocative, and fun.

"Any notes?"

"Some, but nothing major."

He leaned forward, ready to listen.

She started talking and he swiveled to his keyboard to take notes. It didn't take long.

"The big picture," she concluded, "is that you're on the right track, so once you make those tweaks, just keep going."

"Good." Frank had such a charming smile.

Paul had been charming at first. He had been lovely.

She couldn't trust this feeling. How could she possibly believe herself capable of measuring someone else's true nature?

And what about the disparity between how she regarded herself —as a kind, caring, thoughtful person—and her actions? A bitter taste rose in the back of her throat. She swallowed it down. She was likely a riskier bet for Frank than he'd be for her.

Joni returned to the table in the main room where her colleagues quietly worked. Sitting in front of her laptop, she stared at the screen but couldn't focus on it.

Her thoughts spun around something she recalled about Patricia Highsmith, whose work had inspired her at the start of her career and again five years ago when that cunning voice wormed its way back into her imagination and showed her how she was capable of getting rid of Paul.

Highsmith was famous for her charming, criminally minded protagonists. Wondering why she was so good at creating twisted minds, she asked her diary, "Am I a psychopath?"

Her answer: "Yes, but why not?"

Alone in the living room that night, after Chris had gone to bed, Joni sat there gazing through the wall of glass and lost herself in the twinkling darkness of the Manhattan skyline across the river. She couldn't stop asking herself Highsmith's question: "Am I a psychopath?"

No.

She wasn't.

She couldn't be.

She'd done a horrible thing, but it was an aberration.

She would never kill anyone ever again; she wasn't capable of it. (Was she?)

Did that make any difference since she'd already done it once?

When she asked herself if her brother was a psychopath, the answer arrived without hesitation: Yes. Obviously. Of course.

But how could it be that both of them, the two and only siblings in the same family, had discovered within themselves the same capacity for taking a life—and, more to the point, acted on it?

Did it run in families?

What was a psychopath, anyway?

The longer she thought about it, the less she understood, so she dove into the rabbit hole, googling into the night.

There did not seem to be a gene for it.

But it did appear to run in families.

(What did that mean, exactly?)

And, of course, it wasn't that simple.

The complexities were vast, categories endless, definitions protean, with ever-evolving assessment tools offering, at best, a cacophony of interpretation. It was overwhelming.

She took a deep breath, popped a gummy, and followed her gut into the tiered definitions of the OCEAN scale: openness, conscientiousness, extroversion, agreeableness and neuroticism.

From there she dove into the "dark triad personality": Machiavellianism, narcissism, and psychopathy.

Wikipedia: "Psychopathy is considered the most malevolent of the dark triad."

And then the Hare Psychopathy Checklist (revised). She froze, reading it. Trait by trait, there was Marc:

- Glibness/superficial charm
- Pathological lying and deception
- Conning/lack of sincerity
- Lack of remorse or guilt
- Callous/lack of empathy
- Parasitic lifestyle
- History of early behavior problems
- History of juvenile delinquency
- Lack of realistic, long-term plans
- Impulsivity
- Irresponsible behavior
- Frequent marital relationships
- Failure to accept responsibility for own actions

And that was just during childhood when she'd known him longest, and recently in his middle age. Twenty-five years of his adult life were a blank. She wondered what Louisa (or the late Carolyn) would have to say about the traits Joni couldn't vouch for:

- Egocentricity/grandiose sense of self-worth
- Proneness to boredom/low frustration tolerance
- Lack of affect and emotional depth
- Short-tempered/poor behavioral controls
- History of promiscuous sexual relations
- Recidivism
- Other offenses

Joni read and reread the list. Some were clear while others, like juvenile delinquency, were murky. Did Marc's childhood bullying and his emotional and moral transgressions count as crimes? And what about the years since then?

What about their parents?

What about Carolyn Knudson?

How could she, of all people, hold her brother accountable for their deaths—if he'd killed them, if it was true?

The gummy wasn't working. She reached to take more, then stopped. The impulse to numb herself was the same as when she used to drink and drink some more, when there was no limit to how much alcohol she needed to blur the sharp edges of her thoughts and feelings. She didn't want a new addiction. She ziplocked the baggie and tossed it aside.

Panic wound tighter.

Would she ever be able to reconcile what she'd done with who she believed she was? Who she wanted to be?

Would the guilt, the remorse, the confusion, her itch, ever go away?

Was she capable of recognizing herself on a list like that?

How could anyone be visible to themself in the darkness?

She envied Highsmith's clarity, her quick ability to see it and to say it, to actually write it down. "Yes, but why not?" As if she knew exactly who she was and accepted it.

Finally, lying in bed, Joni closed her laptop, eradicating all light. Moonglow reflected off objects on her bedside table: the sleek dark face of her phone, the translucent paperweight she'd brought with her from Malibu. She closed her eyes but her mind wouldn't stop whirring. She wanted, needed, to talk about all this with someone, but who?

Chris? Her beloved daughter.

Val? Her best friend.

Irene? Her trusted therapist.

No one was equipped to hear what she had to say. No one deserved that heavy a load. There was simply no one to whom she could reveal all of it, not in a way that might help her unravel the knot, the question that pulsed at her core and made her inauthentic to herself—the question she'd worked so hard to avoid for five years.

16

Two weeks went by with no news. It felt surreal to Joni, living in an apartment in New York, working in a new place, and no Stella. Every day she and Chris got up, went to work, and came home, as if this new routine could possibly be normal.

One morning, as they left for work, Chris announced, "Look— there's water in the pool." Joni stopped beside her daughter, and it was true: The long-empty rectangle of concrete now glimmered with bluish water.

"And there's Griff," Chris added.

Standing beside the pool, with a woman Joni didn't recognize, was their handsome, silver-haired neighbor, admiring the building's latest completed feature. There would be an email later with the subject line (Joni predicted): "Latest Feature Completed!" Real estate developers loved stating the obvious, building where there was more money than need, over-touting fixtures as "luxury" when you could find them stacked in Home Depot aisles. Joni was glad for the pool but wondered if she'd ever actually use it.

It was early spring but chilly, and Griff wore a light jacket zipped halfway. The young woman with whom he held hands wore her brown hair in a topknot and was dressed for warmer weather in a tight short-sleeved T-shirt, high-waisted jeans, and a bright pedicure, acid green, showing through her sandals. It made Joni think of California, where people would know to wear a sweater if the temperature dipped below sixty-five. Only in New York did she see people out in shorts and tees and sandals at fifty degrees.

"She's pretty," Chris noted.

"She is," Joni agreed.

Neither of them guessed the woman's age out loud, but Joni thought: *late twenties to Griff's sixty plus.* Of course. He was a good-looking older man. And it wasn't their business. And she was too exhausted to pass judgment after last night's inner marathon.

Chris's car arrived to take her to Sunny Day. They kissed goodbye until later.

When Joni arrived at Red Chair it was after ten. Mike was at the table, Zooming with white earbuds plugged into his ears. Other than Sam, Frank's assistant, no one else was in yet, not even Frank, who lived upstairs. The place smelled of coffee. Joni knew she'd drink a lot of it today and that it wouldn't make a dent in her exhaustion.

Blair arrived and set up across from Mike, who picked up his laptop and went outside to finish his meeting in the garden.

A few minutes later Diana rushed in, breathless, apologized for being late and got right to work.

Frank appeared fifteen minutes later with damp skin, obviously fresh from the shower. He wore trim slacks and a dark blue button-down shirt dotted with tiny yellow stars. Joni approved, not that it was any of her business, either.

"Morning," Frank greeted all.

"Hit traffic again?" Sam quipped.

"You know it."

It was their morning routine, a comfort and ballast as Joni clung to a roller coaster of hope and disappointment in her wait for news about Stella. Frank would check in with Joni and her team, stop at the galley kitchen for his coffee, then close himself into his edit room for the rest of the morning. Joni kept waiting for something to happen, to change, but together Frank and Sam held the ship cruising at a steady clip through weather that was always calm. At one point Joni began to wonder where the red chair was—there had to be one somewhere—but held her distance by not asking. There was no red chair anywhere in the office. If there was such a chair, it must have meant something to him since he'd named his company after it. Maybe it was the first chair he and his former wife bought together. Maybe it was upstairs in the house part of the building. Or maybe the ex had it. Or no one had it; it was in a dump somewhere, all the red paint chipped off by now.

Every few days she texted Roddy for an update and his reply was always more or less the same: "Working on it." Or "Hang tight."

Now, Joni only thought of the disappearance in terms of Stella, not Marc. He was a sharp kernel of malevolence lodged in her craw and she wanted him out. She hated him. She didn't care what happened to him. She found herself wishing he'd never been born and sometimes, to comfort herself, pictured a world in which he didn't exist.

One evening when Chris was out somewhere and Joni was alone in the apartment, she found herself indulging in a fantasy of mixing her brother a drink: half whiskey, half antifreeze. The imagined act felt like a first drink after years of sobriety. Delicious. Forbidden. Immense. Everything she'd pent up would come rushing out of her and she'd be light and free. The thing would be done in one definitive moment and he'd be gone. Marc would be gone. He would never hurt her or anyone else again.

Her rational mind switched on and the feeling evaporated.

It would be too obvious if she did it the same way twice.

Then her better instinct kicked in with a feeling of repulsion: She would never, ever, ever stoop to something like that. Not again.

She wasn't that person anymore.

She just wanted Stella back.

That was all she wanted.

In the meantime, she focused on work: The pilot was coming along beautifully. Mike worked on their pitch to networks, looping Joni in as needed and presenting every new draft as it was ready. Afternoons at the Navy Yard plugged Joni into the circuitry of all the other projects happening at Sunny Day. Val was there three days a week and they'd seek each other out for a quick coffee. She relished sharing the latest demands of her star's mother, Esther.

"Watermelon. Cubed, not sliced. No seeds."

"Gluten-free protein bars, some with almonds, some with chocolate chips, no peanuts, no raisins."

"Coconut water in small containers."

"Ripe mangos, but not overripe."

"Hard-boiled eggs cooked for eight minutes, so they're jammy but still cooked through. Peeled. At room temperature."

The list went on. Val was getting good at a vocal staccato that mimicked ETR.

Somehow time flew by before Joni and Val got a chance to be alone together and really talk. Joni had wanted to ask her friend if she was okay, really okay (the bright hair, the new lack of confidence), but it didn't happen until they finally put a date on their calendars to go to dinner, just the two of them.

Joni and Val sat beneath strung lights at an outdoor table on the corner of Henry Street and Atlantic Avenue. Frank had recommended the restaurant and suggested the fried chicken, which they both ordered. It was delicious. They ate with their fingers after fork and knife proved impractical.

"Val," Joni asked. "What's been going on with you?"

"What do you mean?"

"You know what I mean."

Val put down the piece of chicken she was partway through. "Okay. Here goes." She cleaned her fingers on her cloth napkin, and said, "Russ is cheating on me. I think."

As it sank in, Joni realized that it wouldn't have surprised her if Russ turned out to be a bad husband. But she knew better than to say that to her friend. "I can't believe you've been holding that in all this time. Why didn't you tell me? I've been *right here*."

Val tilted her head and sighed as if to say, *Have you, really?* It was true; Joni had been preoccupied with her own worries.

"I haven't been very available, have I?"

"I don't know if that's really it, though," Val answered. "Maybe partly. But I also didn't want to, you know, say it out loud."

Joni got that. Saying something out loud made it real. It was harder to pretend something wasn't happening when you started talking about it to other people.

"I'm here for you," Joni told her friend. "Talk to me."

"Okay." Val straightened in her chair and took a breath. "I came home early from the city on one of my office days, and he was out. He hardly ever goes out anymore, not since he started working at home—he works all the time, and it's not like he's the one running the household errands." She raised a hand. "That would be me."

"Still hanging on to remote work?"

Val nodded. "He said he was taking a walk. A walk. Joni, he drove home in the car."

"Isn't there that state park near you guys?"

"Sure, but on a workday? Who would go all the way there just to take a break on a busy day?"

"I can see it. Workdays aren't the same as they used to be before the pandemic."

"It happened a second time."

A second time rose an alarm. Joni leaned in, listening.

"There's been this awkwardness between us. We don't talk about it, but it's sitting right there, the proverbial elephant."

"Have you asked him if he's seeing someone?"

"Not exactly." With her teeth, Val pulled the meat off a bone, leaving a greasy streak on her chin.

"Val, he can't read your mind. Wipe your chin."

Val took the napkin from her lap and cleaned her face. "Better?"

Joni nodded. "Ask him."

"I'm afraid to."

"Why?"

"I don't want him to leave me."

"He won't."

"How do you know that?"

"I don't, I guess."

"I'm going to be sixty soon. He's five years younger. I'm worried that when he looks at me, he sees an old woman."

"Oh, Val, you're beautiful."

"I'm old."

"Russ loves you."

"He's restless. I can feel it."

"You're strong. No matter what happens, you'll be fine."

"I don't want to end up alone."

"Look, it probably won't happen, but what if he did leave? So what?"

Val stopped eating. "That's a little cold."

"What I mean is, isn't it better to know? And decide what you want? Even if you did end up alone, you wouldn't be alone. I've learned that. You have me. You have Zeke."

"You live in a different state—two different states. And Zeke's leaving for college soon. He's basically gone."

"Well, you have your work to focus on. There's a lot to be said for that."

"I don't *want* my marriage to end," Val said. "I like being married to Russ. I love him."

Joni rearranged her face to stop incredulity from overtaking it. Personally, she didn't understand what Val saw in her husband, she never had. She smiled and nodded and was about to say something to correct course, but before she could speak Val stiffened.

"You know what, Joni? Believe it or not, I don't want to be single. I don't want to be alone." She folded her napkin and laid it beside her plate. "I don't want to end up like you."

An awful silence yawned between them. *Like me*, Joni thought, *end up like me*. She cracked a chicken wing, ate the sliver of meat off the bone with her teeth, then preemptively wiped her face. Tables for two on either side of them chatted happily and sipped pretty cocktails, and Joni wanted one, too. She could do it: raise her chin to the waiter and order a drink. Ignore Val's objection. Ask for another.

Instead, Joni channeled the feeling into an urge to hurt. "I've noticed how insecure you've been lately," she said. "I've never seen you insecure before. Insecurity is so ugly. You should try not to let it show."

Val's jaw dropped. She took out her wallet and put three crisp twenties beneath her water glass. "I have to get going." She stood. Before walking away, she added, "All you do is work, Joni. It's not healthy. And it's worse since the thing with Marc. It's like five years ago all over again, watching you feel blindsided by what's been right in front of you, but instead of processing it, you paper it over with work."

"Process it? I have a therapist. I process it all the time."

"Is it helping?" Val had her hands on her hips now. Neighboring diners were starting to look. "Because from what I can tell, you're carrying some pretty heavy baggage all by yourself. Sometimes I wonder what exactly is inside those bags."

Was this the moment Val would ask Joni outright if she'd poisoned Paul? Right here, at a sidewalk table, in front of all these people?

Joni lowered her voice. "Val, sit down. Please."

Val remained where she was, standing there, looking down with an attitude of power that frightened Joni.

After Paul died, before Joni fled to Bali, Val had whispered a promise in her ear: "If you did it, I'll never tell." She had wondered what Val thought about Paul's death but never knew for sure. The crackling energy Joni saw in Val's eyes now told her what her friend thought. That she was ready to talk about it, eager to talk about it, bursting with it. Joni felt the other diners' eyes on her.

"Why is this happening?" Joni asked. "Why are we fighting? You're my best friend."

Val stared at her.

"Let's go back to my place and talk there. Okay? Please?"

Val opened her mouth as if to speak, then closed it. After a moment, she said, "I have to get home," and walked away.

Joni paid for the meal with her company credit card and left the entire sixty dollars of Val's cash behind as a tip.

Walking home, she wondered if she should call her friend and apologize. She hated this. And it worried her. If Val turned against her, she could do real damage. She took out her phone but before she could click Val's number a text from Roddy popped on the screen.

Joni stopped walking and stared at it.

We located your brother in Mexico, somewhere near El Rosario. We think he's at a campsite. Hang tight.

17

Val gripped the steering wheel so tightly her knuckles were white through the stretched skin of her hands. She thought of the way Joni had cracked that chicken wing and practically sucked the meat off the bone. "Insecurity is so ugly."

It was a mistake to open up. Joni had been prodding her lately, asking how she was doing, picking up that something was off. Val had known the conversation was coming and was eager for it. She needed to talk. But she didn't expect it to go the way it did.

She turned on the radio, but everything irritated her. Music, talk, it didn't matter. She turned it off. The whirring of traffic on either side of her produced a white noise that was almost calming. She thought of Russ and wondered if he was at home or out on one of his "walks" and anxiety flooded her. Her new stash of gummies, the ones she'd bought to replace what she gave Joni, were in the glove compartment. She leaned to open it, and the car swerved. Someone honked, holding down their horn. Val pulled back. She'd have to wait until she got home.

As she was pulling into the exit for Maplewood, her phone rang. It was Joni. Val let it go to voicemail. Joni tried again when Val was pulling into her driveway beside Russ's car, but she was still too upset; she wasn't ready.

Russ was cleaning up the kitchen when she walked in. With Zeke out most of the time, at school or with friends, there wasn't much mess—especially on the days Val worked in person and Russ was alone in the house—and they always left it to the end of the day. The thought of him staying alone in the house irked her. What did he do? Where did he go? Why didn't he ever go to work in the new office space his firm just leased? He claimed he was so busy he sometimes didn't stop for lunch until four o'clock but for all she knew he was taking his "long walks" every time she went out.

Russ dried his hands on a dishtowel and folded it neatly before hanging it over the drawer handle. He turned to her. "Did you see the neighborhood chat tonight?"

"I was out. I was driving. So . . . no." It irritated her that he'd ask that the moment she walked in. "Why?"

"It was on fire. Shelley Nelson saw a prowler. She called the police. They didn't find anyone, though."

"Shelley Nelson?" Val's mouth flattened to an ironic grin. Years ago, Zeke had a playdate with the Nelson kid and came home crying. He'd been accused of taking the boy's best baseball card when he hadn't, and the mother had jumped to her son's defense. "I wouldn't believe anything that woman said."

"Good point. Hopefully it was a false alarm. How was dinner?"

"The food was good."

"Just the food?"

"I don't know what's up with Joni, but she was a little, I'll just say it, bitchy."

One side of Russ's mouth hitched up. He'd always thought Joni was "a little pushy," which was code for "such a bitch." Val had always thought that, deep down, her husband was a tad misogynistic (he couldn't help it; it was baked in; he was a product of his time like the rest of us) in the way he'd characterize Joni's strength as a flaw. But now she wondered if he was right.

"Want a glass of wine?" he asked. "I was just thinking of having one."

"I'd love one. That's another thing: having to not drink around her, even if you want one yourself."

"You had to drive home anyway."

"I know, but that's not the point."

Russ poured them glasses of Rioja from a bottle that was already open. They went to the living room, and she sat on the couch. He settled into an armchair across from her. A twist in her stomach: Not too long ago he would have sat beside her.

"What happened with you and Joni?" he asked.

Val picked up her glass and held it in front of her with both hands as if it could shield her from what she really needed to say to her husband. To ask him. Because Joni was right, damn it. Still. She didn't have to say that: "Insecurity is ugly." She took a sip of wine and was struck by the sourness. The bottle had sat open too long on the counter.

"I'm starting to think Joni might be more like Marc than anyone realizes," she said, watching her husband's pale face for a reaction. He knew all about what Louisa had told them and was as horrified as everyone else.

"What do you mean?"

"Sometimes I've wondered if Joni actually did kill Paul." There. It was out now. She took another sip of wine.

Russ leaned forward. "The police ruled that out, though."

"Maybe they just gave up."

"Huh. I mean, it's pretty crazy that people keep dying around those two."

"Alex doesn't count." Little Alex was hit by a car in front of the house while Joni was inside working. Maybe it did count, in a way. No, no it didn't; she was working, that was all. The accident was a tragic . . . *accident*. A real accident. Not what happened to Paul.

"I know," Russ agreed. "But her husband and his wife. What are the odds?"

"That's the thing."

They sat in silence and drank their sour wine. She felt calmer, better, here with Russ, talking. But she wished he was sitting beside her. The space between her couch and his chair felt gray and heavy and she didn't like it. She leaned forward.

"Listen, I have to ask you something." She picked up her empty glass, wishing there was something in it, then put it back down. "Would you sit next to me, please?"

He placed both hands on his knees, pushed himself up and moved to the couch. Resolute. Nervous. As if he could tell she was about to unpin a grenade. He sat beside her. She swiveled to face him. His blue eyes seemed to darken and she almost said never mind but thought of Joni at the table, cracking that wing.

She steeled herself and asked the question: "Are you having an affair?"

He jolted back as if she'd pushed him. "What?"

She didn't repeat herself. He'd heard her.

"Why are you asking me that?"

She began to feel lightheaded, waiting for an answer, and wished she could unask the question. No. She was glad she'd asked it. Because Joni (damn her) was right.

He inched closer and took her hand. "No. I'm not."

"Where are you really going when you take those long walks? You never even liked taking walks."

"That's true." He lifted her hand and brushed the backs of her fingers against his stubble. The reddish-gray stubble that used to be so thick by five o'clock that if they kissed, she'd get a brush burn. It was softer and thinner now. She hadn't noticed before. He was losing hair, not just on his head but on his face.

"Radiation therapy."

She stared at him. She didn't quite understand—and then she did. "You have cancer?"

"No, I'm doing it for fun." His smile didn't reach his eyes and it broke her heart because she saw, finally saw, how hard he was trying to please her.

"How long?"

"I found out in February. It's stage one, and it's curable. I just have to have these treatments. There's an excellent chance I'll be cured."

"What kind of cancer?"

"Prostate."

"An excellent chance? Not a hundred percent?"

"Nothing's a hundred percent, honey."

Honey. She opened his fingers and kissed his palm. "You do not have cancer. I won't allow it." She kissed his palm again.

"Okay," he said. "Deal." He, too, would rather go back to the theory of long walks.

"Why didn't you tell me?"

He let go a long, deep sigh. "I should have. I know I should have. But I kept thinking about how bad it would be for you to wait through the treatments with me, worrying you'd end up alone. All the stuff with Zeke leaving soon for college. And that Esther woman, at work. You seemed, well, overwhelmed. I wasn't sure you could handle it. I didn't want to dump it onto your plate along with everything else. I planned to tell you when it was over."

There it was: fragile Val, the woman who was so afraid to face the fact that she'd been raped that she kept it secret for decades and bound her best friend to that secrecy. The woman who refused to comment publicly on Paul Lovett's suicide. The woman who was attacked on the witness stand during his accomplice's trial. Val didn't like being protected but now saw that she'd depended on it.

And, yes, Zeke. It was true: She openly dreaded their looming empty nest.

"I can't believe it," she said. "You have cancer. Cancer."

"I'm going to be okay. I promise. I hated not telling you."

"You should have."

That night, they slept in each other's arms.

In the morning, Val had two more missed calls and three texts from Joni.

I'm sorry.

I'm sorry.

I'm so sorry.

It was early, so Val texted back instead of calling.

I'm sorry too. I talked to Russ. He's not having an affair.

Joni put a little heart on that message and answered right away.

The investigator located Marc. That's all I know right now. I'll keep you posted. I'm glad you talked to Russ. I had a feeling it would be ok. xoxoxoxo

Val knew she should pick up the phone and call, but they were in texting mode now, shooting information back and forth, and chances were that Joni hadn't had her morning coffee yet, either.

I'm glad they found Marc. And Stella?

No mention but I assume she's with him. I'm glad Russ isn't cheating.

He has cancer.

The phone rang instantly.

They regaled each other with *sorry* and *love you* and parsed every strand of their emotionally packed evening. With every word she shared with Joni, Val's regret deepened. She wished she could take back what she'd said to Russ last night, those sharp, heavy words that had cut open her insidious vein of doubt about Joni and put it on vivid display.

18

Joni waited all morning to hear from Roddy. Occasionally, convinced that her phone was vibrating in her back pocket, she'd reach for it and stare in disbelief at the blank screen. Blair knew she was waiting for the call and would glance at her before returning to her work, tucking away her own uneasiness. She'd united with Joni in disdain for Marc and a powerful wish for Stella's return. They'd all been taken in by him and shared the pain of betrayal—and shame. Shame for having been too stupid or naïve or blind to see him for who he really was. It was a shame familiar to all women, reflexive and all-consuming even if it was undeserved.

And wasn't it shame—shame and fear—that had held Val back from confronting Russ sooner? She'd been too ashamed of her aging body to ask him why he'd been distant lately, which in hindsight seemed absurd, though, over dinner, Joni had understood exactly what Val was talking about. Another thing women shared was a fear of discovery, since apparently every one of them (us) was a fraud. She looked at Blair across the table, concentrating on her work. There was nothing fraudulent about this smart, diligent, heartfelt young woman.

And all along, it was cancer. Russ had cancer. Cancer. A condition that was all objective fact. Joni tried to wrap her head around that, too. It hadn't occurred to either her or Val that the man could be in trouble.

"Does Zeke know?" Chris had asked as they left the apartment that morning.

"I doubt it. Maybe they'll tell him now that Val knows." Joni looked at Chris, that gentle profile, those clear eyes, a hint of crow's feet just starting to show. The strawberry hair was growing out, showing blond roots. How could her baby be thirty years old? "Do you think it's better for him to know?"

"Yes." Then Chris hesitated. "Maybe. I don't know. I couldn't have handled knowing the truth about my dad at that age."

"At any age."

"Right. Not exactly the same thing."

They'd discussed Paul for hours, days, months, years, a conversation that was like adjusting a telescope in search of focus, and when you thought you'd found it the horizon line would retreat. Joni understood that there was no way a daughter could ever, in a single lifetime, understand how a beloved father was also the kind of man Paul had turned out to be. She'd asked Chris once if she could choose, would she rather never have known?

"Yes," Chris had answered unequivocally.

"Wait," Chris had said that morning, stepping out of the elevator into the lobby and greeting Hector, the day doorman, with a wave. "It's not the same thing. I think they should tell Zeke, but maybe in a few weeks after he graduates. He won't be able to focus on school. This can wait, right? Isn't the prognosis really good?"

Joni nodded. "I guess we'll see what Val and Russ decide."

Roddy finally called after lunch to fill Joni in. She listened eagerly, each drop of information balm on the parched skin of her long waiting.

"He walked through the San Ysidro border crossing into Tijuana three and a half weeks ago. He must have used a fake name because he's not in the records, but CCTV shows him with the dog—that's how we flagged him."

"*Three and a half weeks ago?*"

"We just got our hands on the footage; they're not exactly efficient down there. But we're on him now."

"Stella's in *Mexico*." Joni hadn't imagined that.

"They traveled south along the west coast. There's not a ton of security footage around there but we spotted him in a few places—two gas stations and a convenience store. Yesterday he turned up on footage from a store in El Rosario. He was buying camping supplies. My guy down there checked all the campsites. He was camping at Punta Baja, but bad news on that front—when my guy got there, he was gone."

"Is my dog still with him?"

"Hard to say. But I want you to hang tight, Joni. We're working on it all. We'll find him. And we'll find her."

"I don't care about him." Venomously. She softened her tone: "I just want my dog back."

"Gotcha. We'll keep trying."

Louisa was blunter in her text that arrived moments later: "That fucker! How did he know we were coming?"

Joni wondered that, too. It disturbed her how good her brother was at slipping through the cracks. But then, so was she.

Saturday morning, in the chilly spring sunshine, Joni retraced her steps—their steps, hers and Stella's—from five years ago, when they used to set out together every day. Stella had been the anchor of Joni's lonely, drifting hours while Paul worked long days and sometimes nights at the studio. She cringed, looking back at how unmoored she was then. How had she let that happen to her?

Alex. Losing Alex and the deep plunge after. The plunge into alcohol. Isolation. Fantasy. Eventually, the hard climb out of that drowning pool.

She threaded along the edge of Brooklyn Bridge Park past picnickers, boaters, volleyball games, walkers, runners, and whole families of bicyclists. She realized that she hadn't been on a bike since before Alex was hit by a car riding hers. Part of her wanted to feel that freedom and speed again, whizzing along, peddling, steering, ringing your bell. Another part of her recoiled at the thought.

She kept walking past the wildflower pier, the soccer pier, the music pier, the roller rink pier, and the ice cream pier where people queued for cones and boat rides.

She made her way into Dumbo along Water Street with its cobblestones and renovated industrial-age warehouses shoulder to shoulder with shiny new apartment buildings. She was jolted by a dissonance between familiarity and change. Had there been this many tourists when she lived in neighboring Vinegar Hill? She hadn't been back to the neighborhood since then and this city didn't sit still.

She kept walking.

She turned on Main Street and again on Plymouth. There was an off-leash dog run—was it always there, or was it also new? It looked dark and dank beneath a traffic overpass, more a gesture than an actual respite.

Where was Marc now?

Where was Stella?

A fog of hatred for her brother wormed its way through her body; she felt it in her lungs, like bad air. With each breath, each step forward, it solidified into a toxic pellet that inched its way upward, aimed at her heart.

She kept walking.

At the end of Plymouth Street, she turned onto Little and again onto Evans and there it was: the Commandant's House, the big white mansion with its stately lawn. Her home for a few fateful months. She remembered how Stella used to race into the yard for her first morning pee. Other memories returned in quick flashes: music, meals, bitter words; hours by herself, writing that screenplay she ended up shelving; rye in her morning coffee and her nighttime glass; a ghost of Alex at the door; Paul dead on a curve of the stair.

Why had she come back here?

She shouldn't have.

Turning, she chose another route home, past shops and up the hill into Brooklyn Heights. When she got back to her building, she felt relieved to be firmly back in the present. She had a virtual stack of screenplays to read and decided to work on the terrace since it was such a nice afternoon.

Laughter tinkled up from below, familiar laughter—it was Chris.

Joni put aside her iPad and leaned over the parapet from which she could see that around the newly filled pool there were now several lounge chairs and a few small tables. No cushions yet, no umbrellas, but the emails promised they were forthcoming and that it would be a "fun summer." Chris, Blair, and the young woman they'd seen with Griff were gathered around one of the tables, leaning in, talking, laughing. The sight made Joni happy but a little confused. Blair, on a weekend? Griff's young girlfriend?

Later, Chris explained.

"Haley's not Griff's girlfriend, she's his daughter." Chris stared at her mother, awaiting reaction since they'd both jumped to the wrong conclusion at first sight, misjudging men, as usual, either they were too good or too bad but rarely getting it quite right.

"Oh," was all Joni could think to say. "Okay."

"We're getting together tomorrow with our knitting."

Joni forced herself not to laugh. It was such a quirky generation with their drugs and their crafts, their politics and their teas.

"Nice," was all she said. But she had a thousand questions: How old was Haley? What did she do? Did she live here with her father? Joni kept her mouth shut because she knew from experience that the more she asked Chris about her friends, the less she'd find out. Their crisp professionalism at work did not translate to home. The one thing Joni asked was, "Is Blair knitting with you?"

Chris smiled; they both knew that Blair was too restless for such a sedentary hobby. "She joined a Sunday running club."

"Why was she here?" A second question but allowed since Blair was their colleague.

"We're talking about finding an apartment together."

"Really?"

"Why not?"

"You're her boss. Wouldn't it be . . ." Inappropriate, Joni was about to say but caught herself. ". . . Awkward?"

"We're basically the same age, and we get along. I don't see the problem."

A red flag flew up, but Joni kept quiet after that. More and more, she noticed that her daughter jumped too quickly at decisions. She wondered if she'd have to stay at the helm of Sunny Day longer than she'd hoped.

The knitting took place on their terrace, over herbal tea, to the sweet, warbly sound of a folk singer. Joni punctured the young women's privacy to poke her head out and ask, "Who's that singing?"

Haley put down her needles and turned to answer. "Connie Converse. She was never really discovered, but she was the female Bob Dylan; that's what they're saying now." Haley had lovely blue eyes, pale brown bangs, and a round face. "I'm a singer-songwriter," she announced. "Connie really inspires me."

"I'll look her up," Joni promised, meaning it, already knowing she'd forget.

"Mom," Chris said. "Connie Converse has a good story. We should seriously think about doing something with it."

Chris and Joni had taken to pitching each other like that all the time.

Joni gave her daughter the thumbs-up and disappeared behind the sliding glass door.

By midweek Haley had joined the search for an apartment. At Sunny Day, in the afternoons, Joni noticed that Chris and Blair were letting their boundaries blur. The trio had decided to only look at no-fee apartments so they could avoid a broker's fee that could run into the thousands, which meant their search would take longer. Joni was glad. It would give them all time to see if the dynamic really worked.

She glimpsed the first fissure of tension the following Sunday when the three gathered at the penthouse to set out on a day of open-house hopping. It was the way Chris and Haley leaned together over Chris's phone, the two heads coming so close their hair mingled, that caught Joni's attention. And how Blair looked at them sharply, from the side of her eye, that raised the alarm.

19

Val and Russ sat together on Joni's terrace sofa, holding hands. Russ's free hand gripped a cold beer, but Val had refused alcohol in deference to Joni, which was completely unnecessary and actually bothered Joni a little bit. She wasn't so fragile that she couldn't stand watching other people drink. In fact, she prided herself on her ability not to mind too much. Every encounter with social drinking was an inoculation against the urge to drink alone, which was where Joni had really gone wrong in the heyday of her alcoholism. Sipping her seltzer with its wedge of lemon, Joni admired the quickly evolving pink-to-orange sky behind her friends' heads.

They'd planned on going out to dinner, but it was such a lovely evening they decided to order in and eat on the terrace. Russ had another beer. He was a redhead and always pale, but Joni thought he looked sallower than when she'd last seen him in Maplewood. Val hadn't mentioned that; maybe she was so used to seeing him that she didn't notice. Val had instructed her not to discuss his cancer. They also tried not to talk about their work too much when they were around him; he hadn't been thrilled when Val made the shift from teaching to producing, especially since she'd be working for Joni. Instead, they talked about anything else. The bathroom Val and Russ were planning to renovate. Chris's decision to get her own place in New York and how she was apartment hunting with a neighbor's daughter and Blair.

"Blair?" Val said.

Joni nodded with a sharp, "Yup."

"That's a terrible idea."

"I'm hoping it won't happen. I noticed some tension between the three of them—maybe it'll work itself out."

"Three-ways never work." Russ raised his beer as if to toast an old dead concept.

The women laughed, and Val asked, "And you would know because . . . ?"

"*You* used to say that." He smiled at Val, tossing back the hot potato. "Whenever Zeke came home from a playdate with two other kids."

"Right," Val said. "That's true. It was always a disaster when there were three kids together."

"I remember that, too." Joni recalled the day Chris brought a friend home from school and the kid spent the whole time playing with Alex while Chris sulked in her room.

"What's the other one like?" Val asked. "The neighbor's daughter."

"Haley. She seems nice enough. Young. A singer-songwriter."

Russ rolled his glazed eyes. Joni felt a stab of resentment. Why would he assume the young woman wasn't good enough to succeed? It was rare, yes, but someone always made it past all the obstacles and why not her? Unless she was misreading him. Lately she'd wondered if the filter of her feminism was stuck on a single setting when a shift in perspective might have offered a clearer view. Or maybe the innate misogyny she'd always sensed in Russ was really there.

"Want me to say something to Chris?" Val offered. "I'm assuming you can't."

It was true. Joni and Chris were good colleagues, but they were still mother and daughter. When it came to things like Chris's hair, clothes, friends, and living spaces, Joni had to tread lightly.

"Sure," Joni said. "But not when I'm around."

"It's good for Chris to get her own place," Russ said.

"We had our own place when we were, what?" Val asked Joni. "Twenty-two?"

Joni nodded. "Chris lived with roommates until the pandemic. They say half her generation boomeranged back home."

"They'll never grow up if they don't get out," Val said.

"It's a recipe for disaster," Russ said. "I mean, all kids are afraid of becoming their parents, right? Living with them is how to make it happen."

Joni looked at him: a little drunk, scalp shining through thinning hair, freckles darkening in the twilight. He wasn't aging well, but he had cancer. He must have sensed her attention because he turned to her and looked right into her eyes with a directness that made her uncomfortable.

He added, "The last thing you'd want is for her to become like you and your brother." He smirked and turned to Val, who shot a startled glance at Joni.

"We should put our food order in." Val stood up. "What should we eat?"

But Joni wasn't ready to change the subject. She asked Russ, "What did you mean by that?"

"How about Thai?" Val asked. "Or maybe sushi."

Russ looked at Joni, directly into her eyes again. "Family traits are hardwired," he said. "You can't get around it."

Joni felt her face go slack. Her gaze solidified on his. She stared at him until he began to fidget with a loose button dangling from his shirt. It came off and clicked to the floor. No one picked it up, and that's when Joni knew.

"Sushi," Val said brightly. "Let's do sushi."

"Sushi sounds good," Russ mumbled.

Joni tore her gaze off Russ and got up to place the order, use the bathroom, and compose herself.

When the sushi arrived, she asked Val to help her in the kitchen. Dropping the bag onto the counter, she demanded, "What was that?"

"What?" Val opened a cabinet and took down three plates.

"What Russ said. 'Like you and your brother.'"

"Don't listen to him. He's just . . ." Without finishing her sentence, Val opened the silverware drawer for forks and knives.

"What did you say to Russ about me? Me and Marc. Why did he say that?"

Val gripped the cutlery in both hands and held it in front of her like a multipronged weapon. When Joni reflexively took a step back, Val's eyes hardened.

"The night we had that argument," Joni said, "over dinner. What you said about me and the 'baggage' I was 'carrying alone' and what you thought was in it."

"I was just angry."

"No. Tell me. What exactly do you think is inside my baggage?"

"Forget it."

"We should have talked about this a long time ago, Val. It was a mistake not to. Let's talk about it now."

Val dropped the forks and knives onto the counter with a clatter. "Okay. I'll tell you what I think."

But Joni already knew; she could see it in her friend's face. One of the reasons Val had been a good actress was her capacity for nuanced shifts in her expression, the minuscule movements around her mouth and eyes that told whole stories. Joni watched Val's face as she gathered the courage to speak her thoughts out loud—the slight hardening of her forehead, the stiffening of her lips.

"I think you poisoned Paul. I've always thought so. It's exactly what I would have done if I were you. I basically let you know right away that I thought that, didn't I?"

"I never really knew what you believed," Joni said.

Val folded her arms over her middle. "So, did you?"

"You promised you'd never say anything. But you told Russ, didn't you?"

"I told him what I thought, but it was just a thought." Her face softened with regret. "I was angry and it spilled out."

"Val."

"I'm sorry. I shouldn't have. It was that night, after dinner—I was so mad at you, Joni."

"For calling out your insecurity, you'd throw me under the bus?"

Val glared; the hint of softness was now gone. It was that word: insecurity. Joni had found a button without meaning to push it. She'd never wanted to hurt her friend and yet, that night, they'd gone after each other with a quick viciousness that was new to them.

"You said you didn't want to end up like me," Joni said. "I'm sorry I hurt you but that hurt, too. Why would we hurt each other? Why did we let that happen?"

"You're right," Val said. "We should have talked about this a long time ago. Secrets are toxic. No one knows that better than us."

"No more secrets," Joni promised.

"I never kept any secrets from you, Joni." There it was again, in Val's eyes, the flicker of distrust. "I never needed to."

"But you just kept a secret from me," Joni pointed out. "You talked to Russ. I wouldn't have known if he hadn't blurted that out."

Val's eyes froze on her, as if recognizing the contours of a new danger she'd unleashed.

Joni's thoughts at that moment were too awful to share. It would help her if Russ died of cancer. His curable cancer. He'd likely survive and become righteous in a whole new way. She wished it would spread, poison his whole body, destroy him. There it was, her bad seed, blossoming, inevitable.

In Val's eyes shone a different thought, equally unsayable: What if Joni went after Russ now? What if she got rid of him the way she got rid of Paul? Joni saw a glimmer of her own instinct for self-preservation reflected vividly in Val; felt it, feared it, and was drawn to it.

20

A whole week passed with Joni and Val managing to avoid each other except for one time, on a screen during a staff meeting held on Zoom to gather everyone everywhere. Val kept her camera off so all that was visible of her was a smiling photo from a different time. Joni kept her camera on; as Sunny Day's leader she felt an obligation to be seen. And, on principle, she would no longer allow herself to hide in the invisibility that tempted and shielded and obliterated older women.

But Val was obviously hiding. Hiding from the fear that had animated her eyes the last time they saw each other. Joni knew Val was afraid of her now. And Joni was afraid of Val—more precisely, she was afraid of Russ. Russ, who'd never liked or trusted her. Who now thought she was, like her brother, a kind of disease unto herself. Self-destruction as other-destruction. A lurking danger. Russ, who was like a time bomb out there, a threat Joni had no choice but to rely on Val to contain.

Well, she had a choice.

But not really.

She'd promised herself she would never do that again.

The only choice she felt she could live with was to do nothing, to trust that Val would keep Russ quiet. They'd kept quiet for each other before. They knew how. They were good at it.

But.

Things had changed since their original pact of silence.

The world had developed a capacity to digest certain secrets—Val's, for instance, had gone from hidden shame to book deal—but it would never be ready to hear Joni's without severe punishment. She'd made a colossal mistake and knew it and would bear the burden of remorse for the rest of her life, but she wanted to bear it alone as a free woman; she did not want to rot in prison. The thought of public humiliation, public judgment, and an isolated life behind bars haunted her.

By the weekend she was exhausted, but her brain still churned. On Saturday she headed to Brooklyn Bridge Park with the intention of walking until her body was so drained that her thoughts would (hopefully) slow down at last.

She wasn't sure how long she'd been out when she sat on a bench in the shade for a brief rest. The view was a cityscape: a new building that looked like a Jenga tower, a small plane slicing through cloud-mottled sky. Her eyes saw it all, but her mind didn't register any of it. Her mind wandered to the memory of the antifreeze swirling into a cocktail she'd hoped Paul would drink—how easy that was.

Fentanyl, this time—who wouldn't believe that a man with cancer would want to escape the easy way?

Val—that was who wouldn't believe it.

Joni exhaled so hard and fast it was like she'd been slapped on the back.

She shook loose the digressive thoughts and forced herself to see what was right in front of her: a pretty spring day in an exquisite urban park.

She stood up and resumed her walk. The park was bustling as if the whole city had come out to celebrate the perfect weather.

"Joni!"

Frank Lipstadt stopped walking just ahead of her on the path. She'd been so distracted by her thoughts that she hadn't noticed him coming her way. He wore his usual jeans, sneakers, and T-shirt along with a cobalt baseball cap with a logo she didn't recognize, and he was smiling his amiable smile.

"I hope you're not thinking about the pilot," he said.

She knew that when she was lost in thought her face could betray an intensity that alarmed people. Chris had told her that.

She smiled back at him, shielding her eyes against the sun. "No, just other stuff."

"You're not supposed to worry on your day off." His smile grew and her heart lightened.

"Then when would I worry?"

He laughed.

"I like your hat," she said. "I forgot mine. It's so bright out here."

"I know where there's some shade. Are you on a schedule or do you have some time? I was about to get some pizza but I'm in no rush."

"Nothing until later this afternoon." She had therapy with Irene at four.

He led her to Pier 3 and onto a path that wove into an interior so shady and lush with green it could have been somewhere in the country (if you didn't glance past the treetops at the urban juggernaut beyond). A coolness trickled into her nervous system and she took a deep breath.

The path forked with a choice. To the left, keep walking. To the right, explore.

"What's all that?" she asked.

He led them to the right, into a clearing marked by large, white-painted structures that looked like . . .

"Mushrooms," she said. "Or ship moorings."

"Or sculptures. Context being everything."

Fucking context, she nearly quipped but held her cynical tongue. Frank was a nice guy. And anyway, why not? Ship moorings as art sprouting their way along a widening path that led to a cluster of enormous mirrors.

Frank walked into the mirrors and turned to her. She followed.

Context and metaphor, true loves, begetters of irony. She didn't say that, either.

He planted his hands on his hips and laughed at his multiplied reflections. He stuck out his tongue. He fanned both hands over the top of his head so his fingers fringed down like hair. He stuck a hand on a hip and half-turned like a posing model. Everything he did ignited a replication of his antics that obviously made him happy. Watching him, Joni laughed with simple pleasure, something—she realized in that moment—she hadn't felt in a long time. Off-hours, friendly Frank had a silly side. Her own repeated reflections showed a woman bound by opposing impulses: laughing with her arms tightly crossed. She released her arms but didn't look any more relaxed. If he noticed, he didn't show it. She appreciated that.

Talk tubes sprouted here and there. Standing far from each other, Frank spoke into one and Joni listened.

His echoey voice said, "Pizza?"

She wasn't sure if it was a nuanced question or a plain suggestion. She bellowed back a simple, "Pizza!" Then added, in a whisper, "You saved me from myself just now," and was relieved to understand, by his shrugging shoulders, that he couldn't make out the last part.

They walked for a while longer before heading back to "the mainland," as he called it. She wondered if the park was filled with other hideaways and enclaves she'd never noticed on her beeline walks along the water's edge.

There were plenty of available tables at his favorite pizza place on Atlantic Avenue.

They told each other about their lives. His wife Nancy's sudden departure three years ago to live with another man; their son, Ted, who lived in Syracuse and was studying for a doctorate in neurobiology; their daughter, Frances, who lived with a boyfriend in Asheville, North Carolina, and worked as a yoga teacher and barista. Joni told about the trauma of Alex's long-ago death, Paul's outing and suicide, what it was like being hounded by the press while she hid out in Bali, and the comforts and challenges of living and working with a grown child.

He said, "You left out the part about your first films."

Of course, he knew about that. A long time ago she was briefly famous for the right reasons.

She countered, "And you forgot to tell me all about those Emmy awards in your office."

They nodded knowingly at each other. Neither one of them was interested in touting past successes.

"Well," she said. "I should get going. I've got a Zoom at four."

He glanced at his watch. "Yikes. I've got to walk the dog."

"You have a dog?" Joni had never seen or heard one in all her time working beneath his home.

"His name's McDuff. My kids were obsessed with the McDuff books when they were little." Frank smiled. "He's old and he sleeps most of the time. He can't walk very far."

"I have a dog, too."

Frank lit up. "Doggie playdate?"

Joni smiled and said nothing. She couldn't bring herself to explain why Stella wasn't with her. *My brother is a lying, cheating, murderous psychopath who ran off with my dog.*

After therapy—helpful as always without quite reaching the source of her angst—Joni thought of Frank and clenched her jaw, which ignited the fierce itch she couldn't reach. She picked up the back scratcher she kept on the coffee table and dug at the spot of screaming skin. If she had been a different person at a different time, in a different place and with a different life, she would have let this thing with Frank blossom into whatever it wanted to be. But she wasn't. The mirrors had revealed her inability to let herself go. He may have noticed it, but she was sure he couldn't possibly have fathomed why.

Only Val, who knew everything about her, could understand.

Joni was dangerous; she came from dangerous people.

Every time her thoughts drifted to Russ and what she could do to keep him quiet if she wanted to (which she didn't; she would never, not really) she was reminded of that.

She scratched harder.

She needed to talk, really talk, to someone—to Val. She wished she could force a reconciliation, but how could she? If Val wasn't ready, it could backfire with ramifications it chilled Joni to think about.

When she put the back scratcher down, she noticed blood on its blunt little teeth. Luckily, she was wearing a black shirt today; since she wouldn't be able to put a Band-aid on that spot anyway, she did nothing. A scab would form to crust over any damage.

She thought again of Val. Is that what would happen to them? Would a crust now form to keep them from ever being close again? Wasn't that what happened to most relationships over time? They bloomed, they sustained, they dried up. Old friends drifted out of our spheres and new ones drifted in.

She thought of Chris—Chris and Haley. That seemed to be blossoming into something unexpected, at least for Joni. Apparently, something had shifted for Chris after an early adulthood of dating men followed by several chaste pandemic years locked down with Joni. Now, this. New love—or something. It made sense. She'd wondered how Chris would handle men, dating men, after the revelations about her father. All Joni knew was that her daughter seemed happy, and that made her happy.

Sunday proceeded slowly and without Chris or Stella, Joni felt a new kind of aching loneliness. She busied herself with work. And then, within a single hour, two things happened.

First Chris came home and reported that she, Haley, and Blair were no longer looking for an apartment together; Chris would get her own place and felt good about that. Joni was relieved by the restoration of her daughter's good judgment, so that bullet was dodged.

Then Roddy texted with another update about Marc.

We found him in Bahia Tortugas. This time he's not getting away.

Joni shared the good news with Chris, who texted Blair. Then she dialed Louisa and left a message.

When Louisa called back, what Joni learned knocked her flat.

21

"He did it again," Louisa said. "The Bastard."

"But I just heard from Roddy twenty minutes ago."

"Yeah, well, Roddy shouldn't report good news until after the fact."

"What happened?"

"They found him farther south in Baja . . . Bahia Tortugas. Roddy's guy out there had pictures of him coming and going from some shithole in town called Hotel San Lorenzo."

As Louisa spoke, Joni searched. Hotel San Lorenzo looked pretty bad. Scanning the hotel's amenities, if you could call them that, she saw that it was not dog-friendly and her heart sank.

"Louisa, what happened?"

"He's gone. He packed up and checked out like he knew we were coming."

It took a moment for that to settle before Joni muttered, "Oh my God."

"Exactly. Roddy's texting me right now. Hold on." After Louisa read the message she asked Joni, "Can you hop on Zoom? He wants to talk to us together."

Up until now Roddy had been a name, Roderick McClellan, and a smooth, deep voice. Joni had looked him up—former marine, cop, detective, private investigator—and he passed muster, to say the least. He'd been decorated and lauded. He had five stars and dozens of reviews on Yelp. Yet there wasn't a single photo of a Roddy or Roderick McClellan that matched with his bio. That satisfied Joni; it was a testament to his skill that he'd kept his image offline—crucial in his line of work.

He was waiting in the Zoom room when Joni arrived. She was caught off guard as her assumptions restacked. He wasn't the cliché of some big Irish cop but a slender Korean man in aviator glasses and a pale blue polo shirt. Against a blurred background, his watch stuck in glow mode looked like a flying saucer when he lifted a hand to adjust his glasses.

"Hello," he said, and there it was, the baritone she knew from the phone.

She unmuted herself and said, "Hi, Roddy. At last."

Joni wondered what he thought, how surprised he was when he saw her in her little floating square . . . though presumably he'd looked her up and was familiar with decades of her iterations: the young face of an acclaimed filmmaker, turned distraught as a mother grieved, turned ashamed as a wife distanced herself from a disgraced husband, turned determined as a woman reemerged in charge.

Louisa popped on the screen, hair pulled back into a tight pony-tail, her unadorned Sunday-morning face an enervated wilderness. She was in her kitchen with her stove as backdrop: six burners, two ovens, a pale blue enamel front, darker blue cabinetry on either side, a wide gleaming range hood, a pasta faucet folded against a backsplash of crackled ecru tiles. Joni tried to picture Marc in front of that fancy stove cooking one of his meals. He must have done it hundreds of times, but there was too much dissonance in the image for her to hold it for long.

"We have a situation," Roddy said.

Louisa rolled her eyes. "My life is a situation." Joni felt for her; she'd obviously had a bad night.

"This is a good development," he reassured her, "because now we know what we're dealing with. Your brother's very good at this, Joni."

"Yes," she admitted. "He is."

"I've seen this before," Roddy said. "He leaves right before we get there. He knows we're coming. It's going to keep happening until we find out who's tipping him off. Louisa, how much does Lawrence know about what's going on?"

"Oh, Jesus, nothing. He's a teenager. He doesn't give a shit about me."

That made Joni sad. As a teenager Chris had reeked of diffidence and attitude, but Joni always knew she cared.

"How many friends have you shared this with?" Roddy asked Louisa.

"None. I talk to you, and I talk to Joni and Val. That's it. I'm not proud of what's happening. My friends around here, well . . ." She didn't need to finish that sentence. Divorce was one thing, but an ex who was a murderous conman definitely wouldn't go over at the country club.

"What about you, Joni?" Roddy asked. "And Val? Maybe we should have included her in the call."

Russ. Did he despise her enough to do this to her just for spite regardless of its impact on Louisa? Did he even know how to get in touch with Marc? Joni's thoughts were spinning on the impossibility of having that conversation since she and Val weren't talking when suddenly Val appeared on-screen.

Val sat in her dining room with its burnt red walls and antique sideboard, in front of a window view of her quiet suburban street. She reared when she saw who else was there—Joni, specifically. Without needing to be told, Joni understood that Louisa had shared the link with Val the minute Roddy regretted not having done it himself.

"What's going on?" Val asked.

Roddy explained and asked the same questions.

"No," Val answered. "I mean, the only other person I talked to about this is my husband, but I'm sure he didn't say anything to anyone. Why would he?"

"Can you ask him?" Roddy said.

"Sure, but why would he want to help Marc? They've never even met."

Joni thought of Stella. It wouldn't surprise her if Russ thought she was an unfit pet parent given the presumed family predilection for psychopathy. But why would he favor Marc over her if they were cut from the same cloth? Joni wished she could talk it out with the group, but she couldn't. There were things Val knew that couldn't be discussed here even if they were relevant. Joni felt the web tightening and kept quiet.

"Are you sure they've never met?" Roddy probed.

"Of course I'm sure."

"Talked, maybe? On the phone?"

She insisted, "He doesn't know Marc's number. *I* don't know Marc's number."

Outside, behind her, Russ pushed a mower across the lawn until he was out of view. Every time he reappeared Joni's pulse thrummed.

"The Bastard doesn't have a number," Louisa pointed out. "No one can find him. That's the whole fucking point of this whole fucking debacle."

Roddy said, "He'll be using burner phones. He gives the number to who he wants. Whoever's keeping him updated is in direct touch with him by his choice."

"It isn't me, and it isn't Russ if that's what you're thinking."

"Don't take it personally," Louisa said. "We had to ask."

"For the sake of argument," Roddy said, "let's rule out the leak coming from Louisa or Val." He leaned forward and Joni felt his attention turn to her, the way body language can substitute for the lack of eye contact on Zoom. "What about you, Joni?"

"Chris knows everything. She and Marc were getting close before he left, but it isn't her."

"You're sure?"

"Absolutely."

"I second that," Val chimed in. "No way is it Chris. She was in shock when it started coming out who Marc really was. And then when he took off with Stella, wow."

Joni nodded, hoping Val could read her gratitude through the tiny lenses of their distant cameras.

Other than the people on this call, along with Russ and Chris, Joni was aware of only one other person with inside knowledge of Roddy's hunt for Marc.

Just as it came clear to her, Roddy asked, "What about your assistant?"

"Blair." Joni's stomach sank. "She's an assistant producer. I promoted her."

"How much time does she spend around you?" Roddy asked. "How much does she know?"

"A lot. Everything." Marc, his life, and his wives had been discussed at great length between Joni, Chris, and Blair. "She's got the whole picture. They used to go running together in Malibu."

She recalled the look in Blair's eyes right before the apartment search fizzled when it was clear that Chris and Haley were growing especially close. A look, Joni now realized, she'd seen before when Chris joined Sunny Day and then quickly rose in rank. Blair had worked for them for years, always did a good job and never complained. It was a reminder of how Joni hadn't thought enough about that, how it was typical, expected, for assistants to stay in the background. Joni's mistake of falling into that old trap loomed like a coming wave.

"Okay," Roddy said. "For now, our best assumption is that our leak is Blair. If he knows everything she knows, then he'll be aware that there's more than the divorce at stake when we find him. He'll know we have thoughts about the first wife. Suspicions."

"Why would that matter to him?" Louisa asked. "It went nowhere when the police looked into it. Even if he did kill Carolyn, he probably assumes he's off the hook."

"But the life insurance never paid out, right?"

"Right."

"Presumably the insurance company's been doing its own investigation. Even if they're slow-walking it, it's somewhere in the background. Depending on their findings, the police could reopen their case at any time. So, he's not exactly off the hook. And there could be other things he's running from that we don't know about."

Joni thought of her parents' deaths. She hadn't planned on saying anything about that since it was so long ago and it was just a feeling, possibly an irrational fear, that Marc might have had something to do with it. But if it was true, then he'd be aware that it would occur to her and that her suspicions could trigger an investigation into that as well. And if he'd killed them *and* his first wife, then he'd be more desperate than any of them had assumed. A sickening feeling rose in the pit of her stomach.

"Lately I've been thinking about how my parents died," Joni said. She told them the story. "It was over thirty years ago. We split their estate. Marc never had a career. I didn't want to believe it but more and more it's starting to make sense."

Louisa's hands flew up to her face.

Val's mouth hung open.

"I'm really sorry to hear about that, Joni." Roddy clenched his jaw and nodded somberly. "In my work I start by assuming the best of people. Someone comes to me with a fear or suspicion or just a bad feeling, and I take a look. Sometimes it's nothing and everybody's happy. But once I start finding dirt there's usually more dirt. At that point I assume the worst and go from there. So that's what we do now. We assume he did it all, that he's desperate not to be found, and we go forward carefully—but we don't hesitate."

"The minute I'm off this call," Joni said, "I'm firing Blair." That, at least, was one thing she could control.

"No," Roddy said. "Don't set her loose. We want to keep her close and test her; that's how we'll know it's her."

"How can I keep working with her now?"

"You know how to work with actors, right?"

"Of course."

"This time, you're the actor. Know your goal. Work with it."

"What's the goal?"

"First we discover, then we disable, then we get him."

"Disable how?" Louisa asked.

Roddy lifted his hand to adjust his glasses again, the bright face of his watch like a rising moon. He said, "Here's the plan."

Joni had a rough night. Sleep came in shallow waves before she woke again in a froth of worry.

They had a full day of work tomorrow.

How was she going to "act natural," as Roddy had instructed, when she felt so unmoored?

She was supposed to find an opportunity to casually drop something in, a piece of information that only Blair would be privy to, and wait to see if it reached Marc.

But how was she going to manage that? She was an executive, a producer, a director, not an actor. The more she thought about it the more she doubted she could do it without Blair noticing.

Pale sunshine filtered into her bedroom, that gentle first morning light. She reached to her bedside table for her back scratcher, rolled her face into her pillow in search of darkness, comfort, delay, and dug at the eternal itch.

22

Esther the Relentless wanted a cake for her daughter's birthday so the whole crew could celebrate together. It had to be an organic, gluten-and-sugar-and-caffeine-free chocolate cake with fair trade certified unsweetened coconut flakes. Val had just returned from hunting for organic beeswax birthday candles. She was starving, having skipped her lunch to run the errand personally to make sure it was done exactly right—that morning one of the production assistants had returned with three choices of candles, all wrong. It was absurd for the senior producer to waste time like this but ETR's aftershocks would have been more absurd. The kid was turning thirteen. It was ridiculous but *the show must go on*.

"Would you please order me a tuna sandwich and an iced tea?" Val asked Alan, the *MMI* assistant, as she entered their suite of offices.

"Sure thing." He picked up his phone to tap out the order.

"Where is everyone?"

"Conference room." The party was scheduled for two p.m. and ETR was punctual.

"Am I late?"

"No, but hurry."

In her office she retrieved the overpriced candles from her purse which she'd locked into her desk's bottom drawer. She was desperate for her sandwich but knew she better get to that party on time.

Joni and her gang were making their way down the hall toward the conference room, walking in a loose cluster with Joni and Chris in the lead and Blair right behind them, followed by Mike and Diana. Val stopped walking and resisted an urge to run in the opposite direction. This was the first time they'd seen each other in person since that awful confrontation in Joni's kitchen, both of them angry, facing each other, facing off. They'd hurt each other over that outdoor dinner and retaliated by slinging truths. Now it was out there, the thing that had lingered between them for five years, too hot to touch or even look at.

Joni had killed Paul. She'd admitted it, erasing the *if* that had buffered them for so long.

And now Russ was openly suspicious because Val had (thoughtlessly, in anger) opened her mouth, broken her promise that she'd never tell.

They'd hurt each other the way siblings did, recklessly, enraged. It had taken days for Val to metabolize what she'd seen in Joni's eyes that night: Her friend was terrified. Once Val realized that, it had crystallized a new understanding. It had to be awful to recognize your own capacity for malevolence.

Val was not afraid of Joni, but Joni was afraid of herself. Val saw that now. And it had gotten worse with Marc's appearance and the revelations of who he was and what he'd done.

Val felt awful for her friend to have to live with all that.

All last week, on her office days, she'd managed to avoid Joni and assumed the effort was reciprocal. Now, seeing her friend, former, suspended—*estranged*, that was the word for what they were now— froze her in her tracks. The Zoom call yesterday was an eye-opener and she'd been thinking about their argument ever since, regretting it, wishing she'd never opened her mouth to Russ. On yesterday's call she'd sensed a fragility in Joni that moved her. And with Joni's tendency to blend repression and reactivity in a way that could turn especially combustible, she had to be struggling not to unload on Blair.

Val moved aside to let them pass.

She caught Joni's eye, hoping to transmit confidence, but what she read there was the opposite. Heat. Unsteadiness.

Joni was in trouble.

She walked with a reserved stiffness, like someone trying hard to show that she knew exactly where she was going when she didn't. Her eyebrows were hitched a bit too high on her forehead. Her mouth formed too straight a line. Val knew that working with actors didn't mean you knew how to act yourself; she'd seen directors freeze when they were in front of the camera, trying to show how a scene should be played. Roddy had told Joni to act, and she was acting like someone who couldn't act to save her life.

As soon as the group passed, Val texted Chris, who had to know what was going on and must have noticed Joni's awkwardness: See if you can convince your mom to let me give her some acting tips ASAP.

She watched Chris's head tip down to read the text and her shoulder blades pinch as she resisted the urge to turn around and look at Val. The return message came right away: a thumbs-up.

It would have been better to meet outside the office, somewhere beyond Blair's scope, but this couldn't wait. The cyc stage *MMI* had been using was available, so they met there, far from Blair's purview, against the sloping green backdrop that expunged perspective.

When Val looked at Joni in that sea of green all she saw was a woman stuck in a moment of time. There was no past or future. No crimes or suspicions, no accusations to account for, no damages to heal. There was just a single task and that was to fix Joni in three specific ways so she wouldn't blow it with Blair. So Louisa could serve Marc her divorce papers and maybe he'd get picked up for crimes he'd committed along the way. Whatever else Joni was grappling with—the agony of trying to reconcile her own actions with those of her despicable brother—that was for another day, if ever. She was grateful that Joni agreed to meet with her, was willing to accept her help, to admit that she needed help. Looking at Joni now, Val had no doubt that she still loved her friend and wanted to protect her.

"First thing," Val said, "is to relax your body so you're not so stiff." To demonstrate, she swung her arms around her revolving body, staying in motion.

Joni mirrored her.

"Looser," Val coached. "Pretend there's no gravity. Just move."

Joni flung her arms and moved her legs but kept her feet planted.

"Walk. Hop. Whatever you want. Just move your feet."

Joni now moved through the green space with her entire body.

"I feel silly," Joni said.

"Good." Val smiled. "Now, stop."

Joni stopped.

"You look relaxed."

"I'm definitely not relaxed."

"But you look relaxed; that's what we're after."

Joni nodded. Val sensed that she understood the distinction between her body and her mind, that she had the power to separate them. It was a good start.

"Now shake your face. Like this." Val demonstrated, letting go of her mouth so her lips shook and her skin wobbled. She knew how it looked—ridiculous—and didn't blame Joni for laughing. It was good to hear her laugh. Val shook her face again, then watched Joni try.

"Better. Again. Good."

Joni's face shook like jelly. Now it was Val's turn to laugh.

"Excellent. Hold the sensation of your body and your face being relaxed. Now step up close to me."

Val also stepped up, so now they stood inches apart. Joni emanated a familiar warmth. Val wanted to reach out and hug her to reassure her that she was safe, that Val wouldn't allow Russ to say anything to anyone. She wished she could reassure Joni but how could she when she had no idea if all that was true? She could influence her husband but not control him. Val stood motionless in front of her angry, terrified friend and slowed her breathing until Joni caught on and her own breathing slowed.

Val told her, "Empty yourself of thought."

"Ha."

"Try."

Val watched Joni's outer layer of muscle and skin soften.

"Good. Now remember something that made you happy. Just let the feeling come without thought or effort."

Joni's expression shifted; it was a slight transformation, exactly what Val had hoped to see.

"Now you're sad."

There it was, on Joni's face.

"Now preoccupied."

Joni's forehead clenched.

"Too much. You're showing me worried. Show me preoccupied."

There it was, the small shift Val was looking for.

"Excellent. Now take a deep breath, close your eyes, and let all feeling and thought wash out of you. Now open your eyes. Now walk across the room and turn around to face me. But it's not me, I'm Blair. And it's not today, it's last week. Greet me like it's a regular morning at work and you trust me."

While Joni moved through the green space, Val did the same thing she'd told Joni to do. She turned around and was Blair.

"Morning," Joni said.

"Morning."

"Anything I should know?"

"Hulu green-lit the pilot!"

Joni lit up with genuine delight, then said, "I actually believed you."

Val smiled. "That's great. Just be in the moment and punt. You'll be fine."

"Can we practice how it might go after? Once I find out Blair's the leak?"

"*If* you find out."

"If."

"Try to hold on to that, Joni, because you really don't know for sure. Do you want to rehearse planting the information? Have you thought of what you'll say?"

"Not yet. Right now, I'm more worried about how I'll fire her without losing my shit."

"Okay, let's do that first."

Joni felt a tendril of anxiety touching her, looking for a way in. She breathed into the imagined space between body and mind, inflated it, and pictured a kind of air shaft where anxiety would be vented out and away. It worked. She calmed.

She told Val, "Ready."

Val became Blair again. "Morning."

Joni pictured herself putting down her bag and hanging her sweater over the back of her chair. "Blair, let's go outside and talk for a minute." Outside where it was private. Blair would know what that meant. Immediately, she would understand.

"Okay," Val as Blair said.

They moved a couple of feet along the field of green. Now they were outside, in the front garden at Red Chair. They were sitting, facing each other.

"Blair, I'm—" Joni almost apologized. She caught herself and started over.

"Blair, I realize you and Marc are friends. I also know you've stayed in touch with him this whole time."

Val's face registered alarm, the alarm Blair might feel when she learned she'd been found out. Her head reared.

"I have not been in touch with him!"

Joni almost took the bait but stopped herself. There was no point arguing about what they both knew to be true.

"You're fired," Joni said. "You'll get a month's severance." She'd take the high road. "But I want you to go right now."

"You can't do this to me."

Joni felt a trickle of heat. Do this to her? Was she kidding? She felt her face tightening, lips thinning. Val's eyes—Val as Val—percolated a reminder to pull herself together. Joni took a breath and opened the imaginary space between her body and mind and her anger vented into the ether.

"I didn't do anything to you," she told Blair, Val as Blair, the Blair she knew whose flashes of resentment were so minor they'd dissipate before you bothered to reckon with them, the Blair who succumbed and did what she was told. Joni felt her right eye twitch. Who was she kidding? Deep down she'd always known Blair wanted more.

"I saw that," Val as Val said. "But you caught yourself in time. Well done."

"I hope I can do this," Joni said.

"I know you can."

"Thank you. This has been really helpful."

"Another exercise," Val said. "Then we'll practice planting the info."

Joni shook thought and feeling out of her body then faced Val, ready.

"Tell me your first thought," Val said. "Whatever it is, don't censor it."

"There's no one I can trust." It was the first thing that popped to mind. Joni wasn't sure who she was thinking about when she said that, Blair or Val.

Blair.

She was thinking of Blair.

"Now ask me the same question," Val said. In Joni's eyes she observed another brief struggle as she searched for a footing. It happened sometimes when you were acting, a momentary lapse in confidence when you lost yourself in the scene. It was similar to the disorientation you might feel waking up in a strange room. Val watched Joni find her balance, a settling in her eyes.

Joni said to Val, "Tell me your first thought."

"You can trust me."

"Was that an exercise? That last one?"

Val shook her head. "You *can* trust me, you know."

Joni moved through the rest of the afternoon with a sense of ease that had evaded her that morning when she was so uncomfortable around Blair that she'd actually fled to the bathroom at one point to check her face in the mirror. She'd tried to adjust her features, but it didn't work. Now, after a little coaching, she'd grasped how the shift had to be internalized first. She'd known that in her mind but never in her body, not the way Val had shown her.

She'd felt something, a resistance, melt away as she stood in front of Val. The new distrust had struggled to find a footing inside her; she didn't know how to doubt her old friend. Joni had long found that the older she got, the less she knew, that certainty was as relative and mutable as imagination allowed. She knew Val too well. She just couldn't believe—she didn't want to believe—that her friend was capable of doing her harm.

Blair was different. She could imagine Blair wanting to hurt her simply because there was so much about the young woman Joni didn't know. For so long Joni had rested comfortably in the notion that they were *like family*, but they weren't. They weren't even friends. In many ways Blair was a blank so anything could fit. Unlike her relationship with Val, which was defined by its bonds, her relationship with Blair was defined by its gaps in understanding.

All afternoon Joni avoided Blair. She needed time to practice what Val had taught her. It was helpful, this concept of separating body from mind, locating and sustaining a moving meditation that created a buffer between the nervous system and anxiety. Joni wished she'd learned this skill years ago. It could have saved her so much trouble.

The next morning, she walked into Red Chair feeling prepared.

23

Joni was last to arrive. Mike had his headphones on and was focused on his screen. Diana was in the middle of a call. The room was redolent with the warm, rich notes of Sam's pot of morning coffee. Blair looked up from her laptop and smiled at Joni with the same easygoing friendliness with which she'd greeted her for years. Everything was as usual, yet Joni felt as if she'd stepped into an alternate universe. She forced herself to smile in return before settling in across from Mike.

She felt a stiffness creep into her body, took a breath, and willed it away. She longed to fire the young woman—but not yet. She reminded herself, again and again, that her one task was to confirm that Blair was the leak.

Roddy had advised her to pounce the moment she found the right opportunity. He'd said she'd know it when it came. But all morning, nothing felt right. Twice she caught Blair glancing at her as if wondering what was wrong. Then, after lunch, as they packed up to head over to the Navy Yard, Joni had an idea.

She pulled Blair aside and said, "Let's talk a minute." Maybe she wasn't a good actor, but she knew how to frame a story. She understood the power of deflection. Misdirection. That if she moved the spotlight away from her anxiety-jammed inner air vent she'd be able to get a handle on herself.

They sat alone in the front garden. Blair was clearly uncomfortable, the way she crossed her legs tightly and swung her foot in sharp kicks.

Joni felt like she was on a tightrope and had to get every step exactly right; the slightest breeze could knock her off. She took a deep breath and began. "Things are feeling a little awkward and I thought we should just, you know, talk about it. Clear the air."

"Sure."

"I'm sorry it didn't work out with you and Chris and Haley and the apartment. That's too bad."

Blair exhaled slightly but Joni saw it, a relaxation in her chest. The subject would be the apartment search, not the betrayal.

"It was Chris's idea," Blair explained, making sure it was clear that she herself would never have crossed that boundary. "I mean, we're about the same age, and it's insanely expensive here, so it made sense to get a place together. Except. Well."

"It did make sense," Joni lied. "You've known each other so long. Why not?"

"But. Haley."

"You must have started to feel like a—"

"Third wheel."

Joni nodded. "Exactly. I don't blame you for pulling out."

"I didn't pull out."

Joni's surprise was genuine—she was grateful for an opportunity to express something real. "Oh. I thought . . ." What had she thought? She'd imagined a confrontation, Blair sulking, the arrangement ending. All Chris had told her was that she'd decided to find her own place.

"Chris talked to me first, but I was already going to say something."

"That must have felt really bad."

"Actually, it was kind of a relief. I'm just going to rent a room somewhere. I don't want a lease."

"Where are you staying meanwhile?"

"Still with my friend, but it's tight at her place."

"Apartments are really pricey here," Joni said. "I get the feeling it might be worse than LA."

"I think you're right."

Frank appeared through the building's private door with a small white terrier and stopped when he saw Joni and Blair sitting in the garden. Unable to resist, Joni went over to greet the dog, who tilted his head as she approached.

"Say hello, McDuff," Frank said. McDuff furiously wagged his tail.

"What a cutie." Joni crouched to pet McDuff then watched, smiling, as they left through the gate.

Turning to Blair, she said, "God, I miss Stella. I hope she's okay."

"I know. I'm really sorry. Poor Stella. Poor you." Blair's eyes clouded and for a moment it looked like she might cry.

Joni's jaw wanted to drop but she didn't let it. Had Blair just, in a way, apologized? Was that actual remorse?

And then, out of the blue, Joni saw it: the opportunity Roddy had said she'd recognize when it appeared.

"Well, at least Roddy found my asshole brother again," Joni said, "so at least there's hope."

"Really? Where?"

"Farther south. San Ignacio, this time—staying at a place called Hotel Paraiso—*Hotel Paradise*. As if. It's another crappy motel outside town. Where the hell is he going?"

Blair shook her head as if she wondered the same thing.

One of Joni's hands reflexively clenched. She released it quickly, hoping Blair hadn't noticed. Then, as casually as she could, she slipped in the coin: "Roddy's guy's on his way over there now. Fingers crossed he still has Stella."

Blair held up both hands and crossed two sets of fingers in a display that irked Joni. "I mean, even if a motel isn't dog-friendly, it's Mexico, right? An extra twenty and they don't see the dog." Blair shrugged. "Maybe that's a stereotype, I don't know. I've never actually been to Mexico."

"I have. It's a beautiful country with a rich history. But it depends on where you are, like anywhere."

Blair nodded vaguely, as if she hadn't really heard. "So, should I call a car now?"

"Sure. I'll run to the bathroom and meet you outside."

As Joni turned to go inside, she saw a shadow pass over Blair's face, obscuring her expression. The young woman was on her phone, doing something—summoning a car to take them to the Navy Yard—or maybe something else.

They wouldn't know until Roddy got in touch.

Joni stood in the parking lot at the Navy Yard and stared at Roddy's text, making sure she wasn't misreading it, that her mind wasn't playing tricks. That happened sometimes, especially when she was upset—the omission of a crucial word that changed a sentence's meaning.

Checked out of motel at 2:07 pm put suitcase in car drove away. Sorry no dog.

Joni read it again. *Sorry no dog*. Blair had to know that Stella was no longer with Marc. How long had Stella been out there, abandoned somewhere in Mexico? How far did Marc and Blair plan to take this? What were they up to? Why was Blair still with Joni in New York? Had her promotion changed something, altered their grand plan, whatever it was?

Joni seethed.

Minutes after she'd left Blair in the front garden, Marc packed up and bolted.

This time, though, Roddy's guy followed him.

"Coming?" Mike held open the building's door for Joni.

She looked up from her phone. "Be there in a minute. You guys go ahead."

Joni saw the way Blair glanced at her, the agitation on the young woman's face before she turned to follow Mike and Diana inside. Joni could only imagine what her own face looked like, but she was sure that any shred of acting had sloughed off as she read that message.

She stood alone in the parking lot, the sun ferocious on her face, and she felt blinded. For a moment, she couldn't move.

Because it was true.

It was Blair.

Blair had done this.

Why?

A car pulled into a nearby space, startling her.

She jogged across the lot, out of the sun, into the building's cool lobby and waited for the elevator's light to ding back down the floors from Sunny Day's office where it had just left her colleagues.

The bullpen was quiet, with just a few junior people working in person, as was typical these days. Joni could see from across the room that Blair wasn't at her desk. She wasn't in Joni's office, either. Joni dropped her bag and sweater on her couch and went looking.

Through the glass walls of the small conference room, she saw Mike, Diana, and Chris clustered at one end of the table. Mike and Diana had been working that way lately as if carrying forward the morning seating arrangement they'd grown used to at Red Chair and it wasn't unusual for Chris to pop in for an update on the progress of the developing pitch. Chris spotted her mother approaching and waved hello. Joni waved back.

Coming through the open door, Joni asked, "Anyone seen Blair?"

"What happened?" Chris searched her mother's eyes. But Joni didn't want to spill it all in front of Mike and Diana.

She answered simply, "I need to talk to her."

"I ran into her in the bathroom," Chris said. "She wasn't feeling well. I told her to go home for the rest of the day."

"You told her, or she asked?" The distinction mattered. Everything mattered now.

"She didn't exactly ask. It was more like she told me, and I agreed."

Joni nodded. "Okay. I'll give her a call." She almost added *to see how she's doing* but didn't bother. Soon everyone would know that Blair had been fired, effective immediately, and why.

She'd do it right away and if she couldn't do it in person she'd do it on the phone.

She'd do it in a text.

She'd do it by cutting off her email and every company-related subscription.

She'd do it any and every way she could, and she wouldn't wait.

As Joni stalked the halls, looking for Blair, she braced herself. Gossip would swirl, and stories would build on part fact and part invention. Joni would have to control the narrative if she didn't want it to become about Marc and her and the violence that followed them and oh god, oh god . . .

Dread spun into panic, hardened to anger, and, as the hours wore on and Blair didn't respond to her phone message or either of her texts, melted into an enervated goop.

24

Joni had a pile of work to do and a whole afternoon to do it, but she couldn't focus. All she could think about was Blair—reliable Blair, Paul's Blair, her Blair, their Blair—the Blair she'd relied on so completely that she'd never really thought about her.

She thought about her now. Blair was so young when Paul first hired her—twenty-two or twenty-three, fresh out of college, an art history major. That was, Joni thought . . . ten years ago, the decade when a young person expected their career to blossom.

She tried to recall whether Paul had ever said anything about nurturing Blair's career but couldn't. All she remembered was how much he trusted his stalwart assistant over the years, how they both trusted her. Blair quickly found her footing at Paul's side and by the time he created Sunny Day and planned the move to New York there was no question he'd bring her along.

"She'll come with me," he said. Joni remembered that: Paul in their Malibu kitchen, morning coffee, excited for what he was building, where they were going, how they'd all go together.

"She'll come with me."

Joni didn't recall asking him if he'd discussed it with Blair or decided on his own. He stated it as a given, a fact.

"She'll come with me."

Joni was ashamed to realize how little she'd thought about Blair over the years. Ten years. A whole phase of a lifetime.

Thirty-three. That's how old Blair was now. Just before they left LA, she'd celebrated a birthday.

Thirty-three and she still lived alone, after a broken engagement a few years back.

Thirty-three and a lowly cog in a wheel that never stopped spinning: Sunny Day, Paul's death, Joni's life, Chris's quick ascent in the company.

Joni felt queasy, thinking about that now.

During the height of the pandemic lockdowns, when Joni had returned to California to navigate the company's survival, she brought Chris on as an assistant producer and quickly notched her up through the ranks. They celebrated every elevation with champagne after work—champagne that Blair, in her efficiency, kept on hand.

Chris was now Executive Producer and COO, and Blair, older than Chris, was finally an assistant producer but at the same time effectively still Joni's assistant.

As the day wore on Joni recognized the extent of her mistake in not promoting Blair much sooner. She'd perpetuated Paul's mistake by relying on the young woman as thoughtlessly as he had. The guilt she'd hoped to resolve with the promotion now simmered and clarified, then blackened at the edges.

Blair must have trusted them to recognize her value and felt thwarted when they failed her.

That evening, on her terrace in twilight, darkness gathering, cityscape twinkling, Joni couldn't resist the other feeling that lurked beside her shame for her part in holding Blair back.

It wasn't all her fault.

Blair had failed herself, too; that was a fact. Passivity was never a good strategy. If you wanted something, you had to ask.

No, demand.

As Joni's resentment of Blair's failure to assert herself grew, so did her recognition of the anger that inevitably grew alongside that failure. It was a malignancy, a fierce rage that blinded and drove you and made you do things that were self-serving and unforgivable. It was the aggressive underbelly of entrenched passivity.

Joni knew it well.

How you couldn't bring yourself to take action and at the same time couldn't stop your rage from bubbling over.

But now what?

If Blair had been in touch with Marc all this time, feeding him information so he'd know how to evade them—why?

And why did he take Stella along?

And Blair—what was in it for her? The prize couldn't possibly be the company of a middle-aged, potbellied, money-hungry psychopath. There had to be something else she wanted from all this, but what?

Joni resisted the urge to take a gummy the way she used to fight the urge for a drink. She didn't like to be "too relaxed" (Irene's words) when she appeared for her weekly therapy.

As always, Irene popped on the screen the moment Joni logged in. Clearly, she'd been waiting but made a point not to be first to arrive; maybe it was a billing thing or some arcane insurance rule. Irene always appeared without expression as if prepared to mirror Joni's mood. What Joni saw on her therapist's face the moment it shared the screen with hers was concern.

"What's up?" Irene asked.

Joni wanted to tell Irene that she liked her magenta top, how it was beautiful against her skin. That she liked her hair today, how it was pinned back, allowing her cheekbones to frame her face. That what she knew she had to talk about had left her exhausted, eaten alive from the inside out, and she couldn't.

Joni sighed. "I don't know where to begin."

"Anywhere."

She'd start at the easiest place. "Chris found an apartment. It's on the Lower East Side. She just went to show her friend and sign the lease."

"Her friend . . . ?"

"Haley. The girlfriend. At least, I'm pretty sure that's what it is. *Partner*, I should say."

"You haven't asked?"

"Don't ask, don't tell." Joni forced a smile. "I guess that's also obsolete."

"Totally. This generation's more about not defining."

"Which feels so weird."

Irene nodded.

Joni added, "And isn't exactly easy for a mother."

"How would you feel about Chris and Haley being a thing?"

"Fine. No problem. I like Haley. I just don't like not knowing what's what."

"Not knowing is tough."

"Chris is doing great," Joni said. "If she's found love, I'm happy. And it's good for her that she'll have her own place."

"That's not what's bothering you," Irene said. "But something is. I saw it in your face immediately."

Joni's eyebrows hitched up. "I'm a terrible actor."

Irene smiled in camaraderie. "Me, too."

"I've been trying to act my way through the past couple of days. What a mess."

Every week since Marc had run off with Stella and all his latest lies had fallen away, Joni had updated Irene on the details of what she knew and didn't know. They hadn't spoken since the Zoom bomb about Blair, so Joni filled her in on the latest. Irene listened, rapt, as Joni talked about Blair's betrayal, and her heartbreak that Stella could be lost to her forever. But as usual she held back about the worst of what troubled her: the haunting fear that she and Marc were more alike than not, the panic that what she did to Paul would come out, the cauldron of dread that bubbled constantly below Joni's surface.

"That's a lot," Irene said.

Joni nodded. It was an awful lot—a lot of awful. It really was. For some mysterious reason, hearing Irene say it aloud so simply was helpful. Joni felt her anxiety dial down a couple of notches, an improvement worthy of that gummy she hadn't taken.

"What Blair did," Irene said, "sounds a little like suicide by cop."

It was a startling image. "What do you mean?"

"Think about it."

"You think Blair wanted out?"

"Maybe."

"Then why didn't she quit?"

"Good question."

"This is a ridiculous way to leave a job."

"When we can't bring ourselves to do something on our own, sometimes we self-sabotage."

Self-destruction as other-destruction. There it was again.

By the end of the fifty-five-minute session Joni felt lighter and clearer, as if she'd put down a writhing burden she couldn't tame and could no longer carry. It wasn't solved; it was just set aside.

Chris came home tired but happy.

Joni asked, "How'd it go?"

"Great! I signed the lease. What a day."

"Congratulations." Joni meant it. She was happy for Chris but also sad since she'd be leaving soon. After years of living apart pre-pandemic, Joni had grown used to living with her daughter again. "This will be the first time you've lived in your own place without roommates. How does it feel?"

"Scary. Exciting. I'm ready. I'm glad it worked out this way." Her expression darkened. "You fired Blair?"

"Not yet. I still can't reach her."

"Tomorrow, then."

But Joni had a bad feeling. Blair had never been unreachable for so long. It felt important to finish this, make it official, and send her packing.

"Do you want me to be with you when you do it?" Chris offered.

"Let me think about that."

They shared a late dinner of leftover chicken and salad and discussed how they'd cope without Blair. Once she was officially fired, they'd start searching for a replacement. Roddy's guy would serve Marc the divorce papers, and he'd find Stella, and the turmoil of the past weeks would be behind them. It was part to-do list and part wish list, created by the two women as a scaffolding to keep them upright and strong as the coming days unfolded. Neither broached the possibility that things might not go the way they planned.

They settled in to watch some news, but neither one of them was really watching. They both scrolled their phones while images of a broken world flashed by, narrated by stern voices trying to make sense of it.

Joni couldn't resist checking Blair's social media. Nothing since yesterday. For the first time, she searched years of photos for a glimpse of the life of the person who'd loyally assisted her and, before her,

Paul. It was a gallery of a young woman's twenties but in reverse, starting with lone selfies posted in front of quiet New York sunsets, too many of them, ending in groups of friends at play in Los Angeles. In between was a decade of images of a Millennial young adulthood, highlighting the best moments. For a period of a few years there was a young man, presumably her fiancé, and then he was gone—it hit Joni hard to realize that she'd not only never met the guy but hadn't been particularly interested. The pandemic years looked lonely; she must have been by herself in her studio apartment in Santa Monica. Yes, she was—Joni remembered Blair mentioning it once over Zoom when Joni was just back from Bali, and they were discussing how to get back to work.

Joni put down her phone and thought about Blair and Malibu earlier that spring. How out of nowhere, along came Marc. Friendly Marc. Older and out of shape but fun to be with. Willing, eager, to join Blair on her runs.

Joni could see it now. How a slow drip of disappointment would lower anyone's standards.

The news ended. It was late. Mother and daughter kissed goodnight and went to their rooms.

While Joni was washing up, her phone dinged with an update from Roddy.

Bad news Joni I'm sorry but we lost him in San Quintin there's an airport there we think he got on a flight stay tuned.

How?

Flight to where?

Joni's thoughts raced. She lay in bed and knew she'd never sleep. But she must have, because suddenly it was morning. The room was filled with light. And standing in the doorway, in pajama shorts and the ragged-at-the-collar T-shirt she'd slept in, was Chris, eager as a little girl whose parent wouldn't wake up fast enough.

25

"Stella's microchip pinged the system," Chris announced. "She just turned up in an animal rescue transport from Santa Rosa to Harbor Springs, Michigan. She's in Michigan, Mom—*we can go get her*."

Instantly awake, Joni bolted up and swung her feet to the floor. She grabbed her phone and in minutes found a nine-thirty flight out of LaGuardia that would get them to the Pellston Regional Airport, with one quick flight change, before one-thirty. It was the smallest airport Joni had ever seen, furnished with rough-hewn furniture like a rustic lodge. Shellacked hand-carved signs directed them past the small luggage carousel orbiting a cluster of taxidermized bears, moose heads hanging on the walls, a one-room sheriff's office, and finally, the car rental desk.

Twenty minutes later they pulled into the parking lot at the Humane Society.

There was no one around; the place couldn't have been quieter. Joni and Chris ran to the building's entrance. The front door chimed when they entered, and a woman appeared. She was short and stocky with a wrinkled face mismatched by badly dyed coal-black hair. She had the kindest eyes Joni had ever seen.

"You must be the ladies from New York," the woman greeted them.

"I'm Joni, and this is my daughter, Chris."

"Well, I'm Donna, but you're not here to see me."

They followed her down a hall and through a door to the kennels where the larger animals were kept. There were so many sad-eyed, whimpering, unloved dogs that it hurt to walk past them. Even Stella looked abandoned, curled asleep on a neatly folded blanket beside a bowl of water and a food bowl licked clean. Her fur was matted. She was too thin.

Joni threaded her fingers through the slatted wire and cooed, "Stelladoodle!"

Stella opened her eyes and saw them. She jumped up so fast the crate rattled. Joni pressed her face against the slats and let her pup lick away.

"We checked her out," Donna said. "She's a little scrawny but she seems fine. Just needs a good bath when you get her home. Before you know it, she won't even remember this happened."

Donna was probably right: Stella would likely adapt and forget.

But Joni and Chris would never forget what Marc had put Stella through. What he'd put them all through.

"How did she end up here?" Joni asked.

"Compassion Without Borders—we've been working with them for years. They're an international outfit out of California and we *love* finding homes up here for their rescues. We get a batch from them about once a month. Your Stella came in yesterday—apparently, she was picked up somewhere in Mexico. Can you imagine? It's sad."

"So sad," Joni agreed. But for her, for them, it was a stroke of luck.

"Funny thing," Donna said. "When we scanned her for a chip, we found two."

"That's weird." Chris looked at her mother. "Did you know about that?"

"No." Joni turned to Donna, who shrugged.

"I've seen it before—anytime a dog lands in a shelter it gets chipped. Someone must have chipped her again without checking first. One time we had the sweetest old dog here with three chips. That was a first."

"We got her as a puppy," Joni said. "From a breeder. Do breeders chip before the adoption?"

Donna tried unsuccessfully to suppress her disapproval. Chris also noticed and remarked, "I'd only adopt a rescue, but hey, that's me."

Donna sent them off with both identification numbers and a bag of liver treats.

On the trip home—and it killed Joni to put her beloved double-chipped doodle in cargo, but it was that or a thirteen-hour car ride— they sat side by side, too emotionally exhausted to switch on their flight screens or scroll their phones. They'd bolted so fast that they hadn't brought diversions. Joni knew, though, that even if she'd brought a book along, she wouldn't have been able to concentrate.

"I wish I had my knitting," Chris said. Then she straightened and turned squarely to her mother. "That fucker. I taught him how to knit."

Joni could still see it: Marc and Chris sitting happily together with their knitting, his chunky needles struggling with thick yarn, her slender needles nimble with impossibly delicate strands. She wondered how strong yarn was—if it could be, in certain forms, durable enough to strangle someone with. Her mind wandered to how easy it would be for a middle-aged woman to carry around a craft bag without anyone wondering if it contained something lethal.

She relaxed against her seat and closed her eyes and saw her fingers curl around the imaginary yarn—this yarn, her yarn, was strong as spun steel. She'd wind it around her fingers for a good grip (she'd need gloves), catch Marc at the throat, choke off his air supply. How satisfying that would be.

In her mind, Marc's face turned into Blair's, the freckled cheeks reddening as she struggled to breathe. Joni felt sad watching the light fade out of the young woman's eyes. Then sadness gave way to anger, and she pulled tighter on the wire until the light flickered off. Joni was torn between tears and rage, but how could she help it? Blair had betrayed her; she'd done this to herself.

Then the blond ponytail melted into a balding ginger head and Joni clamped her jaw as she pulled the wire tighter and tighter around Russ's neck. Maybe Val trusted him, but Joni couldn't. He was suspicious of her. He would never be able to hold himself back from telling someone, anyone, the police, that she had possibly, probably, killed her husband five years ago before she left, fled to a country beyond the reach of U.S. laws.

"Mom, are you okay?"

Joni opened her eyes to Chris watching her, a vertical groove pinching her forehead.

"I'm fine. Just spinning a little, but you snapped me out of it."

"You can relax now. We've got our Stelladoodle back."

"We do."

"Uncle Marc's not our problem anymore. Wherever he is, they'll find him, and serve him the papers, and Louisa will get her divorce, and everyone gets to move on. Screw him."

Joni wished it could be that easy. But Marc's transgressions were a mirror that revealed her reflection—she needed to turn that mirror away from herself, to protect herself.

They were both killers who'd gotten away with it.

Joni shuddered, thinking that. She hoped Marc would vanish completely. She could only imagine what he and Blair might have discussed, what he'd share with the police if they caught up with him, that could turn their attention to her.

She reached for Chris's hand and looked out the plane window at a blue-gray sky hovering above a menacing horizon of dark clouds, stretched thin like an angry mouth about to open.

THE PUSH

26

"We should go to the police," Russ said. He used his knife to separate a single layer of flesh from the grilled salmon on his plate, then forked it into his mouth.

"No," Val said. "We can't. Absolutely not."

His gaze settled on her. "You need to see this clearly."

She didn't like his tone: cold, superior. And she didn't like that look in his eyes, trying to pin her down like she was a writhing butterfly. At the same time, she recognized how little she cared what he thought about her. No, that wasn't exactly it; she cared. But now, this forceful pushing back . . . well, it was a new feeling. She pictured herself saying, *If you don't like it, that's your problem.* She'd never spoken to him like that before. She'd always been willing to reconsider her positions and find a compromise. Before he told her about the cancer, her malleability had reached an extreme as she'd teetered on the edge of paralyzing doubt, an edge from which she'd allowed herself to be pulled in any direction if it kept the peace—to keep him at home with her. Well. Now she knew the truth; he wasn't cheating on her; he had cancer, not Big Cancer but Little Cancer, Curable Cancer. He wasn't going anywhere. And now that she'd discovered that she was capable of such a profound self-defeating timidity, such an ugly insecurity, she wasn't going to let it happen again.

Joni was right. Joni, of all people. Her friend, who was capable of so much—of anything, it turned out.

Joni. Who had deliberately poisoned her husband. Who had finally outright admitted it.

It was that clunk of fact that had catalyzed the shift Val recognized within herself now. A new clarity that felt like confidence. Up until now, coping with the possibility had been easier because there was always that comfortable landing pad—*of course Joni didn't kill Paul, she wouldn't, she couldn't, not really*. But Joni *did* kill Paul. It was that simple.

No, not simple.

Definitive.

Clear.

A shifting from one foot to the other and staying there, settling.

The empathy Val felt for her friend soothed her, but she couldn't help wondering if she should be more worried than she was, more afraid of Joni's capacity to remove a thorn from her side even if she had to cross boundaries to do it.

Was Val now a thorn?

Russ would be, for sure.

Why did Joni have to do it? Kill Paul, that monster, when she could have let the law deal with him. She didn't have to do it herself. If she'd controlled herself five years ago, their friendship wouldn't be in this spot now.

Were they even still friends? Even after the acting lesson, Val wasn't sure.

Now, sharing dinner with her husband and discussing this very subject—what to do about Joni and Marc—Val wondered, really wondered, what the siblings *were* capable of.

An old saw ran through her mind: "Keep your friends close and your enemies closer." Who said that? Who else understood what she was going through? There was no one she could talk to about the problem of loving two people who hated each other and fearing them both. Absolutely no one.

But Joni wasn't an enemy. Val loved her. As she thought about it and thought about it, compassion overcame doubt and she felt awful for her friend who was clearly suffering, cornered by fear—fear of herself and now also of Russ.

Still, Val worried about what Joni might do to Russ. Given what she was capable of doing.

Joni had boxed herself in and now they were boxed in with her.

There was also this: Val had lied when she told Joni that Russ was under control. Had she told her that? Or maybe she'd just implied it. In any case, he wasn't.

Val's quest, she decided, lifting a forkful of salmon to her mouth, was to find a place of perfect balance where neither acted on their worst impulse.

She loved them both.

She would challenge them to be their better selves.

Russ took a sip of water, put down his glass, and looked at her like he thought her judgment was off. Somehow, even with all their talking, he'd managed to finish his meal.

"We have to go to the police with this," he said again. "They're dangerous, both of them."

"Marc, maybe. But Joni? No."

"Val, come on."

"No."

"You're colluding if you don't report them."

"Colluding?"

She saw the way he reared so slightly that he hoped she wouldn't notice. Well, she noticed and mirrored his arrogance right back at him. He didn't like it, either.

"Who with?" she asked.

"Both of them."

"I'm not colluding with that asshole."

"With Joni, then."

"Russ, all I told you was that I had a feeling about something. I was angry, and I'd had a couple of glasses of wine, and I said something I shouldn't have said. Feelings aren't facts. If I went to the police about a feeling they'd laugh at me." Luckily, she'd never told him that Joni had confirmed that feeling. She didn't plan to; Joni didn't deserve it. She really didn't.

"I agree with your feeling."

"You agree with my feeling?" Her quick smile was automatic whenever she heard something absurd.

"Your intuition," he tried to clarify but it was really the same thing.

"Come on, honey, be reasonable. You're a reasonable person."

"It's not unreasonable," he said, "to go to the police with these very grave doubts. They could decide to reopen the investigation into Paul's death, see what they find."

"Look," she told him. "You're overreacting. I didn't mean what I said about Joni. And when you repeated it to her that night—wow."

His pale eyebrows shot up and his cheeks flushed with color. He looked healthier and stronger, and she wondered if they should argue more often. "*Wow*, what?"

"*Wow*, I couldn't believe it." The surge of anger surprised and pleased her and became the skin within which her confidence grew. She raised her voice. "What if I blurted out everything we discussed in private when we were with friends? What if I came out and announced,

'Russ had to borrow money *from his parents* to expand his business?' How would you like that?"

He sighed heavily. "Alright. I'm sorry."

"Please don't do that again. Please just keep what's between us, between us."

"I get it." His tone sharpened as if to cut her down.

"You know what? You have a choice to make. You can go to the police and tell them all about your feelings about my feelings about my best friend and her fucked-up brother. Or you can stay married to me." She stood up to clear her plate even though there was still some salmon left. She ate the last bite on her way to the sink.

Russ made a "huh" sound, the sound of air leaving his body. He clearly hadn't expected that of her, and she liked the sense of power it gave her. She had more power than she'd ever realized. Apparently, he was as afraid of losing her as she was of losing him.

"I don't like being told what to do," he said.

She turned to face him, her back to the sink. "I'm not telling you what to do. I'm telling you what I'll do if you do what I don't want you to do."

He got up from the table and walked away, leaving his plate behind.

She turned off the kitchen light and followed him to the living room where he sat in his chair and turned on the TV. The way he scrolled quickly down dozens upon dozens of possibilities without stopping to consider any told her that his mind was working over the choice she'd given him. Eventually he settled on what they always watched at this hour: the news.

But unlike other nights Val did not take her place on the couch. She continued on to the screened-in porch off the living room to sit in the quiet late-spring evening. She loved the sound of crickets, and the fireflies were out in force. When Zeke was little the three of them

used to sit out here together and marvel at the display. She was looking forward to spending some time with her son during his summer
break but wasn't desperate for it—another recognition. It was just a
beginning, but she was learning to do without, to find herself in a space
that felt not empty but vast.

Maybe she'd let her gray come in. Grow racing stripes like Joni's
if she could.

The sound of the news stopped, and the screen door creaked open.

Sitting beside her on the wicker love seat, Russ took her hand
and said, "Okay."

She smiled and repeated, "Okay."

For the first time in months, she felt a balance between them,
holding space on their opposite ends of the marital seesaw, hovering
at an even height. Then her side tipped.

There was one more thing to clear up.

She still hadn't told him that her anger before wasn't only about
this disagreement. There was something else she'd been stewing on
that she needed to say when the moment was right.

Screw it: There would be no right moment.

She told him, "While we're at it, I'll just say this, too. You were
wrong not to tell me about the cancer. You should have told me right
away so I could share it with you and support you and help you through
it. I'm angry at you for thinking I wasn't strong enough. That's what
needed to be told. To me."

"The marriage police." A smile in his tone.

She squeezed his hand. "I feel guilty saying that, but I had to get
it off my chest. In my mind I understand why you didn't tell me, but
in my heart it hurts."

He squeezed back. "It was a mistake. I kind of knew it as it was
happening, but I went with it. I'm sorry."

"This is good," she said. "I like it when we talk like this."

"Yeah," he agreed. "Me, too."

They fell silent and watched the blinking fireflies for a while before drifting into the house and putting the TV back on.

While Russ was searching for a show, she checked her phone and saw that she'd missed an earlier text from Joni: a selfie with Stella.

That's a nice one, Val replied. She assumed that Joni was revisiting old pictures, missing Stella as usual. Then another text arrived.

Taken today!!!

"Oh my God!" Val jumped up, aware of Russ watching her as she hurried out of the room to call Joni. She'd been wanting to call her all day and this was the invitation; she hated how hesitant their estrangement had made them with each other.

She had so many questions.

27

Joni woke with her face buried in a cloud of soft brown fur. Stella smelled of chamomile from the shampoo they'd given her following cuddles and licks, a meal, more cuddles and licks, a snack. For a moment, Joni thought her pup was purring, that soft rolling sound of happiness, but of course she wasn't. Her copious tongue spread across Joni's face once, twice, before she bounded out of bed. Right. She had to pee.

Out they went into the golden morning. Joni wondered if she was dreaming—walking Stella, happy in New York of all places, the same New York she'd once fled for her life. Walking and whole and happy in air so weightless it was as if it didn't exist.

Then the thought of Marc ripped her open.

And she zipped herself right back up.

It was over as far as she was concerned. It had to be.

She had her Stella back. That was all she wanted.

It was just a matter of hearing from Roddy or Louisa or whoever got to her first that Marc had been found, wherever he was now, and served the divorce papers. Then they could collectively pop the proverbial champagne and move on to the next thing. Meantime Joni wouldn't allow herself to think about her rotten brother. She was not a reflection of him. She wouldn't allow herself to think she was. She was better than him. She was.

She wouldn't think about Blair or Russ, either. Every time she thought about them her blood pressure rose, so she wouldn't. She would tunnel her vision forward only and work on her project without thinking about any of them or any of it. She'd done it before. She knew how.

When Joni got home from walking Stella, Chris had already left for work. After breakfast and a shower, she headed out with Stella in tow; she was not yet ready to leave her behind. Their vet had phoned in a prescription for heart medicine to a local vet and Joni stopped to pick it up on the way to Red Chair.

Frank had finished a rough cut of the pilot. A screening had been scheduled for ten and pushed to eleven to accommodate Joni's delay. When she walked in with Stella at her side she expected a cheer to rise from the group, and when it didn't she felt gratified that their efforts to keep the Marc thing private had succeeded. With Blair gone, no one here knew the details. As far as they were concerned Stella had just arrived from LA, fresh from a solo flight in cargo.

Frank was standing at the open door when they appeared at the small screening room downstairs. Sam and Diana went immediately to the sofa closest to the screen while Joni and Mike hung back. Frank dug his hand into his jeans pocket and produced a treat for Stella, who lapped it up. He let her keep on licking when the treat was obviously gone, making them fast friends.

"She's a beauty." He beamed at Joni. "I bet you're glad to finally have her here."

"To say the least."

Joni and Mike settled into the sofa at the back of the room. Her phone bleeped—she'd forgotten to silence it.

"Oops. Sorry." While she switched off the phone, she saw that Roddy had tried calling.

Her pulse lurched. So, they finally got to Marc. She reached down to pet Stella—settled at her feet—to hide her smile.

Frank pushed a button on the console. The room darkened and the audio system eased on. In Frank's rough cut, music arrived first. It was like sinking underwater in a sea of sound, with waves pulsing at you from every direction. The screen silvered and then filled with a black-and-white still image of Barbara and Marianne hauling their boxes across a bustling Midtown street that gathered color and sprung into movement in sync with the soundtrack. It was like past and present, fact and fiction, clasping hands across space and time. Joni loved it.

The cut was just under an hour, perfect for a pilot. When the screen faded to black—where eventually credits would roll—the lights came halfway on, a soft awakening. Joni felt mesmerized. Satisfied. Frank had done excellent work. She had notes, of course, they all would; it was their job to pick the cut apart so it could be even better. The key was not to confuse better with different.

They talked for over an hour. Even Diana, an assistant, jumped in as was expected of anyone who wanted to get ahead. In this business anyone who didn't want to get ahead wasn't tolerated, though it was never a given that the gates would open even for the hungriest. You were expected to fight but not win. Winning was for the most ruthless. The killers. That awful, digressive thought felt like a bloom of ice in Joni's heart. She realized she'd stopped listening to what Diana was saying. But thankfully Sam was taking notes.

"Good," Joni said. "I think we're in good shape. Let's break for lunch then head over to the Navy Yard. We'll meet outside at—" She looked at her phone to see the time. It was after one o'clock. A text from Roddy flashed on the screen too quickly to read. "—Two fifteen," Joni finished her sentence.

She thanked Frank as the others scattered.

"I don't enjoy every project," he said, "but I've had a lot of fun with this one."

"It shows." And then, without thinking, she added, "If we land the pilot and get a season, I hope you'll edit."

His whole face smiled, chin to scalp. "You will, and I'd be honored."

She knew she shouldn't have made that offer without first consulting with the team, but her gut told her it wouldn't be an issue. This must have been how Chris felt when she'd impulsively requested a full bid from Red Chair before first consulting with Joni; it was a sign not of recklessness but the kind of confidence a leader needed.

"Feel like grabbing a bite?" Frank asked.

"Sure. Just give me a minute to catch up." She waved her phone in the air.

She wandered into the hall and scanned her messages. There were forty-seven new emails, nine of which were semi-urgent, and the text from Roddy. She stopped moving long enough to read.

Sorry I missed you I'll be on a flight until two will call you then have some news.

She walked up the stairs with Stella at her heel. In the kitchen she paused long enough to take a deep breath. *Go to hell, Marc. Louisa's got you now. You won't get away with a penny of her money.*

Joni and Frank sat together in the garden with their take-out salads. Joni wished she could tell him that this was a celebration. Instead they basked in satisfaction that the rough cut was a success and delighted in watching Stella and McDuff alternately sniff each other and lay in puddles of sun like old, mismatched friends.

Yes, if the pilot sold (and why wouldn't it?) and a season was ordered (and why wouldn't it be?), it would be a pleasure to work with this kind, talented editor at his homestyle workplace that was almost too good to be real. For a moment she saw herself softening to Frank's charms. Maybe she didn't need to swear off all men. Maybe there were still one or two who deserved a second look.

She reeled herself back in.

A wise woman had once warned her, when she was a young aspiring filmmaker, "Don't shit where you eat." It was crude but it got the point across, especially for women, and especially for women with power. Double standards were sharp on both ends and could be weaponized. Not could but would. Even if you made it to the top, you still weren't wanted there.

She stopped herself from gathering their empty containers; she was a paying client and the post house would take care of it. Standing, she thanked him again for his good work.

At ten-past-two she summoned an Uber. Roddy still hadn't called. She would give him until two-thirty before trying him.

The wait for a pet-friendly car was longer than usual. By the time it arrived the team was gathered on the sidewalk and growing restless. It wouldn't be long before they had a final cut of the pilot. It was bad timing to be ghosted by Blair given how abruptly she'd left without tying up loose ends. They'd have to replace her as soon as possible. Maybe there was someone in-house who could step in—Diana had some ideas. They packed into the car, brainstorming about the pitch, final touches, and scheduling. It was an exciting moment in the process when, after years of writing, pre-production, production, and finally postproduction, a concept was transforming into a reality that surpassed the suspension of disbelief required to make something solid out of what had started as an idea, a vapor.

"We did it, folks," Joni said as they pulled up at the Navy Yard. "This is going to work."

Communal whoops and high-fives swallowed the vibrations of Joni's phone. Only when they were approaching the elevator did she see that Roddy had tried her again.

"Meet you upstairs," she told them.

Roddy answered right away. "Sorry about the phone tag."

Wherever he was, it was noisy. "Where are you?"

"Newark airport. Hold it, here's my car."

She heard him exchange a few words with someone, the slam of a door, the leaned-on horn of a frustrated driver.

"I'm on my way to Colts Neck," Roddy told her.

"Delivering the good news to Louisa in person?" How gallant of him, she thought, if unnecessary.

"Good news?"

"I assume your guy finally caught up with Marc." She allowed a smile into her tone as she pictured the scene: Marc grinding his jaw as the guy thrust the papers into his hand, mission accomplished.

"No. Your brother's gone. We think he's moving under a new alias now. It's like he vanished into thin air. I've never seen anything like it."

A chasm opened inside Joni, a light-sucking darkness.

Where was he now?

Who was he now?

How had he done it—again?

"You're on your way to tell Louisa." Of course, that was it. Joni felt bad for Louisa that it still wasn't over for her.

"I wish," he said. "But I never had a chance."

She didn't understand. "What's going on? You said you had news."

Roddy exhaled loudly. "Louisa was in a car accident last night, turning into her exit off Route 18 on her way home, apparently. She's dead."

28

Like a bird, Joni flew high above the scene and witnessed it from a great distance. There she was, down below, a little speck of a human being, her white sneakers two dots that twitched back and forth on an asphalt grid. A leashed brown dog kept pace. Nearby, a car slotted into the grid, turning the sunshine back on itself in sharp reflective flashes that seemed to reach out and electrify her.

She stopped moving and buried her face in her hands.

She dropped her arms and started moving again, white dots shuddering across the grid.

Another speck hurried toward her, red-haired and arms spread wide.

"Mom!"

Joni flew back to her body to receive her daughter's embrace.

"Are you okay? What's wrong? What happened?"

"Louisa's dead."

Joni felt the pause in Chris's body, the cool air between them as she pulled away. Chris's eyes widened. "Dead?"

"Roddy just told me. It was a car accident. Last night."

"Oh, Mom. Let's go inside." Chris kept their arms clasped all the way up to Joni's corner office. It was chilly; the air conditioning was on though it wasn't hot outside. The closed windows created a bubble of quiet. Joni took a deep breath and felt herself start to calm. She could see the soundstages with their closed doors, people milling around outside, popping quickly in or out so as not to disturb the worlds hidden inside. Was that Val coming out of Stage Five? Joni wasn't sure.

Chris brought her mother a cup of peppermint tea and told her to sit down and quietly have some. Joni obeyed. The tea soothed her. Chris sat beside her on the sofa and shared the stunned silence until the door flung open, and there was Val.

From her face, furrowed, drawn, it was clear that she already knew; Chris must have texted her. She stood with her hands on her hips, pitched forward, looming over them, studying their faces as if trying to understand how this could have happened.

"A crash?" Val asked.

Joni nodded. "At her local exit. Roddy thinks she was on her way home."

"Was she alone in the car?"

Joni hadn't thought about Louisa's son Lawrence. "Oh my God."

"Mom," Chris asked, "was she?"

"Roddy didn't say she wasn't."

"What time did it happen?" Val asked.

"I don't know."

"Where was she coming from that late?"

Joni didn't know.

"Let's get Roddy on the phone." In response to her own directive, Val dialed. She put the call on speaker and placed the phone on the coffee table so they could all hear.

As soon as he said hello, they spewed questions like buckshot. He took them randomly.

"She was alone."

"It happened a little after one a.m."

"She had dinner with a friend then they went to see a movie."

"Her blood alcohol level was within the limit. She might have had a drink earlier in the evening, but her driving wouldn't have been impaired."

"Her son was at his dad's."

"No, we still don't know where Marc is."

"No, the divorce papers weren't signed."

"New Jersey is an equitable divorce state. They weren't separated very long, but I don't know. The lawyers will have to determine what happens now since technically there's no divorce in-process without the signed papers."

"I don't know if she changed her will recently."

"Ladies." Roddy stopped them. "I'm with the local police right now. I'll have to call you back."

Joni asked, "The police? Why?"

"Hang tight," he told them and hung up.

Val sat opposite the couch and the three women looked at each other.

Chris said it first: "Do you think Uncle Marc . . . ?"

Killed Louisa. That's what Chris was about to say and it irked Joni and hurt her that her daughter should come so close to the awful truth of who he was and what he was capable of. Would she also someday see her mother right there beside him, radiant with the same capabilities?

"Hard to say," Joni answered. But she felt no ambivalence. Of course he did it, the bastard. She pictured it: Marc behind Louisa in a car rented under some alias, harassing, road raging, terrifying her, running her off the road.

It wouldn't stop with Louisa. There would be others.

And what about Blair?

She still hadn't surfaced anywhere in any form.

How did a young woman vanish off the face of the earth without leaving even a fragment of a digital trace?

In Joni's dream, she's slumped at a low table sized for children, her hands wet with purple fingerpaint. Then the paint is red. Looming in front of her is a podium behind which a judge sits on a tall director's chair. And the judge's face is pocked because he has cancer; the cancer is eating his skin and his mind and his heart. And the judge is Russ. And Russ slams down his gavel again and again.

Finally she opened her eyes, and it was Chris, knocking on her bedroom door.

"Time to get up."

Russ. He was lodged inside her head. She couldn't trust him not to reopen the question of her guilt. That was Joni's first thought when she rubbed her eyes to check her phone for the time. It was only seven-thirty.

"It's early."

"Haley made us breakfast."

Joni didn't smell anything. She thought of Louisa, dead, run off the road most likely. She thought of Marc and ground her jaw and her itch flared. She couldn't socialize, not this early, not today. She'd stay in bed and work from home. She wouldn't—couldn't—see anyone except Chris until Sunday at the funeral. She'd be able to pull her head together by then. But breakfast with people she barely knew, right now?

"No."

"Mom!" Chris's sharp tone made Joni snap open her eyes. She was awake now, really awake. "She cooked. It was thoughtful of her and kind and generous, and I won't let you screw up my relationship, so get out of bed and get dressed and come on. We're going."

Chris had already walked and fed Stella, who was napping on the couch. Joni checked the twice-a-day pill organizer and saw that she'd also had her morning medicine.

They stepped out of the elevator on the eighth floor and walked to the end of the hall, drawn by the smell of bacon and coffee. The door to 8F was cracked open. Inside, the country breakfast aromas intensified. Joni felt herself relax a notch. Two notches. Griff appeared with his silver hair slicked back from a shower, his face with a freshly shaven gleam. He was barefoot, as was Haley, who appeared in a red apron to welcome them. Joni and Chris slipped off their shoes and followed them inside.

The apartment was modest compared to Joni's penthouse but cheerful. Its south-facing windows bathed the place with light. It took just a minute for Griff to show them around while Haley set the table.

"It was a choice between a small terrace or a second bedroom for Haley. It was a no-brainer." He'd taken the two-bedroom, otherwise Haley wouldn't have been able to afford the city while she got on her feet.

He had a small desk set up in his bedroom where he worked as a "remote therapist," laughing at his choice of words when he realized how bad it sounded.

"Actually," Chris said, "I once had a therapist who constantly overshared about her own life. I prefer my therapists remote."

Griff nodded, smiling. Joni liked his crowded teeth, their slanted overlaps. The recent trend of perfect white smiles had filled her with alarm. Flawlessness was a bad sign; it meant some extreme fault had been covered over and was lurking in the darkness to leap out at you. She thought of Frank, wondered what she didn't see when she looked at him, wondered why his wife bolted and wished she hadn't thought of him at all.

The small table by the window was crowded with bacon, eggs, toast, muffins, berries, yogurt, a porcelain cow milk pitcher, a silver sugar bowl. A calm warmth enveloped them as they crowded in, passed dishes around and filled their plates. Unlike the penthouse view of low buildings, sky, and river, this view's sky was interrupted by denser, taller buildings and a partial view of the Brooklyn Bridge.

The food was delicious.

No one mentioned Louisa's death.

So, this was the way a therapist breakfasted after a shock: gently, deliciously, in good company. She was grateful. An hour later, when they said their goodbyes, she meant it when she thanked them.

Chris stayed behind to help with the dishes. Joni felt much better and decided to go into Red Chair after all. She no longer needed or wanted to hide out alone. She needed people, distraction, and work.

Frank was almost finished with a final cut.

The pitch was nearly polished.

Joni worked all through Friday night and Saturday, trading texts with her team. There was no hard deadline, but it helped her to pretend there was one because then she wouldn't think.

She wouldn't think about Marc or Blair or Russ.

She wouldn't think about her imaginary yarn-wire digging into their throats.

She wouldn't feel the power in imagining how she could end them, the release of imagining they'd no longer be in the world.

She wouldn't recognize the instinct that drove her past limits and bound her to a brother she detested more than feared.

29

Val wasn't surprised by the irritated look on Joni's face when she and Russ appeared in the crisply air-conditioned living room of Louisa's grand art-filled house where mourners had been invited—by Marshall Singer, Lawrence's father, Louisa's first husband—to gather after the funeral. Joni and Chris were standing in front of an ornate fireplace already filled with a stack of logs, ready for next winter. Both held a delicate-looking cup and saucer; everyone did: It was something to do with your hands when you were at a loss. Val and Russ detoured to the dining room where a caterer had arranged platters of luncheon food. Steam rose from their coffee as they made their way back to the gathering and the inevitability of facing Joni together.

She could see it in Joni's eyes, the questions, *Why is Russ here? Why did you bring him? He has nothing to do with this. He isn't needed.*

The answer was that he'd insisted on coming so Val wouldn't have to face a funeral alone. Maybe Val would explain that later to Joni, maybe she wouldn't. Val recognized that she had two lives to live at the moment and she had to live them simultaneously, and when they overlapped, like now, she'd have to navigate between them and hope she wouldn't accidentally set her two beloved bombs off against each other. She wasn't sure what to say to Joni, how to begin, so she said nothing and leaned to kiss her hello.

"I'm having a little trouble absorbing this," Joni said.

Val agreed, opting to hear that as a comment about Louisa's sudden death, not Russ's presence here. She spotted the son, Lawrence, across the room, sitting beside an old woman who might have been his grandmother. Must have been, the way he let her hold his hand between her bony speckled ones. Val had seen him before, once, playing soccer, a shortish sturdy kid with thick dark hair and the first hint of a mustache. He must have shaved it off. He'd also had a haircut. He almost didn't look like the same kid who'd energetically dribbled the ball across the field. Here, minus his mother, he exuded a listless vacancy that made Val fear for her own son. It was shocking how efficiently life could cut you off at the knees before you even got started.

"That's her son," Val said.

Russ, Joni, and Chris looked at Lawrence.

"Poor kid," Joni said.

"Can you believe all this art?" Chris asked. "I didn't know she was a collector."

"Neither did I," Val said. "We didn't really know her."

Joni agreed, "No, we didn't."

Marshall Singer came over to introduce himself and they reciprocated. He was short with a square jaw and full head of salt-and-pepper hair. Lawrence took after him. He hadn't aged as well as Louisa. Val tried to picture them young and in love but couldn't. She'd never known Louisa well but had come to like her. She could picture Louisa with Marc but only because she first met them together at the soccer game. It was the only way she could imagine them together. But she couldn't picture Louisa with Marshall. Neither of her husbands, the one who dumped her or the one who conned her, had deserved her. She was too good for both of them. And now she was dead.

Val's eyes teared.

"I'm sorry for your loss," Marshall said, assuming they'd been close.

"Actually, I didn't know her that well," Val said. "We were just getting to know each other but I liked her. She had some really bad luck."

Marshall nodded.

Cynicism pinched up half of Joni's mouth, lopsiding it. Val recognized the look and braced herself. Chris must have also noticed because that was the moment she chose to edge away.

"Bad luck or bad judgment," Joni said. "Or both?"

"What's your name again?" Marshall asked.

"Joni. Joni Ackerman. My brother was her—"

"Got it. Right. Arno, except that wasn't his real name." Marshall smirked. "I still don't understand how she bought it."

"She bought you," Joni said. "And you weren't real either."

His face smoldered. "I was real. We loved each other. We had a wonderful marriage for a while."

"You returned her for a full refund."

"I didn't get a full refund, though, did I?" His arm extended to present the room, the art, the house, the wealth Louisa had come away with at his expense.

"She was broken when she met my brother. You left her broken. She was a prime target for someone like him."

Marshall retracted his head as if slapped and assessed Joni. Val knew what he was thinking; she felt it and saw it in the slits of his eyes. He wanted to call Joni a nasty woman. A bitch. He was unequipped to spar with her the way another woman would, directly, with spiked words. His impulse was to leap on to his high horse where he could display his dominance. To insult her. But times had changed and he couldn't do that anymore, so he stood there and stared at her.

Val also recognized that her friend was redirecting to Marshall the venom she really wanted to direct at Russ. The words would be different but the intent—to cut him down and disempower him—was the same.

She stepped closer to Joni, hoping her old friend would feel the warmth of her presence, remember their bond, and stand down from the heat of her immediate impulses.

Lawrence came over and his father leaned to receive a whisper. Turning back to the group, he said in a tone dripping with bullshit, "Nice to meet you all. Thanks for coming." Marshall and Lawrence were exactly the same height, Val noticed, as they walked off together and disappeared into another room.

"Well, it was good of him to host this here," Russ said. "For the kid's sake. It can't be easy, wading into his ex-wife's world."

Val and Joni looked at Russ at the same time and in the same way: astounded that he would sympathize with this man who broke Louisa.

Val needed to say something to rein her husband in because if he couldn't see that Joni was still raw and seething and would turn on him in a flash, then she'd have to warn him. But just as she was about to drag him away and set him straight for his own good, the old woman across the room tried to stand up, wobbled, and started to fall.

Joni felt hot, electric, ready to snap. And now Val had rushed off to help the old woman, leaving her alone with Russ, standing there in Louisa's living room.

Louisa's living room.

This was where she'd lived out both her marriages and where she'd tried to return the night her life was cut short. This house. This room. Right here.

And that was the boy who would no longer have her in his life. Who would be left to be molded by the first man who'd demolished his mother. Who would look back and remember the second man who should have loved her but instead used her. Who would wonder what was wrong with his mother that men had opted to damage instead of love her. Who would never trust love again.

Still, she shouldn't have lashed out at Marshall. There was no point. She'd known that but had done it anyway because she couldn't stop herself. She hadn't wanted to stop herself. She hadn't wanted to even try. But she should have; she should have tried. Because now she felt unleashed and she was alone with Russ and what she really wanted to say to him—well, it was a lot.

She saw Val glance at her from across the room. The flash of understanding: Val *saw* her. Saw that, for Joni, Russ was a liability. He was the pin on a grenade that needed to be pushed back in but was slipping out.

Joni crackled, alert. She turned to Russ and stared at him. He stared back, his pale face tightening around that bluish dirty-water gaze of his.

"Why do men always take each other's side?" she asked as if it was a real question.

"Why do women?"

"To survive."

"Is that why you killed Paul?"

"Excuse me?"

"You heard me."

"I know what you think, but you're wrong."

"Am I?"

"If you're so sure, wouldn't you be worried I'd do the same to you if you don't keep your mouth shut?"

Joni watched Russ lurch over to Val and grab her arm and, at the harshness of his touch, saw the tension that lit her friend's body as he dragged her away. He had no right to handle Val that way. Manhandle.

Womanhandle wasn't a word because when a woman handled a man, he tended to be grateful. And if he wasn't, if he was like Paul, he died. At that moment, Joni's rage and remorse melded into a hard truth.

Russ was right to fear her.

And she was right to fear him for what he understood about the danger she posed, loose in the world like her brother.

She had a serious problem.

Two problems: Marc, her lifelong thorn, and now Russ.

She stood alone in the enormous room, sure that everyone had heard everything and didn't dare approach her. But as the moment passed she saw that no one was aware of her. People continued to sip their coffee and nibble on food and admire the art and chat with each other. They were gathered for Louisa, to remember her. Any explosive undertones were playing out discreetly. She was too preoccupied to wonder what others here were thinking about Louisa, her life, her husbands, her wealth, Lawrence's future. There was a lot to process, as Irene would say, slipping out of another session at the strike of fifty-five minutes.

Chris returned with a small plate of tiny sandwiches, chips, and pickle slices. "Here, I made you some lunch."

"You're sweet, feeding me today." Joni took the plate, but her stomach was in knots and she couldn't eat.

"I saw Val and Russ leaving."

"They had to be somewhere."

"How long do you want to stay?"

"I'm ready whenever you are."

"Eat that first, Mom. You're no fun when you're hungry."

"I'm not really hungry." But to please her daughter Joni started on one of the sandwiches—roast beef and kimchi, delicious.

Across the room, Roddy appeared with his starter cup and saucer freshly steaming. She'd imagined him short, but he was tall and lanky. As soon as he spotted her, he headed over.

"How's it going?" he asked.

"Roddy, hi. This is my daughter, Chris."

They nodded their greetings.

"We're about to leave," Joni told him.

"I'm glad I caught you. It's good to meet in person."

"It is," she agreed. "Roddy, I'm curious about something. Did Louisa ever change her will?"

"That's the question of the hour. It was in-process but not complete. But she made a codicil, at least."

"Good." Marc didn't deserve a penny of what Louisa had left behind.

"Well, it'll limit him, but without anything signed, the divorce summons or the will, things are kind of up in the air. Unless there's a criminal case, which would change things."

Joni breathed against a rush of panic. "Are the police investigating him?"

"Nothing's official yet but it's on the radar. They're in touch with Carolyn Knudson's insurance company. There's too much there not to make you wonder: one man, all the aliases, two rich wives who die and, of course, your parents. I'm helping them out all I can but at this point the ball's in their court."

"I hope they get him," Chris said. Joni noticed how quickly her daughter's anger at Marc had shed its ambiguity and solidified, the uncle she'd warmed to and taught to knit and now wanted hunted and dealt with. It amazed and impressed and worried her, the swiftness with which this new generation raised its fist for blood. Unless it was just them, the Ackermans, and an innate predilection for vengeance.

A whole family of psychopaths—is that what they were? The thought horrified Joni but also excited her.

Was it a weakness or a strength?

Patricia Highsmith wasn't torn, and neither were her most devi-ous, powerful, fascinating characters. They knew their power and enacted it and so did she: "Yes, but why not?"

Was that what Highsmith meant? That it made you a monster but was also kind of . . . a gift?

"I hate to say it, he's my brother, but I agree," Joni said. "I hope they get him." But she didn't mean it. If they got him, they might find their way to her. She wanted him gone but not that way.

"Actually," Roddy said, "it might make the difference if they hear from you. The cops seem ready to go but their sergeant thinks they need more than 'hot air.'"

"Hot air?"

"Conjecture. Background from you might tip the balance."

Joni nodded. "I'll think about it. Maybe you could keep looking for him in the meantime? I'll keep paying you whatever Louisa was paying." If Roddy could track him down, she could solve this herself without the police and their messy curiosity. She thought of the wire digging into Marc's throat, breaking skin, drawing blood, the panic in his eyes.

"I don't know," Roddy said. "Your brother's gone. It's like he evaporated. I don't have the tools the cops have to find him. They could get an Interpol warrant, use a facial recognition APB, and have a decent chance of snaring him that way. Think about it."

"Let's do it, Mom." Chris's eyes shone, hungry to advance.

Joni nodded and sighed to express her exhaustion but promised nothing.

It wouldn't be a simple leap from here to there. Joni would have to find a way to explain to Chris the dangers of working with the police without overburdening her with too many damning details. Joni had been, and remained, adamant that Chris never know that her mother had killed her father. It would be too much to carry forward, and Joni now saw that it could be the final push that doomed her to be *just like your mother*—every daughter's nightmare. If Chris knew what Joni had done, she would hate her and emulate her and hate herself. It would be a terrible burden to carry through life. And if Chris ever had a daughter of her own, she'd pass down the taint. And on it would go.

She had to think this through carefully, to consider every angle.

But what if Roddy and Chris were right about urging the police on? Maybe that was how Joni could end the cycle of violence that seemed to be ensnaring her family—by putting Marc in jail. As if he were a bud they could nip off and the underlying vines of Ackerman perniciousness would wither. Would they?

She pictured the police and the lawyers and the courts digging deeper and deeper, unraveling Marc's past, his crimes, figuring her out, her crimes, sending her to prison for murder, unleashing a new level of rage in Chris.

Chris, who was a Lovett like her father. Half an Ackerman. Blessed and cursed by the best and worst of both of them. Talent, brilliance, ruthlessness, and audacity when restraint would serve better. Was she also self-protective in the extreme, like both her parents? The way her father used and harmed others, raped women, and hid it for decades. The way her mother exercised her rage so she could know what it felt like to kill someone, her own husband, and connived a story of suicide that had kept her free . . . so far.

And yet Joni still hung on to the thought that she could come out of all this a *good person*.

Could she?

She felt torn, split down her middle, cleaved by ambiguity and indecision, standing at the fork of two roads both leading to a wrong destination: help the police find a reason to capture Marc and damn herself; say nothing and spend the rest of her life reckoning with her own capacity.

One thing, though, was clear. A mother's love was a mother's love: Joni would die before she let her daughter fall off the track toward a better life than her parents'. A better self.

Whatever was best for Chris, that's what she would do.

30

The unseasonably hot day felt like summer though technically it was still spring. Val had been restless and upset since returning from Colts Neck. When Zeke was little, on a day like this they'd all jump in the car and head to the town pool. But with a whole week free before graduating he'd gone off traveling with a friend—biking up the east coast, what an exciting and ludicrous idea—instead of staying home. They'd always only gone to the pool as a family.

Coming down the stairs to the foyer, she heard sounds from the kitchen where she found Russ pouring himself iced tea.

"Want some?" he asked.

"I feel like going swimming," she said. "Want to go to the pool?"

He stared at her. She knew what he was thinking: *Without Zeke?*

"He's not here but we are," she argued. "Why not?"

"Huh." He took a long drink of his cold tea. "Okay. Why not?"

The pool was crowded with families. All the chairs were taken so they spread their blanket on a free patch of lawn that was half in shade. Because of his fair skin Russ took the shade without asking. Normally she wouldn't have mentioned it; she was also fair, but he burned quicker. Today, though, it got to her. Since they'd left Louisa's house, they hadn't talked about what happened. She didn't want to argue, she wanted to swim. To unwind. If she got worked up she'd never be able to fall asleep tonight and she wanted to catch some rest before getting up at two in the morning to Uber to the airport for a five o'clock flight for a week-long location shoot in Toronto. She didn't want to go away after fighting with her husband. But now. Now, the way he got comfortable in his slice of shade—without considering her—scratched her open. She hadn't realized how thin the veneer over her worry was until it bubbled up.

She settled beside him in the sun and asked, "Aren't you going to tell me what you and Joni talked about?"

He snorted and shook his head. "Look, I don't want to fight."

"Neither do I."

"So let's not talk about it. Ready to get in the water?" He pulled off his shirt. His ribcage laddered visibly under white, hairless skin. Skin that was starting to sag over a concave chest. She wondered if he'd look like that without cancer; if it was illness or aging that was diminishing his body. *Let it go*, she told herself, and she almost did. But then she remembered that this cancer wasn't going to kill him; it was curable. It was just his age showing. He was just as vulnerable to time as she was. And she was strong; she did not need to be protected.

"Tell me," she said.

He grimaced—*you asked for it*—then squared his body to face her cross-legged in the cool of his shade. "She told me that if I didn't 'shut up' she'd 'do the same to me.'"

The *shut up* made Val flinch before the rest sank in. "Do the same?"

"As she did to Paul."

Val took a moment to consider that, then responded, "What did she do to Paul?"

"Oh, great. Here we go."

"What did she tell you?"

"Nothing. Just that if I was so sure she killed Paul, shouldn't I be afraid she'd also 'do the same' to me."

"Did she ask you or tell you?"

"What's the difference?"

"Russ, come on, it makes a huge difference."

He sighed. "I guess she asked me."

"So, it was conjecture."

"Maybe."

"She was needling you. You know Joni."

"Unfortunately."

"She was playing with you because you won't let it go."

"Why should I?" He shifted forward, adamant. "Val, if she killed him, she should face what she deserves. The police should know."

"They already did a whole investigation!" People around them pivoted to look. "Russ," she said more quietly now, "it's history. Case closed. Why can't you move on?"

"I have a bad gut feeling."

"*Feelings aren't facts*," she reminded him.

"Yeah, I know that."

"I realize you don't like her but she's my friend. Can't you please let it go so we can move on? Joni has enough on her plate. And all this shit with Marc—"

"It's a shit pie. Joni has a shit pie on her plate. I wish she'd eat it."

"Russ!" Val whispered fiercely. "You're not well," she reminded him. "Let's focus on that."

He sighed, caught in that gnarly reality.

"And we'll have some time with Zeke this summer before he goes to college. Won't that be great?"

"It will."

"And maybe Esther will decide to go sightseeing in Toronto instead of standing next to me on set the whole time."

He laughed and his eyes brightened. "No way will she go sightseeing." There he was: the person who knew her, the person she'd joined her life with to create a family, the person she loved more than anyone else except her son.

She smiled and took his hand.

"Alright," he said.

"You don't have to see Joni ever again if you don't want to," she promised. "I can keep my friendship separate."

"Good. Thanks."

"But please, don't hate on her."

"I don't 'hate on her.' Who started that? Hate *on* someone. It's ridiculous."

Val laughed. "Language police works. Friend police doesn't."

"Got it."

"Swim?"

31

"Swimming?" Joni spoke loudly so her speakerphone would pick it up across the kitchen. Chris was off with Haley and Joni was preparing herself another lone salad for dinner. "It didn't occur to me to swim."

"You could have. It's so hot out."

"I'm still not used to being in the city and having a pool."

"That was sad at the funeral this morning. And at Louisa's afterward."

"It was. Sad, and other things."

"About that."

Joni dragged a peeler down the side of a carrot and watched the orange curls collect on the marble countertop. She never should have said what she did to Russ, that asshole. He was dangerous. But she was the one who should have kept her mouth shut. She'd probably inflamed him and now here it came.

"Russ is going to back off," Val said. "I talked it over with him and he promised to let it go."

"How am I supposed to believe that? I mean, the way he looks at me—"

"He's just jealous of how much I love you."

Joni put down the peeler and sliced off both ends of the carrot, right on the marble, not caring if she scratched it. If it scratched, it would always be there to remind her to be more careful than she was.

"He still thinks I . . . ?" Killed my husband. Am a killer. Would kill again. Sees me for who I really am. Is too dangerous to let stay loose in the world.

"We had a long talk before we went swimming. I mean, he's stubborn. But I tried to make it clear to him that that question was put to rest a long time ago."

"By the police," Joni reminded her.

"Exactly. So he should just get over this pissy urge he has to talk to the police again because it's just a pissy urge."

"He's a piece of work, your husband." Joni sliced the carrot, cut cut cut on the marble. She thought that Val was pandering to her, calling her own husband's urge "pissy." Joni didn't like being coddled or feared, especially by Val, but if it was the only way to keep this under control then so be it. She realized at that moment that she would do anything to keep him quiet. Anything.

"Joni, though—you've got to stop goading him. I'll have him tamped down and then, when you goad him, he flares up again."

"I hear you," Joni said. "He's your husband. It's tough. I get it."

"Family is complicated," Val agreed.

Joni put down the peeler and blurted, "I'm worried about Chris." Chris was the worry at the bottom of her well of worries, the shimmer of panic that winked and blinked whenever she dared to fathom the possibilities.

"Why? She seems good. Happy."

"She is. But what if Marc . . . If the police . . . If they ask questions and . . . What if Chris finds out everything?"

"They won't," Val insisted. "Stop thinking about it."

"I can't."

"I told you. Russ won't say anything to anyone."

What Joni was going to say, and was glad she didn't, was *I'm afraid of what I might do*. But would she do something this time? She was five years sober—well, four. It was impossible to know for sure, but she doubted she would have gone through with it the night she killed Paul if she hadn't been drunk.

"I have Russ under control," Val promised. "He will not go to the police."

"I hope you're right."

"I have your back, Joni. And I know you have mine. You always have."

That was true. Not once had she betrayed Val when she had a secret to keep. There was no reason to worry now except for Russ. Joni wanted to believe that Russ would mind his own business, but would he? Would he really?

"What time is your flight tomorrow?" Joni asked.

"Five. I'll have to get up at two to make it work," Val groaned. "I'm going straight to the set. Esther wants to get the most out of our first day."

Joni was impressed by the way Val handled her star's demanding mother. She assured her, "It's going to be a great show. Just keep doing what you're doing."

"I'll call you tomorrow night if I can," Val promised. "If not, Tuesday."

"Sounds good."

"Just keep your cool, lady, okay?"

"Who, me?" Joni chuckled.

"Keep your eyes on the prize: Stella's home, and Chris will be fine."

"Chris will be fine," Joni repeated.

"We'll make sure of that," Val promised. "Together."

After the call, her stomach gripped. Her dinner salad was good but it wasn't enough food. She got up from the table and searched the cabinets for something, a snack, anything easy. There was an unopened box of some crackers she liked. She took it to the couch, opened it, and ate cracker after cracker but they didn't fill her. It wasn't that kind of hunger, she realized. The discomfort in her stomach was something else.

She wanted to trust Val, to believe that Russ was ready to let this go. But was he? What if he wasn't?

And then there was Marc, still out there—the dark triad of a little brother she wanted to trust and love but had been harshly reminded she couldn't.

And Blair—what about her? She was gone, too. Both of them, disloyal conspirators, evaporated, thinner than air.

Only Russ was tangibly available, actually gettable—right there in his house, a quick ride away.

Joni's itch flared. *Was* she in control of her impulses, even sober? If the seed was buried inside her, if it *was* her—if she was more than just a (formerly) sloppy drunk but a true psychopath—then she'd be able to do it again with a clear mind.

She closed her eyes and imagined the wire digging into flesh, skin splitting, life leaking away. Her stomach began to unknot.

Val would be gone by three a.m.

Would Zeke be home?

No, Joni remembered: He was away with friends.

Russ would be alone in the house for a whole week.

She could take the train, buy her ticket in cash, go at night so no one would see her when she approached the house.

He would open the door to her; he hated her, but he knew her.

It would be better if it looked like a break-in.

The kitchen door had glass panels—she could break the glass with a rock and open the door that way.

But she would never do it, not in reality. It would be too risky, too obvious. Val would know right away. Even if she were a psychopath, *if*, she could learn not to act on her impulse, couldn't she?

Imagining it, though, felt like a soothing warm bath.

She relaxed her body into the softness of the couch and saw exactly how it could unfold.

She moves carefully, quietly, through the sweet night air, ready to pull an easy smile in case someone comes out of the darkness and sees her—a nice middle-aged woman walking alone at night, not even walking a dog, just walking. A small wave for a passing car. A tilt of her chin for someone on foot. She pushes her hair behind her ears so her gray stripes will show her age, her denuded potential, the invisibility she relies on when she doesn't want to be noticed. She's ready. But, thankfully, no one emerges to see her.

All the lights are off in the Williams's small house, even the light over the front door, which Joni knows from past visits Val always turns on as soon as it's dark. Russ didn't turn on the front light before going to bed but their car is in the driveway, so he's there, alone in his bedroom, possibly already asleep.

She hopes he's asleep.

It will be easier if he doesn't fight her.

At the same time, she wants him to see her, to know it's her, that even if he's right about her he should have kept it to himself. He shouldn't have slammed the door in Joni's face five years ago, the night she tried to visit Val in the hospital. He shouldn't have made that snide remark about her on her penthouse terrace. He shouldn't have manhandled Val. He shouldn't have terrified his wife by keeping his illness a secret and letting her worry it was something else, that he was going to leave her, that she'd be alone. Alone like Joni, letting her age show and her loneliness take root. That worst of all possible fates.

She creeps across the lawn, imagining him realizing his mistakes, wishing he could undo them, recognizing that it's too late.

A silvered ambient light from other houses and a cloud-obscured moon casts the house in a sepia half-visibility that lets her see her way across the property but also feel hidden. She wonders if anyone is looking out their window just then but doesn't allow herself to turn around because she'd appear suspicious.

She is just an older woman, walking alone, veering quietly across a lawn and around the side of a dark house to its sleepy backyard.

If anyone sees her, if anyone asks, she's a friend who is staying over and can't sleep and went out for a walk and is coming in through the kitchen door so the hall light won't wake anyone up.

No one can see the coil of wire tucked away in her purse.

No one can read her mind.

She's just an old friend of the family.

32

Joni roused to a harsh buzzing she couldn't place. The bedroom shades were still open; she'd forgotten to close them before falling asleep. Through the window, she saw that a cherry-red hue infused the night sky over the city, a chemical glow from somewhere—New Jersey, probably—that shouldn't have been so beautiful. She couldn't see many stars through the haze, but the few she could see were fantastic. Sharp diamonds hurling with speed that would kill if they reached you but wouldn't arrive in her lifetime.

That loud buzz again. It was coming from her phone on the bedside table. The intercom app for the building was flashing. She sat up, startled, awake.

She tapped it. "Billy?" If the night doorman was buzzing her in the middle of the night, it had to be important.

"Mrs. Ackerman, sorry to call so late."

"No problem, Billy."

"Valerie Williams is here to see you."

Joni hesitated. Val was supposed to be in Toronto. "Send her up."

Disorientation fogged her brain. Why was Val here this late—or early? Why wasn't she in Toronto? Had a whole week gone by? Was she already back from the shoot? Was it morning, not night? Had they made a plan to meet here?

She stumbled out of bed, unlocked the front door, and went to the kitchen to start a pot of coffee. The apartment was thick with middle-of-the-night quiet. She wondered if her footsteps had woken Chris, then remembered she was at Haley's again. Her thoughts wandered to how things would change when Chris moved out in two weeks. She yawned. Setting the glass carafe in the sink, she turned the water on and waited.

The front door opened and Val burst in, frantic. There were dark swaths under her eyes, her skin was unusually pale and her green blouse was unevenly buttoned. "I've been calling you for hours. Why didn't you answer?" she demanded.

"I was sleeping. What's going on?"

"Zeke was home!"

"Zeke?"

"Tonight. He was at home."

"I thought you told me he was on a bike trip. I don't understand, Val, what—"

"He showed up at home. He's a teenager. They do shit like that."

"Please, slow down and explain what's happening."

"You terrified Russ."

"What do you mean?"

"Oh, please."

Joni turned to shut the tap and empty some of the water out of the overfilled carafe. She could feel Val's gaze burning into her back as she started the coffee. For a moment she wondered if she actually *had* gone to Maplewood instead of just imagining it. This didn't make sense. She wanted to understand. Joni sat at the counter that separated the kitchen from the living room and, with her foot, angled the other stool out for her friend to sit. But Val didn't join her.

"Russ saw you," Val said acidly. "He saw you standing at the kitchen door. He saw you run away."

"But I wasn't there."

"What if it was Zeke? What if whatever you were there for happened to Zeke? Joni, what were you thinking?"

"But I wasn't—"

"Russ *saw* you."

"When?"

"Late. Early. I don't know—it was dark out when he called. I was almost at the airport."

Joni stared at Val. She didn't understand.

"Oh my God," Val said. "I'm so exhausted."

The coffeepot beeped. Joni got up and filled two mugs, prepared Val's with milk, and set it on the counter. She took hers black and sat back down to sip the hot coffee. The first hint of scald on her tongue began to clear her mind.

She had *not* gone to Maplewood, much as she'd wanted to. She could still feel the deliciousness, the irresistibility of her fantasy of stealthily ending Russ's life, her waking dream in which the suspension of disbelief became, for a few moments, more powerful than reality. But it wasn't reality. It was not.

"Val, I wasn't at your house. You actually missed your flight and came all the way here because you thought—"

"Oh, Joni." Val picked up her coffee and took a careful sip, followed by a long one. "I don't have the energy for this. Why don't you just tell the truth? Just say it. Stop pretending." Finally, she slumped onto the stool.

"Why would I go there if you weren't home?"

Val's eyes narrowed. "You know why."

"Whoever he saw, it wasn't me."

"He didn't make it up. He was terrified. He almost called the police."

Alarmed, Joni leaned forward. "Did he?"

"No. I told him not to. I made him promise. But Joni, how could you?"

"I *didn't*. That's the thing—I really didn't."

"You might hate each other but I love him. If you can't leave him alone this whole thing's going to blow up. I won't protect you anymore. I'll choose my family. Do you understand that? I will always choose my family."

Of course she would. So would Joni. But Val didn't need to choose because Joni hadn't done anything wrong. Not this time.

"I would never do anything to Russ. I promised you that and I've always kept my promises, haven't I?"

"But Paul. I can't stop picturing it."

"What happened to Paul was a mistake. I was blind drunk and out of my mind with anger."

"I feel like I'm going to crack in half," Val said. "Russ swears he saw someone at the house. You swear you weren't there. I believe you both." Her eyes lingered on Joni's.

"He saw *someone*? Or he saw *me*?"

Val froze, then squeezed shut her eyes. "He said someone. And I thought . . ."

"Didn't you tell me recently there was a prowler in your neighborhood?"

"Crazy Shelley Nelson thought so." Val sighed. "Oh, shit."

"Maybe Crazy Shelley isn't so crazy," Joni said softly.

"I don't know if I can take this anymore. Everything feels so . . . distorted. I'm starting to feel like I have to choose one of you."

"You don't have to choose." Joni took her friend's hand. If Val chose, she'd choose Russ, and Joni couldn't let that happen. "You can have both of us. I mean, it won't be easy, but—"

"I don't think I can. I tried, but it isn't working."

"Are you going to break up with me?"

Val's eyes sparked at her, sharp black pupils like targets in the pale blue irises. "We're not a couple. We can't break up."

"We're more than a couple," Joni argued. "Better than a couple."

Val nodded. "You're my best friend and I don't want to lose you. But Russ is my husband." Then she shook her head. "I can't stand this."

"Maybe we should just give it some time."

"Maybe."

"We could keep our relationship completely separate."

"I already told him I would. But after last night, tonight—"

"Which didn't happen, Val."

"To him, it did. And to me, it did."

"Let's get some sleep," Joni said. "Chris is at Haley's—you can use her room. We'll talk more tomorrow. Okay?"

"I should probably head to Toronto."

"Now?"

"Esther's always up my ass and if I'm not there she'll go nuts."

"Esther is not the boss of you." Joni smiled.

Val laughed. "Actually, I think she is."

"No. I am. I'm telling you to get some sleep. Tomorrow you can spend some time with Russ and Zeke, then you'll go to Toronto."

"I guess the team could handle it for one day."

"You can remote in if you need to."

"I guess so. But I don't think I could sleep here. It's so noisy in the city; I'm not used to it. I should just go home."

"I have earplugs. They work great. I'll get them."

Within five minutes they were both in bed, determined to sleep, as if you could turn yourself off for an efficient recharge. But Joni couldn't, not after coffee. She looked at the clock: It was 4:16 and she was still wide-awake. She wondered if Val was sleeping. She kept playing the scene over in her mind, reassuring herself that she had *not* gone to Maplewood despite her powerful urge to, she *had* controlled her impulse, challenging herself to unwind. But she couldn't. The urge to take action was still so powerful, right there in her core.

Stella was sound asleep at her side. Joni nestled her face in the soft fur, thinking it might lull her.

4:31.

She told herself to stop looking at the clock.

4:33.

At 4:39 she heard the apartment door crack open. She sat up in bed and listened to the footsteps, trying to tell if they were Val's, leaving, or Chris's, arriving. But they were heavy and slow, unlike either of theirs.

She slipped out of bed.

The hall was dark but just ahead, in the living room, she saw a shadow moving through the ambient light that filtered in through the wall of glass.

She crept forward, not wanting to wake Val in case she was sleeping. In case it was Chris. Though she couldn't understand why Chris would come home in the middle of the night like this unless something had happened between her and Haley.

In the living room Joni's eyes adjusted and the shadow yielded a shape. A man, standing there. A voice she knew too well.

He grinned his grin, half kidding, half menacing, the way one side ticked up and the other held its frown.

Adrenaline surged into her sleepless brain.

"Hey, sister. Been a while."

33

In his grimy jeans and stained T-shirt ripped at the hem, Marc looked like he'd crawled through a sewer. His face was unshaven, and he smelled.

Joni stiffened. There he was, the man of many names and no conscience, uninvited, unwanted. She loathed him unambivalently for the first time in her life.

"Get out of my house," she ordered.

"You mean your *pent*house. La de da." He cocked his head and faked a smile.

"I'm not playing, Marc. Get out."

"Where is she?"

He had to know Blair wasn't here. "Are you kidding me?"

He walked into the living room, awash in silver moonlight that hardened his skin to a metallic sheen. Agitated, he scanned the room, then shifted so he could see into the kitchen.

Joni hurried to the foyer and jabbed the wall intercom to alert the front desk. Billy didn't answer. Cold sluiced through her. How had Marc gotten up here in the first place without a call from the night doorman? Had he done something to Billy? The cold turned to ice and she couldn't move, couldn't think.

Marc poured his hungry attention over her space, her things, the couch and chairs where she and Chris sat and talked, the plaid throw blanket draped over an arm of the couch, the table where they ate, their half-read books and magazines, the basket that held Chris's knitting on a table behind the couch. He pulled the sliding door that joined the penthouse to the terrace and kept pulling until the long panes of glass had stacked and the wall was open to the night sky, cool air rushing in. He stepped onto the terrace and glanced around. Then he turned back into the apartment toward the mouth of the hall that led to the bedrooms.

Did he really think she was hiding Blair? Blair, who had deceived her and helped him—though she still didn't understand why.

She took a step forward. "Get out of my house, you fucking asshole!"

He turned and looked at her with that keen-eyed stare of his, the same way their father used to when they made a mistake for which he didn't intend to forgive them.

"Don't," he said, "talk to me like that."

An inward shrinking, like a tender plant in a blast of sun. But Joni was no tender plant. She gathered herself and said, "Look, Marc, it's the middle of the night. Do you want some money? If I give you money, will you leave?"

"I don't want your money."

Of course he wanted money; he lived for it. "Tell me what you want, then. I'm all ears."

"Sure, let's sit down and have a heart-to-heart." His whole face contracted as if he was about to burst into laughter—or was that rage?

"I mean it." She tried to soften her voice, but the loathing seeped through. "But if you're looking for Blair—"

"Where is she?"

"Why don't you just call her? She won't answer my calls, but something tells me she'll answer yours."

"Not anymore." Frustration shimmered on his face.

"She finally ditched you? Smart move."

"She didn't ditch me, she played me. But you're right—she's smart."

"Played you?" Joni laughed. "How?"

He shook his head like she was a child who would never understand even if he tried to explain.

"Look, Marc," she started. "I've known her a long time and she was never . . ." What? Manipulative? Strategic? Hungry enough to do something stupid? Lonely enough to make bad choices? Desperate for a change? Maybe Blair was all those things. Joni's sense that she never really knew or understood the young woman plunged to a new depth.

Stella's claws clicked along the hardwood floor of the hall leading from the bedrooms. She approached sleepily, stopping at Joni's knee, looking back and forth between sister and brother. Her tail wasn't wagging its usual happy wag, nor was she barking in alarm—she didn't know what to make of this, either.

"Hiya Stellstell." Marc dropped into a crouch and massaged her neck. "Happy to see Uncle Marc?" Her tail started to wag.

Joni felt a new stab of anger at how he'd dragged Stella to Mexico and put them both through hell. "If you had to leave, Marc, that was your business—but why did you take Stella? They found her abandoned! How could you?"

He leaned back and looked up at Joni with an expression of compassion that shifted him back a month, when she might have believed him. "Blair was sick. I didn't know what to do. I didn't want to just leave her."

"She was emaciated and filthy when they found her."

"Poor baby." He gently pet the dog's head.

"Because of *you*," she said, in case it wasn't clear. Was he insane, or malicious, or a combination of both? "You could have knocked on a neighbor's door."

"I didn't think of that."

"Idiot."

He stiffened but didn't respond. Stella's appearance had brought out a softness in him, shame or something that looked like it. Emboldened by the shift, Joni held his gaze and said, "I'll tell you where Blair is," not that she could, "if you tell me something first," because this was her chance, and she had to try.

He grinned. "You never won when we played games."

"Not a game. A fair trade."

"Yeah, right. But why the hell not? He crossed the room and sat down on the couch. "Okay. Shoot."

Gathering herself, she asked, "Mom and Dad. How did they really die?"

He winged his arms atop the cushions, looked away from her, sighed. "You know how they died. Carbon monoxide poisoning."

"Why did the stove leak that night?"

She watched him fist his hands, then open them and flutter his fingers on the back of the couch. He uncrossed his legs and let his knees fall apart. She recognized what he was doing because it was exactly what she would do if she were him: stall, see what tumbled out, assess the risk her adversary posed.

"First Mom and Dad." She held up her fingers to count his crimes at him. "Then wife number one. Then wife number two." She watched him closely for a reaction, to see if she'd hit a nerve.

He pursed his lips and didn't blink and in the icy sheen of her brother's eyes she saw that she was right.

"Now my turn. Where's Blair?"

"Not till you admit you killed our parents for money. Say it."

He smirked.

"You're a grifter. You want money. That's *all* you want."

"As if you don't."

"No, I don't—"

"Because you already have it. Look at the way you live."

"We're going back to bed. Lock the door behind you, please. I'll email you where Blair is when you're gone." She would lock her bedroom door, then lock herself and Stella in the bathroom, call the police, and wait. She'd text Val a warning to do the same. And she'd tell Chris not to come home until the police arrived; she didn't want her daughter walking into this, whatever it was.

"You're full of shit. I don't believe you." He put his hand out for Stella, hoping she'd come over and sniff it, and she did. Then he threaded his fingers under her collar and held tight.

"You're choking her. Please let go."

"Little Miss Please."

"Let go, Marc."

"*Please*, you mean." He grinned. "You were such a kiss-ass growing up, such a 'hard worker.' 'Oh, look at those excellent grades.'"

She hated him. So what if he was her brother? He was worse than a bully; he was evil. People like him, like them, started as children and then grew to this: women, men, bad people who were the dark holes where humanity withered and died. What she had that he lacked was consciousness. She had come to know herself and was engaged in a struggle to resist the worst of her . . . gift. It was a gift. It was a kind of gift to be this cruel.

If she could just get to the kitchen, to the butcher block on the counter that held the sharp knives.

"'Such a genius.' 'What a wunderkind.' 'Only twenty-five and made her first movie.' Oh, excuse me, 'film.'"

But he was too big, too strong, for her to overpower him, even with a knife. And he had Stella. It would never work.

"You couldn't have made that *film* without their money. Admit it."

"I would have raised enough money without the inheritance," she told him. "I didn't need it. You needed it. You've never worked a day in your life. You're a bloodsucker. You opened the burner on the stove before you left that night. You killed them. Say it."

"Yeah," he said. "Why not? I did it. Now you know."

She froze. The hard truth of it clanged around inside her mind like it was an empty can, then spun and landed and fell to rest. Marc had killed their parents for money. Of course he had. He'd killed all of them. Her vicious little brother.

"Where's Blair?" he asked.

"Why do you need to find her so badly?"

"That wasn't the deal. Where is she?"

"Why?"

"She has something of mine."

"Get another one."

"It's irreplaceable."

"Ah." There it was: money, again. Or something worth a lot of it. "What is this irreplaceable thing of yours—or Louisa's? Or mine?"

The tilt of his head, the way he looked at her. Ice slithered up her spine.

He would kill her, too.

He wouldn't hesitate.

"You don't know where she is, do you?"

Joni stared back at him. She hated him. She did.

"You lied. You're the liar. You," he said acidly. "This has been a waste of my time."

He swung an arm toward Chris's knitting basket and yanked out one of her thin steel needles. It slid so abruptly out of the half-finished yellow sweater that it caught the yarn and the sweater began to unravel. Joni felt the snagged yarn as if it was within her, pulling her apart.

He let go of the collar and stood up, holding the needle in his fist. Stella crouched, bared her teeth, and growled at him. He took a step toward Joni. Stella began to bark. He laughed and barked back at her—and she leapt at him.

Val emerged from Chris's room looking disoriented, orange foam earplugs cupped in one palm. "What's going on?" She turned and saw Marc running from Stella. "Is that—"

"Come on!" Joni shouted. And they ran after.

They found him at the far end of the terrace, pressed against the parapet, gripping the needle while Stella barked ferociously.

"Call the police," Joni told Val.

"No police," Marc demanded.

"Are you fucking kidding me? Val! Go!"

Val ran back to Chris's room for her phone and returned with it pressed to her ear, waiting for an answer.

Clenching the needle between his teeth, Marc lowered to his knees, held out both hands for Stella to smell, wiggled his fingers and cooed softly. She quieted and moved closer to sniff him. The moment she was near, he reached out and grabbed her collar. He maneuvered her to the floor and used his bulk to restrain her. With his free hand, he held the needle over the back of her neck like a spear. Heaving, he said, "Do not call them."

The droning squeal of Stella's crying filled Joni with a terror so pure there was no thought. She jumped onto her brother's back. She pulled at him wherever she could get a hold, the bend of his elbow, his armpit. She stiffened her fingers and pecked at his eyes. Nothing moved him. He was solid, hard as stone, a living monument to rage. The knitting needle was back between his teeth so he could use his hand to swat her away.

Val dropped her phone and grabbed his neck, his arm, his torso, both women now trying to wrest him off Stella.

When Val thrust her knee into Marc's crotch, that did it.

He groaned and buckled, red and slicked with sweat.

As Joni fell away, she saw the needle on the ground—it had fallen out of his mouth.

"What is going on here?"

Joni turned and there was Chris, standing in the open space between living room and terrace, hands on hips, scanning the chaos.

Chris picked up the needle. "What is this doing here? Why is Stella like that?"

Catching her breath, Joni said, "He killed *all* of them. He killed our *parents*. He admitted it."

"What the fuck?" Val kicked Marc again, and again he buckled.

Chris clenched the knitting needle and took one step back, and in the single step Joni recognized the powerful force that was her daughter, the quickness with which she metabolized what she'd walked into and how to organize a response.

Marc rose to his feet like a balloon man pumped with air. Joni had seen him enraged before, but never like this. Their eyes had never locked with such force, not even in childhood when cruelty was purest and least resistible. He paused to inhale, then came at her, this sister, this woman who knew too much. But now they all knew, so he'd have to kill all of them. Which would be impossible. Together, they were too strong a force.

Joni felt a hand grip her arm and pull—Chris's hand, or maybe Val's. Joni couldn't tell. All she saw was the funnel of Marc's eyes coming closer. Her body was pulled sidewards. By Val—it was Val pulling her out of harm's way.

Stella crouched and growled, baring her teeth at Marc.

Chris sprang forward and plunged the needle into her uncle's chest.

And time stopped.

Even Stella didn't move.

Chris's hand unclenched and she backed away from Marc, who was frozen in shock, pierced by the knitting needle. Joni saw her daughter leave her body and watched the shell of her stand there, gaping, stunned. Or maybe Joni just wanted, needed, to see it like that. Maybe it was her; maybe she was disembodying. Maybe the sight of her daughter stabbing her uncle was more than her mind could handle, and already she was divesting herself of it. Before it entered memory and became real. Before what it meant, could mean, crystallized in Joni's consciousness.

Blood blossomed on Marc's shirt, dark rivulets worming through the dirty fabric. Joni watched his pupils dilate as his focus unglued itself from her. He fell back against the parapet as his hands grabbed at the needle protruding from his chest.

Joni felt the lowering of her body as Val tried to settle her into a chair. But her mind wouldn't let her body settle. It was as if her mind and body absorbed each other, and one's needs became the other's. It was the most vivid awakening of her life, seeing her daughter answer an urge with an imperative, an urge Joni had once answered and fought ever since. Like the flipping of a switch, the familiar pain shot through her jaw. The itch flared. Now a new sensation appeared: a hectoring soaked her tongue, a taste that was more feeling than flavor, made of a deep thirst, compulsion, and greed.

Joni shook off Val and, standing, her voice flung out: "No way. No Goddamned fucking way."

She strode over to Marc and with the palm of her hand hit the flat end of the needle, pushing it all the way in.

His shoulders crashed onto the top of the parapet and his head whiplashed back, eyes wide, pupils large and dark and empty.

He was dying. He was dead. Joni was sure he was dead. Watching his life drain away, she felt . . . sated. It was the best drink of her life, the iciest and most delicious glass of satisfaction.

Then one of his hands grasped the edge of the parapet and he seemed to inflate again—just a little. But enough. He refused to let her win. She felt the old frustration, anger, and determination gathering— the dance of jaw and itch and thirst. But before she could act, Val rushed over to Marc.

Val crouched down, circled her arms around his knees and lifted his legs. She took a breath and groaned as she lifted them higher, gaining leverage. When she had him equal to the height of the parapet, she groaned again and pushed him over.

There was a long silence.

And then a splash.

34

The first color of sunrise wasn't a color at all. It was an opening, a speck of clarity that blossomed until you could see that first trace of gentle blue, that harbinger of a full-blown day. The rest happened quickly: The baby blue grew vivid and awake, a cerulean so sharp it almost hurt Joni to look at it through the pulled-open wall of glass doors that led to the terrace.

The three women sat in the living room, quiet after the bustle of all the emergency workers who'd swarmed in and eventually left. They needed to stay together a while longer; being alone felt too risky, the way thoughts could sneak up from behind, rear over you in giant waves and then you were drowning.

Marc had killed their parents. Joni's mind wouldn't stop spinning around that: As a teenager, he'd been vicious enough to do that. This tricky little brother whose diaper she'd changed, who she'd loved and played with, then called a bully as if that's all he ever was, a bully who would mature out of it. He'd killed their parents for money. For money. And not just their parents. Carolyn Knudson and Louisa Singer, his wives, both died because he'd wanted their money.

There it was: the first cloud edging in, fluffy white at first, then gray-edged and tremulous. It didn't look like rain, necessarily, but Joni was under no illusion that today would be easy.

After a while Joni told Val and Chris, "I left a message for Candy." Candy Sonnenfeld, the publicist who'd shaped Joni's last climb out of the deep.

"Oh, shit," Chris moaned, burrowed into one end of the sectional couch. Last night she'd come home for her bathing suit so she and Haley could take a moonlight swim "while the rest of the world was asleep," she'd told them earlier. The privacy of it had enticed the young women. She'd come home and walked into an inheritance of violence she'd never known belonged to her. She was stuck on that point: how she'd done something she never knew she was capable of and now her life was ruined. "How is Candy going to spin this one, Mom? I murdered my uncle."

"You didn't murder anyone," Joni argued (again).

"I killed him."

"No," Val interrupted. "I killed him. I pushed him. We all saw it. He was alive when he fell."

"We all killed him," Joni insisted. "And he brought it on himself. It was self-defense. He was attacking Stella with the knitting needle. He came at me. He wanted to kill me—you both saw that. You protected me. Both of you—you saved my life. We had no choice."

"It happened so fast." Val was curled into the opposite section of the couch. "I can't remember any details, just how quiet it was after."

"It was so quiet," Chris agreed. "Oh, God, I'll never forget how it felt when I stabbed him. It was like meat. It was so easy, and then it stopped. I must have hit a bone." She raised her hands to her face.

"Try not to think about it," Joni advised. It *was* like meat. She recalled the effort of pushing past the bone or ligament or whatever the obstacle was before the needle slid all the way in. The satisfaction. She closed her eyes and savored the sensation of hurting Marc back after all the ways in which he'd made her suffer.

"It's too late, Mom."

Joni moved closer to Chris and wrapped her daughter in her arms, insisting, "It's okay, it's okay." But she knew it wouldn't really help. It was true: Chris's life had altered course the moment instinct took over and she drove the knitting needle into her uncle. She'd glimpsed an aspect of herself she'd been unaware of. Joni would help her learn to frame it so she could understand that the brutality, this horrid Ackerman trait that had overtaken her, could be controlled and used as a strength. At least Joni hoped it could. Maybe together they could figure out how.

"I'm already traumatized," Chris said. "I can't stop feeling it. It's like electricity that won't turn off. Do you feel that way too?"

Val's sigh was like a gust of wind, an eternal *yes*.

"You'll turn it off," Joni assured them both. "We all will. You'll see."

Chris's generation made too much of trauma; lately, it had irritated Joni that every obstacle, slight, and setback was characterized as trauma instead of challenge. Challenge was what strengthened you. Walking right into the storm, through it, and coming out the other side was how you got strong. Strength was something to be proud of. Strength was what saved you. But this wasn't the time to say that to Chris.

Val swung her legs off the couch and strode onto the terrace, to the parapet. She stood in the spot where it happened. "I still can't believe it. Even standing right here, it doesn't seem real."

It was true. The terrace looked like the terrace again, not a crime scene from which the police had taken fingerprints and hair samples and infrared photos meant to capture things invisible to the eye. They would do their jobs, as would the lawyers, and then they'd determine,

Joni guessed, that there wasn't enough to build a case. Marc was essentially a fugitive with a sketchy past. The women were only defending themselves—their testimonies would corroborate that, and as they were the only witnesses, there'd be nothing more to go on. Joni was surprised at how little fear she felt, having survived a similar storm once before. She felt clear and strong and ready. And relieved: There was no more Marc to torment her or any other unlucky woman who might have crossed his path.

She wondered if, at some point, grief would overcome her for the baby boy she'd cuddled, whose steps through childhood she'd celebrated until he turned out to be nonstop trouble. Just plain mean. She'd loved him once. Was that love buried somewhere in her? Would it trickle out? Would it rush forward and surprise her? It was hard to imagine she'd ever miss that misery of a man. She only knew that right now, in the bright glare of the aftermath, she felt lighter, freer than she had in a long time.

Holding Chris's hand, Joni reassured them all, "We don't need to worry about this. It was self-defense. We didn't do anything wrong. Keep your minds clear and remember that—it's very important."

Stella appeared in the living room. She looked at Joni and tilted her head, asking for something—a walk. She needed a walk and then she'd need her breakfast. Life had to go on.

"Okay, doodlepie," Joni cooed.

"I'll go out with you," Val said. "Russ is picking me up. He's almost here."

"Wait for me, honey," Joni told Chris. "I'll be back in a minute."

"I can't move," Chris said. "I can't think. I'll be right here."

The ride down in the elevator felt surreal, just another morning when it was anything but. Joni was glad not to run into anyone she knew other than Hector, the day doorman, who was at his post behind the counter in the lobby.

"Good morning," Joni said, searching his face for how he'd react to her. He had to know what happened or at least the basics: A man had fallen to his death in the pool. What else did people know? Did they know, or think they knew, her role in it?

"Good morning, Mrs. Ackerman."

"Billy—?" She didn't know how to ask.

"Billy will be back next week," Hector assured her.

From where? The hospital? Home? What had Marc done to him? How bad was it? She wanted to know everything but worried that asking Hector these questions would open her up to questions and she didn't want that. Not yet. She needed to speak with Candy before she discussed this with anyone else. And call Maris O'Connor—they'd need a lawyer.

The sun must have inched higher in the sky because there was a sudden shift, a brightening, and the air felt warmer. Val stood under the building's awning and told Joni, "I'll wait here."

"Let's talk later. No pressure to go to Toronto."

"I'm too fried to even think about that right now."

With the leash looped over her elbow, Joni reached to hug Val. They held each other tightly for a moment, breathing in sync before letting go.

Joni pulled away first and said, "We're in this together."

"We are," Val murmured. "Yes, we are."

Now Val knew how it felt when you didn't mean to kill someone but you did. When it was too late to go back in time and unpoison a cocktail or unpush a man off a building. It was just too late. You had to go forward. You had to make it work.

Marc had been weakened. They could have found another way to disable him when he'd started to move off the parapet. There were three of them, and they could have overtaken him and held him until the police got there. But they'd each made a different choice. Chris had killed him first. Then Joni had killed him. Then Val had killed him again, actually killed him, the way she'd put her whole body into it and lifted his legs up and over. She'd used all her strength. Joni had watched it happen, and so had Chris, and they all knew.

Joni leaned close and whispered, "I'll never tell."

Val nodded. She understood. They held each other's secrets now.

Joni didn't want to be there when Russ pulled up in the car. She left Val standing under the awning and walked quickly with Stella to the sidewalk and around the side of the building onto Amity Street.

Two squad cars were parked outside the iron fence that separated the pool from the sidewalk. Walking past with Stella, Joni saw that half a dozen police still lingered by the pool. She glanced at them but didn't stop. Yellow tape had been strung around the periphery of the pool. Marc's body had been taken away. The water was pink with his blood.

Her phone rang. It was Candy calling her back. She walked down the quiet street, away from the building, and took the call.

35

Traffic was thick crossing the Brooklyn Bridge at the start of the morning rush hour, but Russ refused to pay for the Battery Tunnel, which would have gotten them to the Holland Tunnel and New Jersey faster. He hated paying tolls when he didn't have to. The Holland Tunnel cost nothing in this direction, so that was one free trip, except for gas. Val was well aware that her husband fixated on details when he was upset. It was a control thing. She said nothing. He could reroute them to his heart's content for whatever reasons he wanted if it kept his mind off the reason for the unexpected drive to pick up his wife in the city at the crack of dawn.

He ground his jaw and stared ahead into the bridge traffic while Val gazed up at the sky. It looked different than the sky from Joni's penthouse though technically it was exactly the same. This sky, Val's view of it from here, sealed inside the family car driven by her protective and loving husband, felt safer. Limited but safer. It was better here. She never wanted to leave his side again.

But she would have to.

In a way, she already had.

In one swift movement, when she pushed Marc to his death, her life had merged inextricably with Joni's. She was Joni's now as much as she was Russ's and as much as she was her own. She didn't know how she'd do it, but she'd have to find a way to live four lives as one: a wife, a mother, a television producer, and an invisible fugitive. Invisible because only three people in the world knew what she'd done—she'd be the kind of fugitive who would spend her life running, but unnoticeably, in circles, inside herself—and it would be their secret. It would be a real balancing act, but if Joni had learned how to do it so could she.

Val glanced at Russ. He had a nice profile, soft yet resolute. She wanted so badly to talk with him. She loved to talk, she needed to talk, but this was one conversation they could never have.

And now it wasn't just out of loyalty to Joni that she'd need to divert Russ from running to the police with his suspicions—it was self-preservation. To save herself, to save him, to save her family, she'd have to find a way to keep quiet and steer him at the same time. She had no idea how she'd do that. She was so exhausted she couldn't think.

As they drove down the off-ramp and turned onto Chambers Street, it occurred to her that Russ hadn't said a single word since he'd pulled up in the car, looked at her, and leaned over to pop open the passenger door from within. Nothing. Not "Get in," or "Hi," or "What happened?" He'd had his own long night after believing he saw Joni at the kitchen door and scaring Val enough to jolt her to New York in the middle of the night.

And then, as if he could read her mind, he told her, "Oh, they caught that prowler last night." He stared at the road. He was embarrassed; she saw it in his refusal to look at her or say more.

When the subject came up again, which eventually it would, she would tell him in no uncertain terms that his "paranoia" about Joni had gone too far and now he had to let it go. She would shame him into backing off. She didn't see any other way.

There were moments in a marriage when you had to stand your ground. You could refuse to discuss the thing again; that was one way. Another way was to try to forget it ever happened and hope he did, too. To pretend it was a bad dream and let the memory fade. Maybe, eventually, one of you would get dementia and the other one would mold the narrative.

Val pictured herself in twenty years, a woman of almost eighty, hair long and gray, crepey skin soft under her grandchildren's tiny fingers. Zeke would have three children, she decided: two girls and a boy. They would cluster on her lap while Russ drooled in the corner, and she'd tell them stories from their past so they could know him through her.

36

Back when Paul first hired Candy Sonnenfeld to handle publicity for Sunny Day, Joni called her a "piece of work."

"Yeah, she's a bitch," he said. "But she's good at what she does."

Turned out she was great at what she did and there was nothing bitchy about her. She was direct and demanding and confident, and one of the most competent people Joni had ever met, but she was also perceptive and kind. During her year in Bali it was Candy, along with Maris O'Connor, Joni's criminal defense attorney, who kept her steady and gave her hope. They were like a pair of ill-fitted yet perfectly synced counselors, prepared with an armory full of facts and reality checks. Maris was instrumental in parsing definitions of culpability and wielding legal concepts proactively to keep Joni from ever getting charged. Candy handled the press, using her vast network of contacts and chits to "keep the hyenas away" from her—them, when the scope of protection came to include Chris. Candy's mandate was to "tell the story" until her version became everyone else's reality. Even Maris came to rely on the publicist's keen sense of timing and presentation. Throughout the process, they all knew that Candy was the star of what she called "the operation."

Candy and her associates rode the internet like cowgirls and swatted down misinformation; well, maybe not misinformation as much as unwelcome information. Candy horse-traded with her media contacts, and they were legion, careful that the *Vanity Fair* "incident" wouldn't be repeated. Candy called it an "incident" because Dallas Miller, the writer, had added his own perspective to the story, questioning how much Joni had or hadn't known about her husband's crimes and setting the internet on fire with supposition. Candy was all over that. Joni's story became Candy's mantra to the world: Paul Lovett had taken his own life in shame, leaving behind a loving (if clueless, at the time) wife and one surviving adult daughter. Anyone who publicly doubted that would have their affiliations, professional or personal, manhandled—womanhandled—by the force that was Candy Sonnenfeld.

And Blair. Joni couldn't forget the role that Blair had played in defending her against Miller and the Naysayers—the band name he might have used to reinvent himself after he was canceled. Joni and Chris, poolside in Bali, had had a good laugh over that one. Blair was her ally, or at least she was back then. Joni was having trouble digesting what had changed between them, and when, and why. If Blair hated her so much, why had she stayed? Was it the promotion that changed her mind? Blair loved her, Joni thought—that was the problem. She was hurt and angry and acted out. Joni knew a little something about that.

Joni trusted her team so much that, when the publicist insisted that she, Chris, and Val voluntarily submit to an "interview" (not interrogation) at the police station instead of at home, she overcame her dread at the thought of it and agreed. Chris also came quickly on board, having seen Candy in action over the years. Maris would not accompany them—a key element of Candy's strategy to demonstrate the women's complete confidence in their innocence—but would Zoom in to the interview.

Val was against it. She insisted that Maris be by their side every step of the way and quoted Russ, who had told her it "would be crazy not to have her there."

"No fricking way," Candy said, and Val reared.

Joni saw it, saw how much her friend disliked the publicist she'd never before met in person.

Of the five women clustered in Joni's Sunny Day office, discussing how to "handle things going forward," Candy was the smallest in body but the biggest in presence. She was tiny, just five feet and a hundred pounds, with a cap of bright blond hair, bloodred enameled fingernails, and scads of gold jewelry. She filled the room with her certainty. She'd kicked off her high heels and her manicured feet were knobby with bunions. Maris was the largest, in both height and girth. She wore her usual neatly tailored pantsuit, a brightly colored blouse—magenta, today—and no makeup. She kept her gunmetal gray hair tucked behind her ears to showcase the glittering diamond stud earrings she always wore. Soon after the women teamed to help Joni five years ago, Candy took that one small detail and fed the press a profile of a lawyer who fought tough, never lost, and always wore the expensive earrings—which she'd bought for herself—as a reminder to the world of her power. It wasn't all true when Candy conjured it and put it out there, but it was true now.

"But," Val argued, her eyes flashing at Joni for help and receiving nothing, "if we go in there without a lawyer and we do the wrong thing or say the wrong thing—"

"You'll be fine walking from the car to the interview room," Maris assured her. "I'll be on-screen before you arrive. Nothing will go wrong. And Candy does have a point about perception."

"But I thought the whole idea of going in through the back door was that there'd be no press," Val argued.

"There won't be," Candy confirmed. "That we can control. But gossip, we can't. What the court officers and staffers see along the way counts whether you like it or not. They're not supposed to talk, but let's face it. Everyone's got a camera in their pocket these days. One tap of a finger and—" Candy shook her head.

"Facebook, Instagram, TikTok, Twitter, they're not our friends," Maris agreed. "X," she corrected herself.

"We don't wanna take chances," Candy said. "If you march in there with an attorney bodyguarding you, especially this attorney, and one staffer goes rogue and snaps it, do you know how it'll look? You'll look scared. I can see the headlines now."

"But—" Val turned to Joni for support.

"I understand how you feel," Joni told her friend. "But this is a tricky business—the way it looks going forward matters at least as much as what happened."

Val looked from woman to woman and shook her head. "That's absurd."

"We're in this together," Joni gently reminded Val. "They really know what they're doing. We need to trust them."

"Fine," Val said with a heavy note of capitulation, a recognition that she'd crossed into Joni's territory of the unthinkable. They were stranded there together now. Joni reached for her friend's hand, her cold hand, and squeezed it warm.

Val stayed over with Joni and Chris so they could arrive together at the 84th Precinct first thing in the morning. On Maris's orders they'd eaten a good breakfast and had only half a cup of coffee each; she wanted them "awake but not over-caffeinated." On Candy's advice they wore "light, summery" colors so they'd look more like "wives and mothers and daughters" instead of the "fricking badass monsters you really are." Candy said that last bit with a laugh—it was meant as a woman-to-woman compliment among professionals who knew the score—but it chilled Joni's blood. The publicist had no idea.

The three women sat on one side of the interview table in dusky pink silk and white linen and floral cotton print, wearing just a little makeup, their hair pulled off their faces. Candy had gotten them this far, and if they didn't feel confident, they pretended they did. Candy had instructed them that there would be cameras in the room, "so hold your shit together, ladies."

As they waited for their questioner to appear, Zoom Maris, on a large screen suspended on the wall to their left, calmly busied herself with paperwork. Every now and then she'd look at her clients with a smile or an encouraging word. Val sat straight with her hands folded on the table. Chris sloughed in her chair and stared at her phone. Joni worried she'd start to sweat in the cool room—and then she did. She breathed deeply to slow her heart rate. She'd been through this before and had hated the way the detective back then, Hipolito McMullen, had studied her whenever they spoke. He'd made her nervous, the way he'd look at her with his probing, seen-it-all gaze. She pictured that craggy middle-aged detective in his pin-striped suit and dark tie walking into the room and her pulse took off.

The door opened and a young Black man, tieless in a pressed white shirt and suit pants, entered the room, sat across from them at the table and put down his file folder. He had short hair and a shaven face rough with ingrown hairs. With elegant hands, he opened the folder. Then he looked up at them and smiled with bright white perfect teeth.

"Good morning," he greeted them. "I'm Detective Jacob Hamilton. This session is being recorded." He stated the date and time. "And you are—"

He looked from woman to woman as they identified themselves, glancing at his file with each name.

Joni wondered what his file said and if it was true when he told them, "There isn't all that much here for me to go on, just a basic description of what happened at your home, Ms. Ackerman, the night of your brother's death. I'll read it aloud into the record of this interview, so you'll know exactly what I know. Then, if you don't mind, I'd like to speak with each of you separately."

They smiled and nodded. Maris confirmed, from on high, that it wouldn't be a problem.

Joni made sure not to betray how uneasy his politeness made her feel. She reminded herself to listen to his words stripped of any presumed intent, to answer with the simple truth, as they'd practiced, and to remember that Maris had their backs.

After he read a brief and accurate description of the bare facts of what had happened to Marc on Joni's terrace, he asked Val and Chris to step out of the room. A guard appeared to accompany them. As they'd practiced, they didn't look at each other. Candy had told them, "Just follow orders like good girls." They all knew how to do that, and they did it well.

When they were alone Detective Hamilton leaned back in his chair, wove his fingers over his belt and said, "In your own words. I'll just listen." He smiled.

Joni explained how Marc had appeared in her living room out of nowhere. That he became violent with her, just like when they were kids. That he grabbed one of Chris's knitting needles out of her basket and chased Stella, the dog, onto the terrace—how terrified she was when he did that. How she ran after them and confronted him. How Val appeared. How Chris appeared. How the rest happened so fast it was a blur. He went after the dog with the knitting needle, and they were all afraid for—"

"Just speak for yourself," the detective reminded her, smiling.

"Of course. I'm sorry. I was afraid he'd hurt Stella. He'd already taken off with her before."

As Joni explained, keeping it as simple as possible, the detective took notes. Part of her ached to spill everything, all the details and nuance, so the detective would understand the context of what happened that night and why. But if she did that, wouldn't her own predilection, her own past, shimmer with clarity as well? She couldn't risk it. They'd have to make what they could of the bare details she offered.

"It all happened so fast. I thought he was going to kill me. The next thing I knew he was staggering backward, holding on to his chest. He was bleeding. The needle was sticking out of his chest. I couldn't believe it."

"How did it get there?"

"I'm not sure. I don't remember doing it but maybe I did. It all happened so fast. I was afraid he was going to kill me." She *knew* he was going to kill her.

"I remember him spinning around, flailing. He fell frontwards over the parapet and kind of bounced off, and I saw that the needle was all the way in. It was awful. And then, then he fell backward. He tried to stop himself from falling but it made it worse. Maybe he tripped on something—I don't know—but the next thing I knew he went over the parapet. Just . . . went over."

She stopped talking; her story was done. They sat there looking at each other for a moment. The detective had lovely brown eyes with short, curled lashes.

Chris was next.

Joni waited with Val in another room next door. Then she waited with Chris when Val went in. They didn't speak with each other while they waited, assuming there were cameras everywhere. Maris had impressed that on them: "Be quiet, be pleasant, be invisible."

Finally, they all gathered in the first room opposite Detective Hamilton, who thanked them for their cooperation. He seemed relaxed as he turned through the pages inside his folder, checking to see if there was anything else.

"I think we're good for now. Ms. Ackerman, you can sign for your brother's things at the front desk."

Joni hadn't expected that. She glanced up at the screen, at Maris, who said, "Thank you, detective. Looks like we're all done here."

"Yup, we're good." He nodded. "Thanks again. We know where to reach you if we need anything. This concludes the interview at 12:02 p.m."

As he rose to leave, Chris said, "On TV, they always press a button to start and stop the tape when they state the official time."

The detective laughed lightly. "No button here. Our tape keeps rolling and we slice out what we need."

"Splice," Chris corrected him. "Or cut."

Detective Hamilton crooked her a wry smile. "Appreciate the correction."

"Me, too. I mean, since we make TV shows. We always want to get it right."

On their way out, they stopped to collect a large black garbage bag with Marc's belongings. Its weight surprised Joni. An officer escorted them out the way they came in, depositing them on a sidewalk at the back of the precinct facing a brick housing project. Trash cans waiting for pickup lined the curb. The morning was warmer than when they'd entered, the sky a flawless blue.

Joni's phone rang with a call from Candy, who asked, "Everyone there?"

"We're outside the courthouse," Joni said.

"Put me on speaker." The three women huddled around the phone to hear Candy announce, "Just talked to Maris. Mission accomplished. She'll call you later, but just so you know, she's not worried."

"It wasn't so bad," Val admitted.

"The detective seemed nice," Chris told Candy.

"Yeah," Joni agreed, "I have a good feeling about it." She didn't, but she wasn't going to share her anxiety. She needed her daughter and friend to believe they were safe, to hold on to that belief and to keep holding it, and if things went their way it would become true.

When the call was over, Val asked Joni and Chris, "But what if we're wrong?" She looked too pale in the clear morning sunshine. Her hair was dry and frizzy, and her middle part had grown gray. Joni wished she could truthfully promise her friend that nothing that had happened on the terrace that night would change them. But how could she?

"One day at a time," Joni reminded them and reminded herself.

Chris sighed. "I'm starting to understand what that actually means."

"So." Joni pretended to collapse under the bag's weight. "What am I supposed to do with this crap? Why is it so heavy?"

Chris unknotted the bag and a mildewy stink blasted out. Marc's clothes were still damp.

"Jesus," Joni said. "That's awful."

There was a public trash can at the corner. Piece by piece, she threw away her brother's smelly clothes: jeans, T-shirt, underpants, socks, sneakers.

At the bottom was a Ziploc baggie sealed with Marc's wallet. She plucked out the bank cards and was about to toss the rest when she noticed the outline of something, a small key, shoved down one of the leather slots. She forced it out and turned it over in her hand. It was a safety-deposit box key. The moment she saw it her mind spun. It meant something—it had to mean something. But what?

Maris had made it clear to Joni that, as her brother had died intestate and she was his only surviving next of kin, she would have access to everything now—all his records, anything and everything he possessed. The paperwork was already in process. Once it was official, Joni could look for trails and follow them for answers.

37

Two weeks later, an Uber dropped Joni on Montana Avenue in Santa Monica, right in front of the bank. She looked at the squat, freestanding building and—something about the structure's rounded corners and the verve of its big red sign—thought of the Dairy Queen their mother used to take them to sometimes, if she was sober. Her favorite was a cherry-dip vanilla swirl cone. Even now, thinking of it, she could taste it on her tongue, that first hard, bright lick. Marc would get a cone with a chocolate vanilla twist smothered in sprinkles and drip it all over the car seat, and when they got home, and their father found out, he'd take a beating for it. Every time.

She got out of the car and thanked the driver when he lifted her small suitcase out of the trunk. She'd come straight from the airport and would only stay a couple of days before heading back to New York—well, depending on what she learned about the safety-deposit box that she'd discovered was located at this Santa Monica bank.

Joni had read all of Marc and Blair's text messages and knew from one scant mention that they'd taken this box together soon after he'd arrived in Malibu. His bank, phone, and email records had answered some of her questions—Marc had stolen something, Blair had discovered it, and she'd pressured him into sharing the bounty. But once things had gotten gnarly and he'd stopped logging into his accounts in lieu of burner phones, all the trails dropped off. Joni had scoured her bank and investment accounts and knew that none of her money was missing, and Marc never had access to Louisa's money, so she guessed that what he'd stolen was tangible. But there was more she needed to understand. What had he stolen, and from whom?

She pulled her suitcase through the corner door of the small bank. There was a beige linoleum floor and stained dropped ceiling, flashes of red signage, cooled air, and lines of Hollywood beauties, young and old, waiting for one of the two tellers. Yes, she was back in LA, her adopted town, where ambition came to meet indifference. A strange feeling took her by surprise: She missed New York, where people left home without makeup, no one cared, and everything mattered.

A security guard directed her to a flight of stairs leading down to the basement.

At the bottom of the staircase another security guard stood in front of a locked door. Joni showed him the key. He led her into a hallway where a once-pretty woman with shoulder-length bleached hair and pink lipstick sat at a desk.

"Your name?" the woman asked. Her silk scarf looked expensive, though it was worn at the edges. How long had she been sitting here, waiting for the role that would change her life?

"Joni Ackerman. My brother has a box here—Marc Ackerman." As she'd been instructed when she called, she gave the woman her ID, copies of Marc's death certificate, and an Affidavit of Next of Kin showing that she was the administrator of his estate.

The woman checked the documents. Her tired blue-gray eyes flashed at Joni. "I'm sorry for your loss. Do you have the key?"

"I do."

The woman stood and gestured for Joni to follow her.

They walked down a short hall to another door. The woman moved her scarf to the side. Around her neck hung a bead chain from which dangled three keys and a laminated card with a barcode. She used one of the keys to unlock the door.

Directly in front of them was a vault door so immense it almost didn't look real. Joni had seen one like this only once before, when she'd briefly had a safety-deposit box at a different bank before realizing she didn't really need one. She watched the woman turn another key, hold her barcode tag in front of a small, flashing screen that switched from red to green, and then punch in numbers that triggered the heavy bolts inside the door to slide open.

The inside of the vault was lined from floor to ceiling with three different sizes of numbered hatches, each with a keyhole. In the center of the small room was a scratched metal table. The woman pushed aside a rolling staircase and went to one of the medium doors. She opened it with one of her keys, slid out a long, lidded box, and placed it on the table.

"I'll be just outside," the woman said. "Take as much time as you need."

"Thank you."

Alone in the vault, Joni slid in her key and turned it. The long top hinged open at the short end. She held it up and looked inside.

The box was empty, as she'd suspected it would be.

Blair had gotten here first.

And that was never the plan, or Marc wouldn't have come searching for her at Joni's, desperate, enraged.

Had Blair changed the plan midway through—after Joni finally gave her what she'd wanted (but never asked for) and promoted her? And then, when they found her out, she bolted and took it all for herself, whatever it was they'd stashed here.

Joni returned to the desk and waited while the woman replaced the box and secured the vault.

Back at her desk, the woman smiled at Joni. "Anything else I can do for you?"

"Maybe. I'm just wondering something. The other person signed on to the box—when was she last here?" Joni smiled. "Blair was my brother's girlfriend. She's been having a hard time and she's been hard to reach. We're trying to get everything straight for the lawyers so we can settle the estate. I'm just wondering if you could tell me the exact day."

The woman checked the computer and told Joni the date: it was right after Joni last saw Blair.

"And my brother? When was he last here?"

"The following week—a Monday."

The day before he died.

So, when Blair didn't join Marc in Mexico, he bolted. Then went to the bank, to the box, and found it empty. Then flew to New York. To Joni's. Looking for Blair. Who had the irreplaceable valuable thing he needed to finance the next phase of his life.

"Are you okay?" the woman asked.

"It's stuffy down here." Joni realized she was sweating and wiped her forehead with the back of her hand.

"It is if you're not used to it."

"Thank you," Joni said.

"You're welcome."

Joni held her breath all the way back up the stairs and through the bank and onto the sidewalk with its blinding California sunshine. She dragged her suitcase into a slice of shade beneath the bank's red awning and waited for a car to take her home.

The house on Idlewild Way looked strange and she stood a moment wondering what was different. The door and windows were closed. The trash cans were tucked neatly against the side of the house. The front path and driveway were swept clean. Then she saw the goddess head flowerpot in the cactus bed beneath her office window, its hollow skull split into three jagged shards. The plants burgeoned where they'd landed, still plump with flowers, and strands of monstrously fast-growing ivy had already started their creep up the side of the house like they were trying to get back in. She ripped the ivy out at the roots, picked up the broken pieces of flowerpot, and dumped it all into the trash can on her way inside.

The first thing she did was check the safe in her bedroom closet. All her jewelry was still there, along with the silver candlesticks her great-grandparents had hauled out of old Russia's Pale of Settlement when they ran for their lives.

Cabinet by cabinet, drawer by drawer, she checked the house for missing valuables.

Everything was in its place.

Joni sat alone in her house and wondered if there was any point in spending another night here. She missed Chris and Stella; they were her home, and they were in New York.

She sat alone in the quiet of her house, the home she'd built with Paul, where they'd raised their family and built their careers—where he'd built his career and she'd foundered—the place of precious memories and unthinkable loss.

She sat alone in this silent place, where a thick layer of dust had settled everywhere while she was gone, and wondered what Marc and Blair might have hidden in that safety-deposit box.

Whatever it was, it was valuable.

And Blair had it now, all to herself.

And she was long gone.

38

Roddy had texted earlier that he had some news and to hold tight; he'd call around noon. Joni waited in the penthouse living room, parked on the couch like when she was a teenager and hoped a boy would call on a phone tethered to a wire connected to the wall. Beside her, Chris's knitting needles clacked restlessly, creating a ribbed hem with the last of the yellow yarn.

When the phone rang, Chris paused and her eyes met her mother's. In those eyes Joni saw a hunger for anything and everything that might help her make sense of what had happened to them. Chris, the plotter and planner, capable, ready. In that instant Joni realized that her daughter's mastery of detail was a hypervigilance that had started after Alex's accident and intensified with her father's death. That was why, if she dropped a stitch in her knitting, she always went back to find it and always took the trouble to weave it back up the ladder so the fabric would be whole in the end. Joni had seen her unravel inches of fabric and hours of work, if necessary, to make that happen. Her industriousness made her formidable and must have felt like torture—it was a reminder that a woman's strength was a scaffolding of hard-won scar tissue.

Joni offered her daughter a loving smile and put the call on speaker.

Chris laid her knitting in her lap and listened intently.

They hurried through hellos and niceties, having not spoken since Louisa's funeral. Then Roddy said, "I heard about your brother. My condolences."

"Thanks, but you know how I felt about him, so . . ."

"Right. Anyway, there's something I think you'll be interested in knowing. I got it from a cop friend of mine about a police report that just got filed."

"Well, if anyone could commit crimes from the grave, it's Marc."

"Nah. This one he did while he was still alive. Marshall Singer's been getting Louisa's estate in order. He brought in an auction house and they're working up an estimate so they can liquidate. She had an art collection worth a fortune. Most of it was in storage, and guess what?"

A light went off in Joni: of course. "Something's missing."

"He cut a small but valuable painting right out of the frame."

"How do they know it was Marc?"

"Security footage at the facility—he arrives and leaves with a shiny black suitcase with its tags still on. He was authorized to come and go so no one questioned it. But the date is right before he took off for Malibu, so it fits. Can't remember the artist's name, someone I never heard of, but they say it's worth about five million. So, there you go."

"Wow."

"No one had any idea the painting was gone. Louisa thought she was tracking him down for her divorce papers. Little did she know."

"Maybe it's for the best," Joni said. "It's one more thing she didn't have to be angry about." Then Joni told him what she'd learned—the empty safety-deposit box, a plan between Marc and Blair that went awry.

"It's not easy fencing art, especially expensive art like that," Roddy said.

"Blair majored in art history. Maybe she thinks that'll give her a leg up." It occurred to Joni that Blair might have used that as leverage to convince Marc to share the money they'd get for the painting. That and a threat to turn him in if he didn't agree.

Roddy chuckled. "Maybe it will. Maybe it won't. I majored in economics and much good it did me."

"I was an English Lit major," Joni said. "It actually did kind of sink in." For better or worse.

"They'll find her eventually."

Joni hoped they wouldn't. The thought surprised her; obviously, she should have wanted Blair caught. Caught and convicted for whatever she'd be charged with for helping Marc get away with robbing another wife. But deep down she found herself hoping that the young woman could get something for the canvas and slink away into obscurity. She'd succeeded at something she connived on her own. She'd beaten Marc at his game—and as good as delivered him to Joni's door so finally someone, all of them together, could take that fucker down.

"Thanks for letting me know, Roddy," Joni said.

"One more thing," he said. "And here's the best part."

She sat forward. "Yes?"

"They won't be pressing charges."

Joni held her breath. "Who told you that?"

"My cop friend."

"He's sure?"

"Positive. The DA doesn't like cases they don't think they can win. There's too much going against your brother. No jury would believe he wasn't a threat."

"It was self-defense," Joni said. "That's what we explained to them."

"Yup."

"Thanks for letting me know. I'm so relieved."

"You got it. Stay in touch if you need anything."

"I will."

Joni put down her phone, went over to Chris and hugged her. "I told you. It's going to be okay."

"Oh my God," Chris said. "Oh my God."

"We have to tell Val."

There was a loud smack and the crowd roared. Val tried to keep her eye on the ball as it sailed over left field, but she lost it. Men in pinstriped white uniforms ran. A man in a red uniform leaped toward the sky with his paw—it looked like a paw to Val, in all honesty—reaching upward. The ball sailed into the stand of spectators and the roar amplified. Someone in the stands caught the ball, igniting a froth of joy. The pounding music got louder. The digital advertising banners that lined the inner periphery of the stadium switched to a flashing zipper: HOME RUN HOME RUN HOME RUN. On the field, men in pinstripes promenaded from base to base and the giant display tallied the score.

Val pressed her hands over her ears and waited for the noise to subside. Russ sat between them. Zeke leaned over to shake his head at his mother. If she hated it so much, why did she come with them? Why didn't she stay home like she usually did when they went to a game?

Val smiled at her son. This wasn't exactly her cup of tea, but she didn't want to be anywhere else. Lately, the only times she felt safe were when she was with her family.

She realized her phone was buzzing inside her purse. ETR had been on her about a perceived scheduling conflict that Val kept reminding her wouldn't be a problem. She knew from experience that avoiding the call would make things worse.

"Be right back," she shouted to Russ and Zeke. They didn't seem to hear her or notice as she got up and headed up the aisle to find someplace quiet to talk. Another red player was at bat.

Hurrying into the women's room, Val looked at her phone and saw that it was Joni. She didn't want to talk to Joni. She wanted to forget all that. But she couldn't refuse a call from the woman who knew her worst secret.

"I have amazing news," Joni announced. "Where are you? It's so loud."

Val realized that the bathroom wasn't as quiet as she'd thought; it was just quieter than the stadium.

"At a baseball game with Russ and Zeke. What news?"

"They're not pressing charges!" Joni's tone was all emphasis. "Roddy just told me. He heard it from a cop friend who heard it from the source."

Val couldn't believe it. She wasn't sure if she should believe anything Joni said anymore. Joni, who'd been working so hard to gaslight her about what she did to Marc. As if there was a universe in which she hadn't killed him. She'd killed him. And she was finding it difficult to live with that.

"Are you sure?" Val asked.

"Roddy's sure," Joni said. "They're not pressing charges because there isn't a case. I told you, sweetie—there isn't a case."

Joni called her "sweetie," like a child, like she now needed care and coaxing to learn how to live in Joni's complicated, twisted balancing act of a world. How to be potent and invisible at the same time—a wolf in sheep's clothing. That was both of them now.

"That's incredible," Val said. "I can't believe it."

"Believe it."

"Joni, I feel so . . ."

"I know, I know. I've been there. It gets easier, you'll see. Trust me."

"Okay," Val said. She had to trust Joni now. If they didn't keep each other close and trust each other, they'd both be unspeakably alone. They'd have no one who could possibly understand. Chris, maybe, but she was young. They had to protect her. She asked, "Does Chris know?"

"Yes. She's here with me."

"I hope she understands she isn't at fault, not really."

"Enjoy the game," Joni said. She couldn't respond about Chris since she was right there.

"Enjoy may not be the word for it."

They laughed.

"Thanks for telling me," Val said. "We need to talk about Chris, though. Later. We need to protect her."

"We do," Joni agreed.

"I can imagine what's going through her mind. I mean, I don't have to imagine it, I know."

"I hear you loud and clear. Trust me, we're on the exact same page."

Chris resumed her knitting, the needles now gliding slowly and quietly, thoughtfully, in command of every stitch.

"Blair hated us," she said to Joni. "The whole time. It gives me the creeps to think about it."

"I don't think she really hated us. I think she was frustrated and confused."

"I thought she was on our team."

"I should have promoted her a long time ago."

"A person like her is never satisfied, though. I mean, someone who would do something like that."

Joni wasn't so sure. "I think it was more like 'death by a thousand cuts.'"

"She's not dead," Chris argued. "But she should be. And by the way, a knitting needle is a great way to kill someone if you don't miss. Right through the heart."

"Don't talk like that."

Please please don't. Don't talk like that or think like that or revisit the rush you felt when you drove the needle into your uncle. The certainty you felt that you had no choice; it had to be done and you could do it. You would. You did.

Joni knew this was just the beginning of the steering she'd have to do if there was any chance of saving Chris from herself. Daughters usually didn't want to be like their mothers. And sometimes mothers didn't want their daughters to be like them, either.

"But it's true."

"She was a sweet girl when Paul hired her." Joni remembered Blair back then, just twenty-three, bright and open, ready to devour life.

"Did you think I was sweet once, too?" Chris stopped knitting, looked up over her needles and grinned.

"I still think you're sweet," Joni said. It wasn't exactly true. Chris was sweet and sour and bittersweet, the way all women were and needed to be to survive. But maybe Chris's balance was tilted slightly to the bitter and the sour, the way Joni's was. Joni told her, "You're sweet, and you're lovely, and you're good, and you're kind."

"Wow, Mom." Chris started knitting again. "Now I know for a fact that you're full of shit."

39

It was crowded in Red Chair's sound-mix room that doubled as a screening room, but Joni wanted as many trusted eyeballs as possible to review the final edit before starting on sound and color and the locked cut that would be used for pitching to studios. It would be ready soon. She and Mike had already started soft pitching, spreading the word of what was coming, and a few key players were already on the hook, eagerly awaiting a chance to see the pilot. Joni's hope was for a bidding war. The thought of it excited her. They could come away with an order for a first season, but that was a lot to hope for. She forced herself back to earth, back to the room.

Joni and Frank perched on tall director's chairs by the mixing board. Sam and Mike sat on the small sofa against the wall. Chris, Val, and Diana shared the couch close to the screen. Frank pushed a button and all at once the lights dimmed, the large screen bloomed with images, and the poet's voice eased to full volume.

Circa 1950s Manhattan, against the crisp silver tones of memory, two young women in skirt suits haul a hand trolley stacked with album-sized boxes across a busy Midtown street. A voice-over of Dylan Thomas reciting *A Child's Christmas in Wales* blends with street sounds:

horns, shouting, laughter, and voices. Then, two voices distinct from the others crystallize in the easy dialogue of close friends peppering each other with questions and demands.

"Are we crazy for doing this?" Barbara asks.

"Probably." Marianne laughs. "Pull! The light's about to change."

A traffic light injects into the black-and-white a circle of red turning to green and the scene pops alive with color like Dorothy stepping into Oz. The friends pull, laugh, and dodge pedestrians as they drag their load across the sidewalk and through the doors of an office building. The first title card splashes onto the screen: *Hear Me Out.*

Two women in their early twenties, blocking out the noise, getting things done.

Joni had been like that too when she was young. It pleased her that she'd captured the mix of excitement and doggedness here, even if she herself could no longer go forth in the world with such pure conviction. Back then, love and success were dreams on a dim horizon. She'd accomplished both. And yet she hadn't, not how she'd imagined it, because when they arrived they were rotten with unthinkable compromise.

When it was over, Frank clicked the button and the lights raised. His expression was impassive—he knew how to hold a poker face until the audience had spoken.

"Notes?" he asked, all business.

The room was silent. Then Chris turned around to face them in the back and pronounced, "Nailed it."

"It's really good," Mike agreed.

"I love it, "Diana said.

"I've always loved it," Sam said. It was true: She'd sat in on several rough edit reviews and never had a note. Of all of them, she was closest to their "perfect audience" in that she wasn't a practitioner of the craft and wouldn't have known how to pick it apart even if she'd wanted to. What she saw, she saw, and either she liked it or she didn't.

Val said, "I wish I could think of something productive to say other than wow. But . . . wow."

Joni felt satisfied. "Okay," she said. "Good job. It's done."

"We won't lock until tomorrow," Frank said. "In case you think of something overnight."

"No," Joni told him. "This is it. Lock. Get started on the sound mix and color and let's call it a day."

Frank allowed himself a small smile. "If you're sure—okay. But we'll still wait until tomorrow."

Laughter bubbled through the room as everyone gathered their things and filed out. Joni held back until she was alone with Frank. There was something she wanted to say to him, but she didn't know how to say it. She liked him. She didn't believe anyone could be that nice—his ex-wife would doubtless have a lot to say if they ever sat face-to-face. But still, Joni liked him.

Their eyes caught. His smile expanded. They looked at each other, thinking things neither one had the wherewithal to carry all the way through a sentence in this late chapter of their lives.

"Can I just ask one question?" Joni ventured.

"I knew there'd be something." He crossed his arms. "Shoot."

"Where's the red chair?"

His arms relaxed and one hand reached into his back pocket for his phone.

"My daughter has it in her apartment in Asheville. She says sitting on it helps her relax. Here, I'll show you a picture of it. It's a good chair. We've had it forever and it could use a little paint."

He swiped through photos until he found the one he wanted to show her.

There it was: an archly smiling daughter about Chris's age—but with long brown hair like Joni's was years and years ago, back in college, when she first met Val—sitting on a faded but sturdy red chair that had been in the family so long it had become a part of them.

"So," Joni said, "it's a real thing."

"Real being relative. It exists. It used to mean something to me. Now I don't have it anymore."

"But she does."

"And it means something to her." Frank shrugged. "To be honest, it's just an old chair to me now—and the name of my business."

"Sunny Day," she said, shaking her head, half smiling. "I don't even remember why we called it that." A lie: She remembered clearly. She and Paul had woken up to another golden California morning and seized on it for the name of Paul's new company. Then they got out of bed and went about their business.

"I've got to get going," Frank said. "But . . . is Stella free for a playdate sometime soon? McDuff wants to know."

"Free is a big word."

"Interested?" he tried.

Joni smiled. It was a *maybe* smile. A *probably* smile. A smile that said most likely.

"Available?"

"McDuff has quite the vocabulary."

Frank laughed.

Her impulse for friendship, for love, was powerful but so was that sharp feeling of satisfaction when she breached a dangerous boundary. She wasn't sure if the two could coexist or if she was willing to sacrifice Frank to the experiment of finding out.

But he was waiting for an answer and she couldn't help herself.

"Yes. Why not?"

Acknowledgments

I am so grateful to everyone who worked with me in nurturing this novel as it grew into the book you now hold in your hands. To my wonderful agent Dan Conaway, for opening the right door to the right editor at the right publisher. To my talented editor Joe Brosnan, for ushering me in and then, with grace and sensitivity, guiding this novel to its true heart. And to all the brilliant people at Grove Atlantic, for everything they did and do day in and day out to bring this and other invaluable works into the hands of readers: Morgan Entrekin, Judy Hottensen, Deb Seager, Sal Destro, Cassie McSorley, Alicia Burns, Natalie Church, Jenny Choi, Mike Richards, Gretchen Mergenthaler, Michael Mah, Margaret Moore, and James Iocobelli. Also at Writers House, thanks to Chaim Lipskar, Sydnee Harlan, and everyone else who has a hand in the flow of work from author to publisher.

And finally, as always, to Oliver Lief. For reading and rereading. For talking and listening. For three decades, and counting, of love. For knowing how to make me laugh.